THE
BROTHERHOOD

BY THE AUTHOR

THE COUNTDOWN INSTALMENTS

Kiss Of The Mandarins
The Warehouse
Never Go Back
The Deception Covenant
Endgame

ORIGIN TALES

The Brotherhood
Rise of the ACF

VLADIMIR SERIES

Vladimir's Diary
Red Empire
Fifty Years to Paradise

OTHER WORKS

The Prophecy Illusion
Trinity
Vampires And Victims
Baltimore

THE BROTHER HOOD

MARTIN M. MCSHANE

The Book Guild Ltd

First published in Great Britain in 2018 by
The Book Guild Ltd
9 Priory Business Park
Wistow Road, Kibworth
Leicestershire, LE8 0RX
Freephone: 0800 999 2982
www.bookguild.co.uk
Email: info@bookguild.co.uk
Twitter: @bookguild

This is a work of fiction and is entirely a product of the author's imagination.
Anyresemblance or similarity to names, places, characters, incidents or events
or to any actual person, living, dead or undead is entirely coincidental.

Typeset in Adobe Garamond Pro

Printed and bound in Great Britain by
CPI Group (UK) Ltd, Croydon, CR0 4YY

ISBN 978 1913913 076

British Library Cataloguing in Publication Data.
A catalogue record for this book is available from the British Library.

Never was anything great achieved without danger.

PROLOGUE

Between the twelfth and sixteenth centuries orders of knights formed for the purposes of protecting ordinary people against the injustices inflicted upon them by their feudal lords and to fight wars for the glory of Church and State. The code of chivalry these orders of knights lived by was based on the words and deeds of William Marshal, 1st Earl of Pembroke, and remained in place, virtually unchanged, for centuries.

Over time, orders of knights became powerful in their own right. Whereas they remained popular among the peasantry, they were feared, loathed and despised by emperors, kings, aristocrats and the Church. The knightly orders often found themselves at odds with the clergy as many deemed them to be familiars of monarchs and feudal overlords; doing their dirty work by subjugating the poor for payment of tribute in gold, property and lands.

Popes in particular came to despise orders of knights because of the influence they had over their flocks. Ordinary people loved the knights so much that they took note of what they said above the words of all others. Pope Clement V was heard to say, 'They are too numerous, too powerful and too popular and must be done away with'. By his time, though, the number of knights within orders was so huge that not even warring popes could hope to defeat them. Something else was needed; other means were called for.

It was during the reign of Pope Clement V that King Philip IV of France found himself in substantial debt to the Holy Order of Knights. It was a difficult situation Philip found himself in. On the one hand, he wanted to rid himself of his debts by killing all those he owed money to; but on the other hand, if he attacked any of the orders of knights he would be destroyed, as to attack one order was to attack them all. There was another factor though, and one of great concern. Many nobles and minor state monarchs, eager to win favour with orders of knights, would most likely side with them against Philip, possibly out of them detesting the French king, but certainly out of fear of retribution by the orders of knights themselves. Before he could begin to resolve the situation, Philip first needed holy blessings from the head of the Church. Happily for him, this was Pope Clement V, avowed enemy of the orders of knights. This is called 'situational determinism': in times of great need, connections come to exist that make ambitious schemes possible.

In early 1307, Philip IV sought a private audience with Pope Clement V to discuss the sticky financial situation he was in with the Holy Order of Knights. He could not believe how well this meeting went. Not only did Pope Clement bless Philip's scheme to kill off the Holy Order of Knights, but he also gave him his blessing to kill off as many other orders as he wished. In addition, right there and then, Pope Clement raised his right hand, made the sign of the cross over Philip and absolved him of all past and future sins against orders of knights, thus assuring him of a place at God's side in heaven. Philip wanted to ask Pope Clement to include the Dutch and the English in the bargain, but didn't want to push his luck. As Philip knelt to kiss the papal ring of office, Clement bent to whisper to him that a tribute of twenty thousand gold crowns was necessary before holy absolution could be finalised. Despite the vastness of the sum it was considerably less than his debt to the Holy Order of Knights, so Philip agreed to Pope Clement's terms. For a brief moment, as he knelt there, Philip considered assassinating Clement and placing his own man at the head of the Church but, as with all 'nearly men' of history, his nerve failed him.

To execute his scheme, Philip hired mercenaries from across Europe and beyond. Their role was to assassinate the knights of the Holy Order during celebrations for the upcoming engagement of his daughter, Isabella, to King Edward II of England. In planning for his daughter's big day, Philip encouraged his nobles to kill their enemies so that they may steal their lands, serfs and other possessions. After the killing was done, Philip taxed the nobles' ill-gotten gains. This amassed him a fortune, which he used as dowry to secure the marriage of his daughter to the English King Edward. It was in Philip's mind to have Edward murdered and so gain the English throne through his daughter, but she was an intelligent, ruthless and ambitious young woman and wanted to rule England in her own right. It was not for nothing that she became known as the She-Wolf of France.

Philip IV of France died, supposedly from a stroke, seven years after his daughter's marriage to Edward II. Rumours abounded in both the English and French courts that Isabella had murdered her father by poison but this was never proven.

The stage was set for Queen Isabella to shape English history in a way it hadn't been since the time of William The Conqueror.

POITIERS CASTLE

Half-starved and on the point of collapse after weeks of rain-soaked riding, the ragged company of horsemen raced through the blinding storm toward the column of knights. Howling and hollering like savages, they dared the lightning to strike them as they scribed circles in the air with their Spanish steel swords. From his mount at the head of the riders, the sergeant-at-arms screamed out, "My Lords! My Lords… we're here!… at last we're here! Poitiers castle is beyond yonder bluff." This news raised a loud cheer from the knights. Dismounting, the sergeant-at-arms approached Sir Guillaume le Fey, Lord Master of the Holy Order of Knights, and kneeling one-kneed in the mud and with his head bowed to his chest, he said, "My Lord Knight, praise be to God in heaven, we have arrived at Poitiers castle at last!"

The Holy Order of Knights had travelled many hundreds of leagues to reach Poitiers castle and, just like their entourage, they were cold, wet, weary and hungry. They had arrived barely in time for the feast ordered by King Philip IV to celebrate the betrothal of his daughter, Princess Isabella, to King Edward II of England. More than anything, though, what was on the knights' minds was shelter. They badly needed to get out of the storm that had raged above them without let-up for weeks on end, draining them of all their strength. Many of the knights believed the weather was an omen of foreboding trying to prevent them from ever reaching Poitiers Castle... but here they were, arrived at last, and only just in time.

★

Following the announcement of the betrothal of Princess Isabella of France to King Edward II of England, knights of the Holy Order were compelled to participate in celebrations of the upcoming nuptials. This particular faction of the Holy Order of Knights was ordered to attend Poitiers Castle while others were directed to venues in northern and eastern France, the southern German states, and the Low Countries. Those few knights who could not make the journey were ordered to attend cathedrals to complete four days of prayers and devotions. Each of them paying to the Church a tribute equal to that of renting a trading space in the inner cloisters for a year.

★

"Pray, tell me, Esquire William, how much farther have we to go?" asked Sir Guillaume le Fey of William Clay, eldest of four English brothers who had served the order of knights faithfully for over four years. Though esquires were on the lowest rung of English nobility, people rightly addressed them by their title.

"We have yet one and a half leagues to travel before we reach Poitiers castle, my Lord," replied William Clay.

"In this foul weather it will be an hour yet before we arrive there," remarked Sir Guillaume to himself.

"My Lord, according to the sergeant-at-arms, over yonder hill lies a road that will take us directly to the castle's gates."

"What think you of that, eh, Sir Michael?" spoke Sir Henri Desjardin to his brother knight and closest friend, Sir Michael de Gel. "Only a little farther and you can rest and recover your

2

strength." Sir Michael had been wounded, many feared mortally, protecting the honour of a peasant girl who had been selected for *jus primae noctis* by her family's feudal lord. Sir Michael had received his wound after turning his back on the French nobleman who'd submitted without entering combat. Though badly injured, Sir Michael had still had the strength in his arm to despatch Lord Beaumont with a single swing of his broadsword.

"*Jus primae noctis* is a filthy and abhorrent rite that even the basest beasts do not perform. It is a sin in the eyes of God and man," sputtered the pious Sir Estienne de Quincey, one of the order's supposedly celibate knights. However, everybody knew Sir Estienne to be a notorious boy-lover who could be heard praying nightly in his tent for the strength to resist the carnal urges that had forced him from his marital home.

"It is too much," interjected Sir Tihon Panshin, "that Philip demand we travel so far just to celebrate his daughter's engagement. In the doing of, we lost two brother knights along the road, with a third at death's door… and all without recompense! What says Philip of the money? When will he pay what he owes?" demanded the knight.

"Sir Tihon, it would be insulting and impolite to broach a debt of honour, let alone one concerning a fortune, at such an occasion. Let your outburst concerning Philip's debt be the last until we leave this place." Sir Tihon bowed in acceptance of Sir Guillaume's order. "And let that go for each of you!" shouted Sir Guillaume to the column of knights. "You are all bound to silence in everything concerning Philip's debt to us… or anybody else's debt, for that matter. If there is any dissent then let it out now." None of the knights moved a muscle. "Then let us go forward together as brother knights. Lead on to Poitiers Castle, Sergeant-at-Arms."

And so, an hour after the first sighting of Poitiers Castle by the sergeant-at-arms, the last of the knights passed along the causeway and through the gatehouse to come to a halt in the enclosed courtyard in front of the castle's keep. It seemed strange to the knights that there were no soldiers guarding the castle's entrance, nor were any to be seen on the battlements atop the stone walls. Arrow slits were unmanned and there was no fiery oil ready to pour over unwelcome visitors in the death holes above the gatehouse. An uneasy feeling crept over the knights and their entourage.

Inside the castle's walls, the knights were greeted by a motley line of grovelling serfs, at the head of which was the 'chief serf', a self-proclaimed title. The chief serf bowed low, removed his threadbare cap, and welcomed the master of the Holy Order of Knights. He apologised for the absence of the castle's owner, Count Colbert, saying that he had been called away on the King's business but would be back in time for the celebratory banquet in honour of the engagement of Isabella to Edward. "In the meantime," continued the Chief Serf, "your knights and servants are to billet in the west wing." The chief serf bowed low again and replaced his cap.

Sir Guillaume ordered the column of knights to dismount and for the grooms to take their horses to the stables to feed, water, dry and brush them before they fed, watered, dried and brushed themselves; such was the value of the knights' mounts compared with that of the grooms. The esquire brothers, being middlemen, oversaw the serfs so that they did not shirk their work. The sergeant-at-arms ordered his men to stand guard at the stables and four of them to mount the battlements to be on guard for treachery, which he had sensed from the moment he entered the castle. He shared his concerns with Sir Guillaume, who revealed that he had similar concerns about the situation they found themselves in and ordered the sergeant to speak discreetly to each of the knights to tell them to keep their swords close to hand. The knights didn't in fact need telling; none of them had any intention of being separated from their weapons by more than an arm's length.

★

"My Lord, a messenger has arrived with news of Count Colbert's progress," spoke the chief serf grovellingly to Sir Guillaume. "He reports that the Count has been detained in his business and will not arrive back at the castle until sunset tomorrow at the earliest. The Count bids you and your entourage enjoy the hospitality of his castle and commands me to prepare a banquet in honour of you and your Holy Order of Knights. I have instructed the kitchen to prepare a lavish feast and the keeper of the Count's caves to bring forth barrels of Count Colbert's finest wines." The chief serf bowed low, waiting for Sir Guillaume's permission to leave his presence.

"It is most unfortunate that your master will not be joining us this evening but we thank him for the kindness of his hospitality. You have my leave to go about your business." Sir Guillaume felt the way that the chief serf had referred to Count Colbert was akin to somebody unfamiliar with him.

Back with his knights, Sir Guillaume informed them of the delay of Count Colbert and of his suspicions surrounding the way the snivelling serf had spoken of his so-called master. He warned his knights to be on their guard as he sensed some treachery was afoot. One of the grooms was granted leave to convey Sir Guillaume's message to Sir Michael de Gel, who was in the care of the esquire brothers in the upper part of the west wing, the brave knight having descended into a fever. The sergeant-at-arms took Sir Guillaume's message to his men standing guard on the battlements. The entire Holy Order of Knights and their entourage were on a high state of vigilance. They were a long way from home and feeling like rats caught in a trap.

That evening when the knights and their entourage entered the great banqueting hall of Poitiers Castle, Sir Guillaume le Fey was surprised to see a priest sat in the middle seat at the top table. The good father stood as the knights entered the hall. He made the sign of the cross over each knight as they knelt one-kneed to kiss the back of his proffered hand. As the esquire brothers kissed the priest's hand, he leaned forward and whispered to them to retire to their quarters as their attendance was not required at the banquet. The brothers bowed low to Sir Guillaume before departing the great banqueting hall. Robert and Thomas Clay, the two younger esquire brothers, felt insulted and humiliated by the priest's treatment of them, but William and John, the elder pair, accepted the situation without complaint or ill feeling as they thought the priest's conduct and treatment of them was appropriate to their station. The sergeant-at-arms, his soldiers and the various grooms, serfs and camp followers were despatched to eat in the basement, while Sir Michael de Gel wasn't well enough to join the feast.

Before the knights tasted a crumb of food the priest led the assembly in prayer, thanking God for the bounty before them, after which each knight mumbled private devotions and crossed themselves. "A toast!" shouted the chief serf. "Bring forth the barrels from the Count's wine caves." He clapped his hands and two barrels of wine were rolled into the banqueting hall. The chief serf passed a spout into one of the barrels and poured himself a tasting cup. He washed the red liquid around his mouth and declared, "A fine wine, an excellent wine!" Having tasted the wine to demonstrate that all was right with it, the serving serfs filled the toasting cups and passed them around the knights sitting at the banqueting tables.

"Let us all stand and make a toast to Princess Isabella's forthcoming marriage!" demanded the priest. Everybody stood and emptied their cups. The wine was indeed excellent, as the chief serf had said. After several more toasts, food was served. As the courses came one after the other, the toasts in between them got more and more rowdy and lewd.

"I have heard rumour that the English king, being a boy-lover," this snide remark brought raucous laughing and hollering, and a banging of fists on tables from the knights, "has yet to bed a woman, and so let us all toast to the power of Isabella, who will bring him to his manhood in the eyes of God." The knights raised their drinking cups downing their contents in one.

"I cannot make the toast… my cup is dry," slur-shouted a drunken Sir Tihon Panshin. "You there… open the other barrel… immediately. Do you hear me? Immediately, I say!" The chief serf passed a spout into the second barrel and poured all the knights a cup of wine for their next vulgar toast.

In the basement dining room, the sergeant-at-arms ordered three of his soldiers and a serf to accompany him in taking food and wine to Sir Michael de Gel and the esquire brothers who were caring for him. Intending on keeping the knight and the esquire brothers company, the men took food and wine enough for themselves also. After ascending the stone spiral staircase, the men came to halt at the landing leading to the esquire brothers' quarters. The sergeant banged on the stout oak door with the pommel of his sword and demanded to be admitted. William Clay, the eldest of the esquire brothers, opened the door and welcomed the sergeant and thanked him for the food and wine that he and his men had brought for them.

The soldiers laid the feast out on a table and after a short prayer, which neither Robert Clay nor Thomas Clay joined in with, invited everybody to partake of the repast. A plate was made up for Sir Michael, who sat up in his cot bed with the support of a nest of cushions at his back. Despite his enfeebled state, Sir Michael offered up a toast to Princess Isabella and her future husband, King Edward II. William Clay, on behalf of his brothers, declined

7

the offer of wine and took up four cups of water to make the toast. This caused sideways glances and muttering from the company of soldiers.

"Forgive us our abstinence," spoke William Clay to the soldiers, "we do not partake of wine or beer, nor anything else that brings on drunkenness."

"Such is at odds with our piety," added John Clay, the second eldest of the esquire brothers, always in his big brother's shadow.

"Aye," uttered Robert Clay, the third eldest esquire brother, without any enthusiasm whatsoever.

"Not so with me," laughed Thomas Clay, the youngest of the esquire brothers. "My brother soldiers, I'll gladly join you in a toast to our future queen." Thomas chucked the water on the floor and held out his cup for the sergeant-at-arms to fill with wine.

"Brother, what will our mother think of your behaviour?" spoke William.

"Nothing, if you don't tell her!" laughed Thomas with a sly glance at the oldest brother.

"Leave the lad be," spoke Robert Clay in support of the youngest brother. "You and John have piety enough for us all."

"You are too soft with him, William," said John, who loved all his brothers but knew his place as second son. A second son who would inherit nothing of the family estate. Though John loved William, he hated him for being the eldest male child and in dark moments wished him ill fortune.

"If I am too soft with Thomas it is out of love for him, our dearest little brother. He has time to change his ways and it is better he is left to find the path to righteousness himself rather than be dragged along it against his will."

"Nay, I agree with John," spoke Robert jokingly to stir the pot. "William, you, as eldest, are far too soft on Thomas; too soft, I say."

"Dear brothers... please do not argue on my part. I have made up my mind and you yours. Let us toast, in our own ways, to the future happiness of Isabella and Edward." The esquire brothers, the soldiers, the serf and the wounded knight spoke as one in their toast, then downed the contents of the toasting cups and commenced their meal.

After they had finished eating and drinking the sergeant-at-arms excused himself from the company, saying that he was going to check on the guard on the battlements and then look in on the knights' celebrations. The group took that to mean he was going to partake of some wine with the knights. They laughed and bade the sergeant farewell, saying they'd see him the next time they'd see him, and laughed again.

A few minutes after the sergeant left, those remaining in the room heard him screaming the word 'treachery' over and over again until his cries were suddenly cut off. All in the room fell silent, staring wide-eyed at one another and wondering what the screaming meant. Sir Michael de Gel, being the leader of the group by his station, rose up on his nest of cushions and tried reaching for his sword.

"Stay here, all of you… I'll… I'll…" Sir Michael, unable to finish his sentence, collapsed onto the floor.

"Sir Michael… Sir Michael!" yelled William Clay, shaking the prostrate body of the knight. John Clay knelt at the knight's side, placed his cheek next to Sir Michael's mouth and, pronouncing him still alive, placed a cushion under his head.

"Brother William, what shall we do?" asked John Clay of the eldest brother. "What could have befallen the sergeant for him to scream and shout so?"

"Treachery has befallen our sergeant. That's what has happened to him," growled Samuel Black in grim monotone. "You heard it yourselves… and if we stay here, we too shall fall victim to that same treachery." All heads turned to look at William Clay to seek his guidance as the eldest esquire brother.

"Young Master Black is right. We must abandon this room, for all must know we are in it," spoke William Clay in agreement with Samuel Black.

"But the door is stout, Master Clay, none can enter without considerable effort," said one of the soldiers.

"Aye, he is right," agreed John and Robert Clay in unison.

"We should take up our arms and discover for ourselves what the trouble is," voiced young Thomas Clay.

"No, little brother, no!" shouted William Clay, shaking his head. "We will not be taking up arms until we know the situation we find ourselves in. What has happened? We do not know, and until we have some knowledge we must conceal ourselves as best we can and only fight if…" William Clay's words were broken off at the sound of yelling and rampaging in the corridor at the bottom of the stone spiral staircase that led to their room. "Let us find a safe place. Be quick, be quick about you," yelled William Clay as he bent to pick up Sir Michael de Gel from the floor, but he was brushed aside by Samuel Black, who lifted the knight up with one mighty heave.

"I will follow where you lead, my Lord Esquire," said Samuel. "I will obey you in all your directions but I pray you make haste and lead us from here without delay." The group filed out of the room behind William Clay.

★

When the sergeant-at-arms had left to check on his men he made his way to the courtyard but when he couldn't see any of the soldiers he'd posted to stand guard on the battlements he became suspicious. The sergeant did not call out to the missing men; instead he backed into the shadows, pressing his body as close as he could to the battlement walls. He then climbed the stone steps leading to the battlements, all the while looking around for the slightest sign of movement.

As he arrived at the top step, the sergeant spied a shadowy shape pulling at something laying on the floor. After his eyes adjusted to the darkness, the sergeant saw the shadowy shape was a man tugging at the prostrate body of one of his soldiers. He was removing the soldier's chain mail. The fallen soldier's eyes met the sergeant's across the shadows. Hope was lost when the sergeant saw the soldier's eyes, though open, were lifeless. Drawing a fat-bladed short sword from its scabbard, the sergeant was about to pounce on the scavenger when a voice from behind froze him to the spot.

"Hey Henri, look, there's another one there on the steps... is that four or five?" The man made his way up the stone stairs to come to stand behind the crouching sergeant. The man grabbed the sergeant roughly and as he turned him over he realised the body was still alive. Before he could utter a cry, the sergeant slit the man's throat through to the spine with his short sword. Alerted by the sound of scuffling, the scavenger came toward the stone stairs.

"Hey! Hey, Eduard... get up! Are you drunk?" he hissed, slapping his compatriot on the back of his helmet. "Get to work before I..." These were Henri's last words before passing from this life at the point of the sergeant's sword.

The sergeant-at-arms knew he must return with haste to Sir Michael de Gel's quarters to tell all there what had happened to his men and of his fear for the fate of the knights of the Holy Order. As the sergeant's foot left the last tread of the stone stairs he stopped to listen for any signs of danger. The only sounds he heard were coming from the great banqueting hall and they filled him with dread. They were sounds he'd heard many times before. They were the sounds soldiers make when going about the business of looting dead bodies. Then, just above the sergeant's head, came a clattering noise... then another. Before he could work out what had made the noise, an arrow pierced the sergeant's back. He screamed out in terror and pain, "Treachery… treachery… treachery!" A second arrow and then a third found their mark. The sergeant stumbled out into the middle of the courtyard, demanding to face his unseen foes. From the shadows emerged a dozen soldiers, their swords drawn. They formed a tightening circle around the sergeant. In his left hand, the sergeant held his fat-bladed short sword and in his right, a long, slender assassin's dagger. Neither had ever let him down until that night as both slipped from his weakening grip. As his dagger clattered to the ground, the sergeant rushed at the men encircling him. Before he made three strides they cut him down. They kicked the sergeant to his knees before throwing him to the ground. *Shame, shame and thrice shame… my eternal shame!* were the sergeant's last earthly thoughts.

As the mercenaries stripped his lifeless body, one of them picked up the sergeant's fat-bladed short sword.

"Look you all, the blade has blood on it!"

"Who's blood is it?"

"How the hell should I know?"

"Go and see who's missing."

"You can go to hell, I want my time picking the knights' bodies… there'll be nothing left by the time we're finished out here."

"The priest said there are more of them in the tower over yonder. If we don't find them the Count will be…"

"'You must find them and kill them all'… is what the priest said, those are our orders."

"They'll surely have something worthwhile on them… will they not?" suggested one of the mercenaries.

"According to the priest they are but feeble camp followers, so it should not need more than three to despatch them… Jacques, pick two others and get you gone! Don't worry, we'll keep some of the pickings for you," said the captain, who then went to join his comrades in the banqueting hall.

The soldiers made their way to the tower where the so-called camp followers, 'fugitives from God's justice', were said to be hiding out. They did not believe their captain for a minute when he said they were feeble. "Even a feeble man with a sword can kill you... let us be careful, brothers." None of them were happy with the arrangements and they cast their minds back to a few hours earlier when they'd arrived in the woods half a league from Poitiers Castle. They'd been ordered to dismount and tie the horses. "Secure them well," the captain had said, "we don't want them wandering off." As the mercenaries dismounted, one of them stumbled and fell, breaking his leg. After the captain inspected the man's injured leg he ordered him put back on his horse. "Your day here is done," he said, "You must leave our company." The man replied, "But what about my share? I've come so far... I can still..." But the captain was not swayed, "There is no share for them that cannot do the work, boy!" he replied roughly and laughing he slapped the horse's rump sending man and horse speeding off into the night. "Right then, captain... will that be more shares for the rest of us?" enquired the other mercenaries. "That is right, my boys; the fewer we are the more reward we will receive... so do your work well and tarry you not." After ten days, the man who'd broken his leg died in his mother's arms while in the grip of an agonising fever brought on by incurable infection.

★

William Clay held up his hand to halt and silence those following him down the stone spiral staircase as the noise of those searching for them got nearer. He ordered the line to reverse direction. The column turned around and headed back up the staircase. When they reached the landing outside the door to their former quarters, William led the line on up the stairs in the hope there would be somewhere for them to hide. As they made their way the ceiling got lower and lower. William felt that they were about to be trapped in a blind end at the top of the stairwell. By the time they ran out of steps, the ceiling was no more than four feet above the final stone stair. William passed the message down the line that they were at a blind end and could go no further. Thomas, who was bringing up the rear of the column, removed his sword from its scabbard and pressing his body hard against the wall of the stairwell he waited in ambush of those coming up behind them. His plan was simple: as soon as the pursuers caught sight of him he would run the first man through and push him down on top of the others. He hoped they might all break their necks in the fall.

When the mercenaries gained the landing they silently eased the stout oak door open before running inside the room, their swords at the ready. They soon realised nobody was there. Thomas heard one of their pursuers saying that the priest had told the mercenaries where to find them and he was angry that they weren't there. Another pursuer said they must continue with their search. When the mercenaries were half a turn of the spiral staircase from discovering Thomas Clay they realised the ceiling height was dropping and they were heading into a blind end. He turned to the others and said they should abandon their search and return to the great banqueting hall otherwise there would be no pickings left for them.

"But what shall we tell the captain?"

"We'll tell him that we found the men right where the priest said we'd find them and we killed them all."

"But what if they are later discovered?"

"We'll say they must be a different band of men... or give some other excuse," laughed the mercenary in an attempt to cover up the weakness of his plan.

"But there's no blood on our swords."

"We'll say that we strangled them... with our bare hands. After all, they're only feeble camp followers."

"Good idea. Now let us return to the banqueting hall and tell the captain we killed the sodomites with our bare hands."

As the mercenaries turned to return back down the stone staircase, Jacques thrust his sword clean through the back of the man in front of him. Looking down at the sight of the sword protruding through his chest, the mercenary screamed an oath and cursed his murderer. The mercenary's body soon became yielding as his blood pressure plummeted. His knees buckled as he tumbled down the stone stairs, coming to rest on the landing below.

"The story about us strangling so many men wasn't a good one... the Captain'd see right through it," said Jacques.

"You're right, brother... you're right," agreed the other mercenary while nervously wondering if he was next.

"Dip your sword in Audric's blood... wash your face and hands in it too," said Jacques to his remaining compatriot. "We'll tell the captain of the fight the camp followers put up and how we overcame them despite them killing poor Audric. He won't care... the fewer of us the greater the shares will be."

After the mercenaries departed the tower, Thomas Clay led the group back to the landing. On it lay the soldier's body in a pool of blood. He was dead. Each stepped over the body and entered the room.

"What did they mean when they called us sodomites?"

"Well, little brother, there are some men who prefer the company of other men in their bed..."

"I know what a sodomite is, brother; what I meant was why did he call us sodomites when we are not?" Suddenly there was a distant cheer. No doubt the news of their demise had been delivered to the great banqueting hall.

"We should pay no regard to what they said about us being sodomites... such slanders are used to enflame passions in battle."

15

"What should we do now, brothers? They are too many for us to fight and in any case, we only have but two swords. We should find a place to hide and wait them out. If we go wandering around the castle we're sure to be discovered."

"Why wander the castle when we have a perfectly safe hideout here? They believe us dead and so are unlikely to return."

"Samuel is right. Lock and bar the door and trust that no one returns. I should think they won't remain long as their work is done."

"I say we should go and meet them but quietly… pick them off one by one until the numbers are more even and then—"

"Thomas, young tender apple of our dear mother's eye, we are neither knights nor fighting men. We are God's servants and through our holy devotions, we seek everlasting life in the hereafter of His kingdom," uttered the pious William. "No, brother, we shall remain behind this stout oak door and pray that the men do not return."

"But brother, we have three soldiers with us! Good fighting men!"

"Aye, three, Thomas… but against how many? But no, let the soldiers speak for themselves… What say you, soldiers?"

"Lord Esquire, we submit to your wisdom and leadership and will follow how you direct us to act," spoke Samuel Black, the strongest and bravest of the soldiers. Having done so, none would speak against him.

"It is decided then. We will wait until the men have departed the castle and then we will emerge from our hiding place and discover what we shall discover."

"The priest! The priest is behind this. Did you not hear, they said when they—"

"What? You say the priest is behind this, Thomas?"

"Aye, I do. William, did you not hear the man when he said that the priest had told them where to find us?"

"I heard nothing of the kind, brother, and I demand you desist speaking so," demanded William Clay. "We shall have no such talk about a man of God here." Most in the group nodded their assent. "We will wait as agreed and when the men have left the castle we will—"

"What shall we do while we wait, brother William? Play us some games?" mocked Thomas Clay scornfully.

"Perhaps eat us a hearty meal?" added Robert Clay, equally scornfully. "And William, I say to you: do not ever put your piety upon me. I declare that the priest who greeted the knights is behind this. See how he…"

"Enough, Robert, enough," begged John Clay. "Do not attack William's piety. He carries the burden for us all."

"I see your lapdog still speaks up for you, brother," sneered Robert Clay. "It is of no use, John; he will get all when Mother passes. No matter what grovelling you do, you will never get a crumb from the table once he is master of it." This outburst of Robert Clay's was followed with an uncomfortable silence.

Waiting for the right time to emerge from their hiding place, the group occupied themselves in caring for Sir Michael de Gel, moistening his lips with drops of life-giving holy water from a bottle said to come from the spring of eternal life at Jerusalem.

★

After an hour of silence William Clay put his ear to the door of the room. Discerning no sounds, he opened the door and listened again. The echoing curve of the stone spiral staircase only returned more silence. William closed the door and said to the others that he, being the eldest of the esquire brothers, would venture a little beyond the room and return with news of any disturbances in the area below. This he did, but he had nothing to report upon his return. He said that he believed the men must have left the castle and that he would make his way to the great banqueting hall to investigate further. Young Thomas Clay strapped a sword to his belt and made to leave the room with his brother. William Clay put his hand on his little brother's shoulder and told him that this was something best done by himself alone. He said the intention was to spy, not to fight. Thomas argued furiously to go with the eldest brother but William would not be swayed and he made the rest of the group swear to keep his little brother safe inside the room. And so William Clay left the comparative safety of the room to investigate the fate of the knights of the Holy Order while the rest of the group prevented Thomas Clay from following William.

The further from the room William got, the bolder he became, as there was no sign of the men. It appeared that they had, in fact, left the castle. There was not a sound to be heard anywhere at all. Walking along the main corridor toward the great banqueting hall, William thought he heard faint sounds but put them down to rodents. Reaching the door to the great banqueting hall, William eased it open a crack... just a crack... to see inside.

The sight that greeted William Clay made him want to tear out his eyes and burn them in hell's fires. It was a vision of pure horror that he saw. The knights were laid all about the floor of the banqueting hall. They had been cut to pieces; there was blood everywhere. Most of their clothing and belongings had been removed. Sprawled on top of the knights were, William presumed, their assassins. He could not fully comprehend the scene so he entered the banqueting hall to walk among the bodies. The faces of the knights appeared animated at times by the flickering flames of the dying fire.

Some of the assassins began to move. William stared in disbelief as they stretched themselves awake. *How can this be?* he thought. In their semi-conscious state, the assassins asked William for help to raise them from the floor... some asked him for the mercy of God... others for another goblet of wine. *How can the assassins be alive and yet the all knights dead? Surely they would've killed at least some of them?* What William was unaware of was that the second barrel of wine served up by the chief serf had contained a powerful sleeping draught. The knights' suspicions were not aroused because they had seen him drink from the first barrel, and so by the time they were ready for the second barrel they were giddy enough in drink to have lost their sense of caution. But what fools the assassins were. Murder, even the murder of those who cannot fight back, is thirsty work and so the assassins had themselves a drinking party, emptying the knights' cups and even pouring themselves drugged wine from the second barrel.

William made to leave the scene of carnage before the assassins fully recovered their senses. As he turned he saw three men spreading out to attack him. Peering beyond the men, William saw Thomas, the most loved but most undisciplined of the esquire brothers, sneaking up behind them, sword in hand.

"What have you done here tonight?" demanded William Clay of the assassins.

"The King's work, which we will finish with you," shouted their captain in reply.

"But why is this the King's work? We are but God's humble servants, so why do you act so?"

"God's humble servants?" mocked the captain. "We know you for what you are. You are plunderers, murderers and sodomites, and our King has ordered you all killed."

"Your King acts so because he wishes to absolve himself from his debt to these good knights who you have murdered."

"No matter, it will be simple to add you and your purse to their number."

William now fully understood the assassins' intentions.

"Sir, I am a good Christian man who has made many sacrifices for the glory of God, the Church and our kings. Please, I beg you, as good Christian men, do not finish your work with me." The assassins moved to close on their prey. As they did so, Thomas Clay made his presence known with a little cough.

Now that they were outflanked the assassins became hesitant. They looked to their captain, who assured them that all was still in their favour, but worse was to come for them. The rest of William's group emerged from the shadows to show their true number. With the boot now on the other foot, the assassins threw themselves penitent to the floor, their hands clasped together, their eyes raised to the heavens as they muttered prayers to beg God's mercy. The group advanced and removed the swords from the assassins. Samuel Black picked up a fat-bladed sword from the floor that he recognised as belonging to the sergeant-at-arms. He regarded his reflection in the sword for a couple of seconds and then, with madness in his eyes, plunged it up to the hilt into the nearest assassin, where the neck meets the shoulder, in a two-handed strike. The assassin died instantly. The remaining assassins jumped to their feet but were cut down before they made three strides. Samuel Black drew a knife from his scabbard and grabbing the hair of a semi-conscious assassin, pulled up his head and sliced his throat wide open. He looked to the others to do likewise.

"Hold!" screamed William Clay. "Hold, I say! For if you murder these men it will be on your consciences for all eternity, and come the day of judgement you will be judged as murderers." The group stopped and looked to Samuel Black for guidance. He told them to do as their consciences dictated but he wasn't going to worry about the day of judgement; he was going to dispense his own judgement that godless day. The esquire brothers looked on to witness the revengers lifting heads and slitting throat after throat.

Sickened at the sight of the slaughter, Thomas Clay threw himself on top of Samuel Black's next victim, shouting, "Enough, Samuel, enough." The assassin Thomas was protecting turned beneath him and, wrapping an arm around him to hold him tight, pushed a dagger through Thomas' heart from behind. The youngest Clay brother's eyes met William's as he spoke in the plaintive voice of somebody who knows they are doomed. "Help me... help me, my brother... help meeeeee." But William knew his beautiful little brother, his perfect little brother, was beyond his help and would soon be in the safe keeping of the Lord God Almighty. Outraged, the group moved as one on the assassin. William Clay held out an arm to halt them. The group fell still and deadly silent. The assassin stood and, in a move lacking compassion for his defender, he threw young Thomas Clay's body to the ground. While keeping his eyes fixed on the assassin, William Clay stooped and picked up a sword. He tested its balance with air swishes, completing circle after circle until satisfied that it would serve its purpose well. The retreating assassin stumbled as he backed away, which caused him to glance behind to see what it was that had tripped him. As he looked forward again, justice was delivered upon him by William Clay's sword. The entire group took up arms and finished off the remaining assassins. Some of them woke before their ends and begged, crying out for mercy, but there was no mercy to be had from the revengers of young Thomas Clay.

★

As they surveyed the scene, the likes of which none had ever seen before, the group debated what they should do next. Some of them, out of respect for the fallen knights, wanted to hold a service and then bury the knights with honours befitting such men. Others were for fleeing the castle with all haste.

"We must leave this place at once. As soon as the assassins are overdue others will come looking for them, and we might not be so fortunate in defeating them," uttered Robert Clay with the support of Samuel Black. William Clay remained silent throughout. He sat with his chin resting on the palms of his hands, staring into space and thinking, *What have I done? What have I done? How will God judge my actions here today?* Things were becoming heated when a tiny voice bade them to cease their arguing. The group turned and was surprised to see Sir Michael de Gel leaning on the doorframe of the great banqueting hall.

"Those of you who are for fleeing this place with all haste are right to act so. We can do nothing for so many dead. Their suffering is over while ours continues. We must all leave this godforsaken place at once if we are to stand a chance of survival."

"But where shall we go, Sir Michael? Where can we flee to? Where can we take refuge? All the country will be out for us. They believe we are plunderers, murderers and sodomites. They will not allow such beasts to live."

"They will think no such thing. The reputation of the Holy Order of Knights cannot be tarnished by mere words. Through our acts, the whole country knows us for what we really are, and you must all have faith in the goodness of the ordinary people. They will help us and they will protect us."

"What about the Church, Sir Michael, what about the Church? The Church controls the people and the priest who was here—"

"Be you silent, brother!" yelled William Clay. "I will hear none of these wild accusations against a man of God."

"But brother, it is as plain as the nose on your face," argued Robert Clay, "that the priest was party to this, if not behind the whole thing. Look around you, brother. Do you see the priest's body? Do you? No brother, you do not. You are wrong, brother, you are wrong; the priest was in this up to his pock-marked scalp."

"Esquire William, I am with your brother in this," said Sir Michael de Gel. "The Church are familiars of the rich and powerful, always eager to do dark work for payment of tribute in gold."

"How can you speak so, Sir Michael?"

"I speak so because it is true, Esquire William. The Church is more interested in the accumulation of earthly wealth than preparing souls to receive everlasting glory in God's good heaven. Look you at the way the Church rents spaces to guilds, by which they profit. They bring money men into the Church and offer them a guaranteed place in heaven in exchange for an inheritance after they pass from this life. It is common for these crow priests, as they are called, to hang around the death beds of the wealthy, for weeks on end if necessary, to obtain signature of transfer of deeds for their lands and possessions. If the dying already be benefactors then priests are nowhere to be seen when the time of their passing comes, leaving the wealthy to die as paupers do die."

"But the Church does many good works, Sir Knight. It gives comfort and succour to—"

"Not all clergymen are evil, Esquire William; some are good, honest men, holy men, who do good deeds daily enraptured by their love for God and all His creations. But enough, good William, enough. We spend too much time in deliberations. We must flee Poitiers Castle before the arrival of the dawn."

"What about Thomas?" muttered Robert Clay. "I will not leave him here for his body to be devoured by rodents or cleaned out by scavengers."

"Aye brother, but we cannot take him back to England with us."

"Who says we're going back to England?" exclaimed Robert Clay.

"But we must, brother, we must. We three must now return to England to bear the news to our mother that her youngest lies dead in France." The esquire brothers instantly felt deep inside of them the consequence of delivering that news to their mother, but they would not turn from their duty to her or Thomas.

Carefully taking up the body of young Thomas Clay, the group filed in respectful silence to the woods beyond the castle's walls and in the starry night, took their swords and dug a grave in the frost-hardened earth, deep enough to keep his mortal remains from scavenging animals. They wrapped Thomas' body in sheets of linen and covers of leather and placed him under layers of plates of armour before filling the grave-pit with earth and rocks.

William Clay, his head bowed, made to say a prayer over his brother's resting place, but no words would come. Instead, streams of tears flowed from William's eyes, which froze upon contact with the cold hard earth. A hand came to rest on the shoulder of the eldest esquire brother and the voice of Samuel Black spoke the prayer that William Clay could not speak. After saying the prayer, the congregation returned 'Amen' in perfect chorus.

As the mourners made to leave the graveside, William Clay threw himself on the mound of frozen earth covering Thomas' body and howling a bestial cry of grief he tore at the frost-hardened ground with bare fingers until they ran thick with blood. John made to comfort his older brother but the others held him back. When William had dug but a few inches, he laid atop the grave covering himself with the earth he'd dug, as though wanting to join Thomas. Again John made to move to comfort his older brother, but again the others held him back, sensing that William's feelings of guilt over Thomas' death lay heavy on his shoulders and needed purging. Then, shivering, William Clay stood over Thomas' grave and, removing his shirt and tunic, took a knife and carved a bloody cross into his bare chest before falling to his knees. Kneeling, William prayed a silent, loving, brotherly prayer to his fine little brother, his perfect little brother.

William swore not to look upon Thomas' grave again until he returned to France to take him home. Mounting his horse, the eldest Clay brother crossed himself while muttering the Trinitarian. Watching William perform his devotions sickened Robert to his stomach. He believed there could be no God because He did nothing to prevent such things as they had witnessed that night. John, as ever, followed William in all his dealings and doings, never raising objection or fault with him.

Leaving the scene, feelings of deep guilt ran through Robert. He loved Thomas more than he loved his other brothers but had always been jealous of him, often making silent wishes for him to get his comeuppance over some transgression or other, but he always got away with everything... *everything*. Thomas would smile his cheeky smile and laugh his roguish laugh and everything was forgiven. Robert had always desired the same love and adoration that people lavished on Thomas without a second thought with him being the youngest of the brothers, the baby brother... the baby brother who took the attention Robert craved. Robert now lamented the unholy incantations of ill omen he'd practised against Thomas when lying alone in the dead of night.

"Did Thomas die because I offended God? Is God, He who made the heavens and the Earth, so easily offended? Curse Him if He is so... curse Him! In which case, I say there can be no God!"

★

Some hours passed before the grief-stricken group felt they could speak of their plans for keeping from King Philip's men.

"Sir Michael, have you any thoughts as to how we can proceed to remain at liberty and alive?"

"I do. Firstly, though, I must find out how many of my brother knights survived Philip's purge. I will travel to the Low Countries as I am certain to find a welcome there. Then I will—"

"But Sir Michael, you are not well enough to travel... you can hardly stay on your horse."

"I have been through greater trials than this. I will make it so long as I have my trusty guard with me. What say you?" asked Sir Michael of the soldiers. "Will you remain at my side?" The soldiers and the serf replied that they would remain at Sir Michael's side until death separated them. "And you, my faithful esquires, you must be bound for England bearing the news of your sad loss to your mother. You shall be safe enough in England… unless the Church comes after you."

"Why would the Church come after us in England?" asked William Clay of the knight.

"Don't be so green, brother," snorted Robert Clay in derision. "There will be a price on our heads that the Church will mean to collect."

"Dear Robert, I beg of you not to speak so, especially if we are ever again in the presence of our mother. She is a pious woman and will not tolerate such talk."

"Brother William, I would not affront our mother so with my speech but my mind is my own, and I have a mind that is now, and forever will be, set against the Church."

William Clay knew it was pointless to discuss this matter further with his – now youngest – brother but he would pray for his immortal soul regardless.

"Sir Michael, how would you counsel us in making our journey to England?"

"Before this day is out, we must end our company to go our separate ways. My advice to you is to travel only at night and to keep off the roads as much as is possible… and, most importantly, keep out of trouble. Trouble attracts the attentions of sheriffs, soldiers and captains of the King's Guard. Make for St Malo and there you can employ a boat captain to sail you to England. That way you will avoid the Cherbourg Peninsula where, little doubt, the King's soldiers will seek you."

"How far is it to St Malo?" asked John Clay.

"It is over two hundreds of Roman miles."

"I cannot conceive how far such a distance as that is."

"Brother, it is about the same distance as from our home to the port of Dover."

"But if we cannot travel by day, nor on roads, how long will the journey take us?"

"It matters not the amount of time but that you make it home safely. If it takes a year, what will that matter so long as you make it back to your family?"

"Dressed as we are, we will not blend in with town or country or village folk. How can we travel dressed so? We will be recognised and turned over to the King's men."

"Or the Church, brother, as we stand accused of the sin of sodomy."

"You must live on your wits... and in doing so you will inevitably commit the sin of theft, as none of us has money with which to buy food, clothes, or any of the necessaries required to sustain life. Stealing from the Church is easiest and best as they have everything they need and more besides. They shan't miss the little that you take."

"We cannot steal from the Church, Sir Michael; to do so would surely make the sin of stealing even greater?"

"Speak for yourself, brother. I will do whatever is necessary to see my England again. I would even steal from a blind beggar." John Clay scoffed at Robert's teasing of the righteous William.

"I will say to you this, William Clay," said Sir Michael de Gel in ominous tones. "Before your journey is ended, you will do more sinning than just stealing from a church... much more. You have already committed murder and, I dare to say, you will do so again before you see your home. Remember; stay out of trouble, keep off the roads, only travel at night, and eat your horses one at a time." At this last remark, Sir Michael coughed a choking laugh and waved away the attention of those trying to care for him.

"I doubt he'll last more than a few days," whispered Samuel Black to the Clays, who nodded in agreement.

The band of brothers rode together until noon, when they literally and figuratively came to a parting in their road. Sir Michael, the soldiers and the serf took the right-hand fork, the esquire brothers the left. "Happy travels and safe arrivals!"

THE ABBEY AND THE INN

After riding as a four for so many years, the esquire brothers couldn't settle into riding as a three. They missed Thomas' incessant chatter, the absence of which was a constant reminder to them of the loss of their youngest brother. The three esquire brothers rode together in silence, each brother lost in contemplation, recalling to mind the times they'd spent with Thomas. It wasn't long before feelings of guilt entered their thoughts, feelings brought on by how badly they'd sometimes treated Thomas due to his immodest and unruly nature. *How that lad loved the girls!* was a common theme in their remembrances of Thomas. Robert Clay, being the most understanding of the brothers, and therefore having the least reason to harbour feelings of guilt, spoke first.

"John, William, do you remember the time when Thomas—" Just speaking Thomas' name out aloud choked Robert's voice, and it was some time before he could continue. "Do you remember the time when Thomas put a wooden disc into the collection box at our church and took out silver coins, claiming them to be change from a gold crown?" All the brothers laughed at that remembrance.
"Aye brother, I do…"
"As do I, brother, as do I," mumbled William, lost in his own thoughts.

"He looked so innocent, so angelic-faced, when our mother asked him where the silver coins had come from… '*From God, Mother, they came to me as a gift from God,*' he replied." The brothers laughed at their recollection of Thomas' words to their mother, though each recalled them differently, as people do under such circumstances.

"But he confessed all later."

"Aye, and told our mother that he'd taken the coins to give to a poor husbandless mother in the next parish because the Church had denounced her and nobody would give her help for fear of being denounced themselves."

"I remember our mother gathering Thomas up in her arms and hugging and kissing him for his goodness toward others, but then chastising him for stealing from the box of God's servants."

"Do you recall what his answer to our mother was?"

"Who could forget it?" laughed Robert Clay. "He said to her, '*I'm certain God wouldn't miss a few silver coins amongst all the hundreds He's given each Sunday; He wouldn't object to me helping one of His flock. And besides, Mother, are we not all God's servants doing His works?*' I was astonished that one so young could come up so readily with such an answer."

"The Devil drives when needs must," said William Clay.

"What do you mean by that, brother?" snapped Robert Clay.

"Thomas came up with his answer because he… You do know who the woman was that Thomas gave the money to, don't you?" The brothers returned a blank look. "Elizabeth Cranwell!" They looked aghast as a realisation suddenly dawned on them.

"But isn't she a…?"

"Yes brother, she is. I think we should change the subject… Do you remember the time when Thomas went to…" Recalling Thomas' adventures over the years, the brothers were reminded that, despite his young age, Elizabeth Cranwell was not the only, or first, woman Thomas had given money to in exchange for sex.

Continuing northwards, the esquire brothers talked of their memories of their impish little brother; most were happy memories, though some were sad and others poignant. While continuing their reminiscences, they came upon a rural abbey. It was immediately clear to the brothers that the abbey was of the type that served a large agricultural community. The brothers debated whether or not to approach the clergy of the abbey to ask for their help, as they most likely wouldn't yet have heard of the slaughter at Poitiers Castle. William Clay, being the eldest brother, decided they would put their trust in God and go and ask if the holy men would assist them in their hour of need. He believed that the clergymen would offer them food and shelter and the brothers, in return, would perform some deed in payment and join the good friars during their services of devotions to God. Robert Clay, on the other hand, was all for making a speedy getaway from the whole area and suggested they follow Thomas' example by liberating the Church of some of its money so they could purchase food and clothing to disguise themselves. William was aghast at Robert's suggestion and made to ride toward the wall surrounding the abbey when John Clay called out for him to halt.

"Hold, brother. See there... there, sitting in the shadows of the cloisters, it is the priest from Poitiers Castle. Look now. He handles some of the knights' possessions."

"With my hand on my sword, I swear I will kill him before this hour is out," threatened Robert.

"Hold, brother. Remember Sir William's advice that we stay out of trouble? We shall give the abbey a miss and seek help elsewhere."

"If we send the Crow Priest to his maker, none at the abbey will know it was us. With him gone, we can get all the necessities for our journey by laying claim to his ill-gotten loot."

"Little brother," spoke William Clay. Robert Clay winced at these words; he was now the 'little brother' he'd always wanted to be. "I say again, remember what Sir Michael said: stay out of trouble, stay off the roads and only travel at night. Though how we will do this with horses in tow, I do not know. Perhaps we should eat them for food and skin them for clothing."

"Brothers, do you think Sir Michael will trouble himself to follow his own advice? No, he will not! Of course he will not. He will be doing as we should now do. We should ride ahead of the news of the slaughter at Poitiers Castle. If we ride hard, the news cannot overtake us. We will ride direct to St Malo and there employ a boat captain to sail us to England."

"These are dangerous times, brother. Travelling with a column of forty knights is one thing, but three Englishmen travelling alone is another. If discovered, we will be taken into custody. While we are imprisoned the news of the slaughter at Poitiers Castle will certainly overtake us."

"Brothers, listen to me… I have a scheme in mind: we sell our horses to get the money we need for food and clothing, and we should still have some left to pay for seats on coaches, and so travel incognito to St Malo," suggested John Clay, his chest puffed out, sounding very pleased with his strategy.

The other brothers were not convinced. For over an hour they debated the best way to proceed in their escape from France. Unable to reach agreement, they resolved to contemplate their options in silence rather than enrage one another further. With the daylight almost gone, the brothers sat in silence and ate what little food they had, and then huddled together against the cold to await the morning.

With revenge on his mind, Robert Clay remained awake, waiting for his brothers to fall asleep. There they were, just a short distance from where the Crow Priest lay, just a short distance away from revenging the death of his little brother. In his mind's eye, Robert imagined himself reaching the abbey, locating the crow priest and taking him somewhere quiet, somewhere private, and giving him a send-off from this life that his eternal soul would never recover from. He wanted to inflict every kind of horror on him but understood that these cravings were at odds with him and his brothers making a clean getaway. In his plan, in addition to killing the Crow Priest, Robert allowed ten minutes to locate food, clothing and, if any was to be found lying around, money. As he lay on his rolled-out jerkin, his only shield against the cold earth, Robert began to have doubts about his plan. *Perhaps my scheme is too bold... but I will begin and see how far it takes me.*

In the early hours, when sleep is at its deepest, Robert Clay slipped from beneath makeshift bedclothes, stole past the tied-up horses, and in the moonlight made his way crunching on the frosty ground to the abbey. He deeply desired to kill the Crow Priest but he was not insensible to the fact that he and his brothers were in desperate need of food, clothing and money in order to make their escape from France. As Robert crouched behind the abbey's boundary wall, he resolved that he would only kill the Crow Priest if the opportunity presented itself, and that the prime purpose of the raid was to steal food, clothing and money... *And whatever else I might come across that will be useful in our flight. The* Crow Priest *might have to wait for another day to receive my justice.*

Unfamiliar with the layout of the abbey, Robert walked around its outside to get an idea of the layout. He decided upon entry via a small, low-linteled side door. Grabbing its iron hoop handle, he attempted to turn it. It would not move. The door was locked. That the abbey's doors might be locked hadn't occurred to Robert. He cursed his bad luck. Walking away to seek an alternate point of entry, Robert heard the door open behind him. Turning around, he saw an old priest, his entire body cased within the aperture of the tiny doorframe. His first thought was to run. His second was, *How small the priest is.* His third thought was to draw his sword, run the priest through and gain entry to the abbey. The priest didn't seem at all surprised to come across Robert.

"Can I help you, my son?" asked the diminutive priest. Robert didn't know how to answer. "I saw you crossing the outer fields. I don't sleep very well and was walking in the open cloister when I first spied you. You were moving as though you didn't want to be seen. Is it your intention to rob the abbey?"

"No Father, no, of course not," lied Robert through teeth chattering in the cold. "I am a stranger in these parts and it isn't safe for strangers travelling alone. These are dangerous times, Father, very dangerous times."

"These are indeed dangerous times, my son. You look cold and hungry. Come inside. Let me give you something to eat and perhaps a cloak to keep you warm. The Abbey is as cold as the grave; you'll need something better than you have on to stay warm in here."

As the men walked together in silence along the cold flagstone corridors of the abbey, the priest made a motion to Robert to keep quiet by pressing a finger to his lips, and then rested his head on his hands to mime sleep. He then gently pushed a door slightly ajar for Robert to see inside. It was a dormitory and there, lying on the cot nearest the door, was the Crow Priest; he was fast asleep. He looked so innocent lying there, though Robert could easily slit his throat while he slept and nobody would be any the wiser until the morning. He understood that in doing so he'd have to kill the old priest too. This was something he wasn't prepared for and so he continued on past the door of the priests' dormitory, leaving the dreaming Crow Priest to whatever fate might have in store for him. The old priest made a beckoning, hurrying motion toward Robert as they entered a room. It was the kitchen. After preparing him a plate of meat and bread, the old priest told Robert to remain where he was and that he'd bring him some warm clothes. As soon as the priest left the kitchen, Robert gathered up as much food as he could, rolling the victuals in kitchen cloths, before making his way to the front of the abbey. Before exiting through the chapel door, Robert noticed a box on a high shelf with a message next to it that read 'For the poor and needy'. Regarding his and his brothers' situation as needy, Robert put all the coins into his pocket. Below the collection box, hanging on wooden pegs or draped over the handles of farming implements, were monks' hooded cowls, dozens of them; for use, no doubt, by the priests and their flock for farming in inclement weather. Being the perfect thing for disguising them, Robert grabbed four cowls. He was beyond the abbey boundary walls before he realised he only needed three cowls. Now angered and saddened by thoughts of Thomas, Robert cursed his lack of mettle in not killing the Crow Priest when he'd had the chance, but swore righteous revenge on him.

★

At the esquire brothers' encampment, William and John Clay awoke and were alarmed at discovering Robert's absence. For a minute they considered that he had deserted them following their disagreement of the previous day but then they saw his horse still tied to a tree alongside their own horses. Fearful that Robert had gone to the abbey to seek revenge against the Crow Priest, the brothers argued as to whether they should go and try to find him. They decided against this course of action and were about to break camp when Robert returned. Angry at their now-youngest brother for going missing, they demanded to know where he'd been. Robert threw food wrapped in kitchen cloths and monks' cowls onto the forest floor and calmly told them that he'd been to the abbey. A picture began to emerge in William's and John's minds that neither was happy with.

"Tell me, brother, tell me exactly: what did you do at the abbey?" demanded William Clay, fearing the worst.

"I went there to procure us some food and clothes and anything else useful that I might come across that could help us in our escape from France."

"To get food and clothes, and not to kill the Crow Priest?"

"I thought about it but decided it would be insensible of me to do so." William and John were impressed with Robert's self-control, his self-discipline, and said so. "I saw him... the Crow Priest... he was sleeping in a dormitory with other priests. It would've been so easy to slit his throat while he slept but seeing him sleeping... he looked so innocent. Besides, if I'd have killed him, I would've had to kill the old priest too and I didn't want to do that."

"The old priest?"

"Yes, he let me into the abbey and showed me into the kitchens, where I was able to procure us some food."

"And the clothes?"

"I happened upon them while I was helping myself to the contents of a poor box." William and John knew exactly to what Robert was referring: penury geld for the impoverished of the parish.

"When we are at our home, Robert, you must send the abbey twice what you took," said William Clay, using his sternest voice.

"Brother, if we ever see our home again I will be happy to send the abbey ten times what I took. Now, for the time being at least, we have food, money and these hooded cowls to warm us and disguise us... which means that neither of you has to commit the sin of stealing," laughed Robert toward his pious older brothers. "Has the argument been settled, brothers?"

"Which argument?"

"Do we ride ahead of the news of the slaughter at Poitiers Castle or do we not?"

"We do, brother, we do," chorused William and John.

After a meagre breakfast, the Esquire brothers gathered up their belongings, broke camp, saddled their horses and gained the road heading north. Mindful that they still had nearly two hundred Roman miles to travel, they set off at a gentle gallop so as to put some distance between them and any pursuers and preserve their horses.

★

Back in the abbey, the old priest was disappointed at Robert's disappearance and his having taken so much food with him, let alone emptying the poor box; he had yet to discover the missing monks' cowls. Disappointed as he was by Robert's behaviour, the old priest realised the young man's need must've been great and so he didn't condemn him as a thief or begrudge him taking what he had. Not wanting to alarm the visiting priest from the King's court, the old priest didn't mention the night's events to him or anybody else. If any alarm was raised over the missing items, the old priest would simply say that he had distributed them among the poor; 'which is our calling, is it not, brothers?', he would say if called upon to do so.

★

The esquire brothers reached a point half distance between Poitiers and Angers before they stopped to eat and rest their horses. With most of the daylight hours gone, and the prospect of a long cold night ahead of them, they looked for a suitable spot to set up camp for the evening. Dismounting their tired horses, they smelled smoke before they saw it rising above the trees in the failing light. Was the smoke from an encampment? Perhaps a village or a hamlet? The brothers had to know and, being wary of discovery, they agreed that John, being a most agile and skilful hunter, would set out to discover the source of the smoke.

While William and Robert waited with the horses ready for immediate flight, John carefully and quietly made his way through the dense wood in the direction of the smoke. Alert and with his sword in his hand, he was ready for any eventuality. Using the point of his sword to part bushes, John pressed deeper and deeper into the forest. After what he estimated to be about two hundred yards, John froze in his tracks. Just ahead of him, probably just beyond the next bush, were at least three voices engaged in quiet, mumbling conversation. Then, to John's left and right, other conversations sprung up and were moving toward his location. His only source of retreat was the path he had arrived by. Suddenly a bell rang out and a voice yelled, "C'mon in. No need to rush, there's beds aplenty for them that needs them." At that announcement, the voices moved toward the caller-outer. A couple of men advancing through the bushes came upon John from the rear.

"Begging your pardon, Sir," said one, "we didn't mean to interrupt your functions."

John at first didn't know how he should reply, but believing politeness being the best first response, he eventually said, "That is perfectly alright, gentlemen, I was not at my toilet, I was hunting for a rabbit. Do you not see my sword drawn in my hand?"

"We do, Sir, but in these parts, which lie near the heath over yonder, the holding of your sword in your hand while at toilet is not uncommon when exposing your lower extremities... if you get my meaning, Sir?"

"I do, kind brother, I do and I thank you for the advice... and... and warning. The call about the beds, what does it mean?"

"I take it you're a stranger to these parts?"

"Indeed I am, good brothers."

"The call means the inn is open for business. What with the

curfew and all, and the inns being restricted in their openings, there's a fine line between shelter and a flogging."

"Inns restricted in their hours of opening? I have never heard the like."

"It's to do with the feudal lord in these parts, Sir. He went into the inn business and would've closed them all down had there not been the need to be indoors by curfew time. The clergy are their watchdogs; they know all the gathering places."

"When exactly is curfew?"

"Now, Sir, right now. As soon as the inn is open then it's the curfew. Come, we must all be away and inside." John thanked the men and, making an excuse, dashed through the woods to warn his brothers about the curfew.

When John reached the brothers' camp, crashing and falling through the undergrowth as he was, William and Robert had drawn their swords in anticipation of a fight. John quickly recounted his tale and suggested they make all haste to the inn to evade punishment for breaking the curfew. William was not convinced this was such a wise course of action, preferring instead to remain hidden in the woods. Robert was of the same mind as John but, far from being concerned about curfew, he was concerned for his own comfort, saying that, "The chance to sleep in a bed should not be given up easily." A horn sounded, followed by loud shouts from the woods. The brothers knew enough about hunting to understand what was going on; beaters were abroad and were driving their quarry to some point where, no doubt, hunters would be waiting in ambush.

John led the way to the inn. Having determined that the beaters were moving from east to west, their only chance of avoiding capture was to head west, then north, and then to head southeast to come at the inn from the rear. Making their way through dense woodland on horseback was not easy but the brothers were loath to leave their mounts behind. Leading the way, John Clay cleared a path for his brothers through the woods. Fortunately, the woods to the west and north were not as dense as the woods to the east, and so the brothers outpaced the beaters and made it to the inn without incident. After stabling the horses, the brothers entered the inn through a side door. As they made their way into the main hall, all went quiet, every head turning in the brothers' direction. John, upon seeing the men he'd encountered in the woods, raised his voice in greeting to them; a greeting that they returned with a smile and some banter. With greetings made, received and returned without alarm, the rest of the inn's guests resumed their chatter, drinking, arguing, gambling, cock-fighting and eating. John, like William, thought, *'Tis a lively hostelry*, while the inn put Robert in mind of similar establishments he'd visited with Thomas.

John Clay approached the innkeeper, a woman of about forty, though it was hard to tell her age due to her apparel, lack of cleanliness, hair and teeth. He enquired about beds for the night but, before she could answer, a hand on John Clay's shoulder turned him around. It was the hand of a priest. He who was responsible for recording, reporting and fining latecomers who arrived after curfew, which was how the innkeeper introduced him to John Clay, who then made light of his late arrival, claiming a lameness in his horse's front leg. John mimed a lame animal limping along to supplement his lack of French. William and Robert wondered what was going on. *Why is our brother engaging a priest in mime?* they thought, while simultaneously gripping the handle of their swords. Each was prepared to fight their way out of the crowded inn rather than be taken to receive the judgement of the King's court.

"Aye, we would have been here in time for the bell had it not been for my horse. He is not very lame but we still have a way to travel yet and I didn't want to worsen the poor animal's condition."

"Be that as it may, the law is the law and the time of curfew is not negotiable."

"What then, good priest? A fine? Surely not more than a fine… a small fine, perhaps?" pleaded John, showing the priest a thumb and index finger barely apart. "We are not rich merchants but poor travellers making our way home, and any penalty will go hard on our family."

"Where is home?" asked the priest.

"At the present time, good priest, we are making our way to a small village to the east of St Malo. It is a new village."

"How is it called, my son?"

"You may not have heard of it, good priest…" John Clay stalled for time, trying to recall the name of some village near St Malo he'd heard of previously. "It's… as I said, it's a newly built village… and it's called… forgive me, good priest, but I cannot bring it to mind as we are yet to visit our mother there, but we shall know it when we are near."

"I know the area around St Malo very well, having been a parish priest around there for more than ten years. I'm sure I will know the name of your village, my son, if you will give me a clue."

"Indeed, good priest, indeed, but as I say it is a new… very, very new village. It takes its name from the crossroads situated nearby," said John, knowing many French villages are named after nearby crossroads. "It's called… *something* la Croix… or la Croix *something*…"

"La Croix Marago?"

"The very same, good priest, the very same!"

"Now that is very interesting, my son, very interesting indeed." The priest's tone made John Clay nervous. Believing that the priest had tricked him with a made-up village, John Clay unclasped his cloak in order to gain quick access to the knife tucked into his belt, should the developing situation demand he spill the priest's blood. "Yes, very interesting indeed, my son. I shouldn't really tell you this, but…" the priest looked about nervously, "but the deeds to the whole area were purchased under threat to the peasantry by a favourite of the King. Please do not ask me to put a name to him but suffice it to say he is a relation of His Majesty." The priest ended with a nod, a tapping of the side of his nose with a forefinger and a wink of his right eye.

"Really? That must be why the rent is so high!" gnashed John Clay, thumping his hand on the bar to demonstrate his anger at the make-believe high rent and causing the innkeeper to jump.

"Well, my son, enough gossip about those who must not be named. We have our business to attend to. It is a serious matter, being in contravention of an order of curfew... a very serious matter indeed," said the priest, nodding his head once more, winking again and this time smacking his lips together.

"Go on, Father John, go on," laughed the innkeeper, "leave the poor man be."

"Good priest, my name is John also," admitted John Clay, immediately wishing he hadn't given the priest his real name.

"Sir, Father John is just angling for a cider. That is the price he demands all latecomers must pay. He shouldn't do it but he's a good man and passes only sufficient fines to Count Colbert to satisfy him that he's doing his job. But he must have your name for the reckoning."

"My name?"

"Yes, good sir, your name for the good priest so he can add it to the reckoning," said the innkeeper with a cheerful note in her voice.

"Ah yes, of course, the reckoning... for the reckoning. My name is John, as you know, John... full name, John Belcher." William and Robert nearly choked at their brother using the name of their detested neighbour back home. "Now, Inn-keep, a cider for the good priest and three more for me and my brothers." John Clay concluded his business with the innkeeper, arranging three beds for the night in a shared room, and ordered a large bowl of mutton and vegetable broth with bread to dip.

After the esquire brothers finished their meal, William and John retired to their beds while Robert remained in the dining hall to keep an eye on events. Being on the run, he was eager to learn if anybody had yet heard anything of the slaughter at Poitiers Castle. Unlikely as that was, Robert wanted to make certain, so he engaged a couple of travellers in conversation. Being travellers from the north, they could not, of course, have heard anything yet of Poitiers Castle. Robert moved about the dining hall casually eavesdropping on conversations, most of which seemed to be concerned with trade or salacious gossip, so he finished up the last drop of his cider and went to join his brothers. William and John were both fast asleep in their cots when Robert entered the dormitory room. *They look so peaceful and innocent in their sleep*, thought Robert, *just like the Crow Priest*. He'd leave his brothers to sleep and wait until morning to make his report that he'd heard no talk of the slaughter at Poitiers Castle.

★

On the road, twenty odd miles behind the esquire brothers, a contingent of King's Knights were making camp. Their purpose was to apprehend fugitives from the slaughter at Poitiers Castle and bring them before the King's justice. A mile further on and they would come to the fork in the road where the esquire brothers and Sir Michael de Gel had parted company; Sir Michael and his entourage having taken the right fork and the esquire brothers the left. If fate was kind to the esquire brothers, all the pursuers would take the right-hand fork; if fate was moderately kind, the pursuers would split their number and follow both roads; if fate were cruel, then all the pursuers would take the same road as the esquire brothers had taken, and in coming upon them there could only be one outcome.

★

The next morning, as the frost lay thick on the ground, the esquire brothers were grateful they had stayed at the inn. During breakfast, John Clay suggested that they might consider staying another day, 'or two to gather our strength before continuing on our journey'. William and Robert opposed John's suggestion, saying their need to quit France as quickly as possible far outweighed their present need for comfort. William lectured John on the difficulties that lay ahead, not least that of hiring a boat captain willing to take them to England. John reluctantly acquiesced to his brothers but left the dining hall in a huff to attend to saddling the horses for the next stage of their journey. After speaking with the innkeeper, who was suspicious of the esquire brothers after earwigging on their conversations, William Clay gleaned from her that the road between Angers, their next planned resting point, and Rennes, was plagued by "outlaws from England... so they say. If you are heading further north than Angers then you might be better travelling by the Laval road."

"Will that add distance to our journey?" asked Robert of his eldest brother.

"Mistress Innkeeper says it will add about twenty Roman miles. She asked me about our final destination, which I skilfully avoided divulging to her," spoke William Clay, smiling a smug smile.

"But I mentioned our destination to her last evening," said Robert.

"Aye, strange then that she made no mention to you of outlaws roaming between Angers and Rennes."

"Maybe their conversation did not steer that way, brother," added John Clay with a knowing look at which William Clay sighed a sigh of exasperation.

"No, brother, no! A thousand times no!" yelled Robert in denial. "I would not ever put myself to her in that way; her breath is like that of Satan's arse."

"Dear brother, do not say such things of a woman!" spoke William in reprimand of his youngest brother.

"I say we ignore Mistress Innkeeper's advice and go via Rennes to St Malo. I, for one, would rather trust to English outlaws than, say, put my trust in a priest!"

"Brother, your railing against the clergy is becoming tiresome and I, for one, no longer wish to hear it, so keep you to your own counsel in such matters."

"You say much, brother, but you do little," added John. "You had the chance to revenge Thomas by killing the Crow Priest but you could not do it because a look of innocence dressed his sleeping face. Also, dear brother, consider the helpful goodness of the old priest at the abbey. And look at the leniency of the priest at the inn; he could've handed us in but he took a cider instead. No, brother Robert, no, your railing against the Church is idle talk and unfounded, and thus it should end as I too will entertain no further ill-speak against our holy Church." Robert Clay mounted his horse and set off at a slow gallop ahead of his brothers, of whom his liking, if not love for, was wearing thin.

★

The brothers rode the whole day at a steady pace to preserve their horses, should they need to race against pursuit. Under Robert's ill-temper they rode in almost total silence. William and John thought Robert's behaviour impudent but didn't make any such remark because his rages were legendary. They let him ride on ahead of them to give his head time to cool down. The brothers made excellent time in reaching the outskirts of Angers. *It is remarkable what can be achieved in the grip of angry silence,* thought William Clay. John Clay's humour with Robert was not improved by a day of riding and when they stopped to consider where they should spend the night, he peevishly said he cared not, 'so long as Robert is happy'. Robert ignored his brother's jibe and, desiring no argument, rode on to a nearby hill to look for a suitable place to make camp. In Robert's absence William reprimanded John, warning him that the last thing they needed was to be divided between themselves at that time. At this reproach, John broke down in tears.

"I am not as good or as holy as you are, brother. When Robert told of letting slip the chance of killing the crow priest, it gave me a cramp in my gut… I had wanted him to say to us that he'd killed the crow priest as revenge for Thomas' death and for betraying the Holy Order of Knights. Oh God in Heaven, William, how I miss Thomas." John's shoulders rose and fell in time with his heaving sobs.

"Brother, none can be certain that the priest played any part in Thomas' death or the slaughter of the brother knights, so how can you think so about killing him?"

"Brother… did you not hear Thomas say that he heard the assassins tell that it was the priest who told them where we were to be found? And when we gained the banqueting hall, the priest was nowhere to be seen… then we spied him in the open cloister of the abbey, clawing through the knights' possessions. What other explanation can there be, other than that he was behind their betrayal and Thomas' death?" Unwilling to continue the debate, William rode to Robert at the top of the hill, from where they spied a small farmstead a short distance from Angers' gates. They resolved to approach the farm to seek overnight shelter and if the farmer was unwilling to provide them shelter, they would camp in the woods rather than risk another night at an inn where their presence may be recorded.

As the brothers approached the track to the farmhouse, William Clay spotted a token carved on a fencepost. It was a symbol for the Holy Order of Knights, albeit inverted. He believed this a good sign and would bring it up with the farmer if necessary. On reaching the farmyard, a voice shouted from the barn demanding that the esquire brothers state their business or leave by the way they had arrived. After ordering his brothers to remain in their saddles, William Clay approached the barn.

The pointed end of a pitchfork emerged from the interior of the barn before William Clay spied the farmer holding it. He offered his hand as a gesture of trust but the farmer declined it, repeating that William should state his business or leave by the same way as he and his companions had arrived. Bowing low, William told the farmer that he and his brothers were weary travellers looking for shelter before curfew set in. He was surprised to hear that there was no curfew around Angers, and William and his brothers were free to leave the farmer's land to seek accommodation elsewhere. Desperate not to spend another night at an inn, William said to the farmer that he would pay well for food and a night's shelter in his barn. The farmer asked William why, if he was able to pay well, was he not seeking accommodation in an inn. William's reply was that he expected to pay less for barn accommodation. The farmer laughed but insisted that accommodating the brothers was not possible. He bade them farewell and wished them a good onward journey. Turning to leave, William asked the farmer about the moss-covered symbol carved into the fencepost. The farmer denied all knowledge of its existence. William offered to point it out to him, adding that he and his brothers were faithful servants of the same Holy Order of Knights betokened by the symbol on the post, and asked him how it had managed to get itself carved, albeit inverted, on his fencepost. At the mention of the Holy Order of Knights, the farmer's attitude changed. He asked the brothers for proof of what they claimed, which they provided by way of hand signs, to which the farmer responded with complementary signals. With a beckoning hand, the farmer hurried the esquire brothers inside the barn, where he told them to unsaddle their horses.

"Forgive my earlier behaviour, my brothers, it is best to be cautious these days," said the farmer. "It is hard to know who you can trust. There are rumours that the King means to destroy the Holy Order of Knights by branding them and their associates as plunderers, murderers and sodomites."

"We have had that notorious slander made on us, good farmer."

"My name is Bertan Defray and I have long been a supporter of the Holy Order of Knights, as many are in these parts; but be careful telling people of your devotion to them as Count Colbert has spies everywhere and is ever on the lookout for ways to please his King." The esquire brothers introduced themselves but did not tell the farmer of the slaughter at Poitiers Castle nor anything of their flight from France. The farmer, to the credit of common sense, did not ask any questions other than those necessary to accommodate the esquire brothers for the night.

★

On their arrival at the branch in the road where the esquire brothers and Sir Michael de Gel and his entourage had gone their separate ways, the pursuing King's Knights similarly divided their forces according to the number of hoof prints traced on the ground. They divined that those who'd taken the right-hand fork were riding with the fugitive knight of the Holy Order, while the left-hand fork had been taken by three riders who were likely, according to their information, to be of little consequence but needed to be brought to justice all the same. Thus the esquire brothers had five of the King's Knights set upon pursuing them and Sir Michael and his group, ten. Being experienced in the pursuit of fugitives and riding fine horses, the King's Knights travelled faster than the esquire brothers. Before the day was out, the King's Knights came to the inn in the woods where the brothers had spent the previous night. Questioning the innkeeper, they learned that the brothers were bound for St Malo via Angers and were taking the Laval road to avoid the outlaw-ridden forests on the Angers to Rennes road. The King's Knights made up some miles on the esquire brothers before setting their camp for the night; this despite two of the knights wanting to take a bed at the inn in the woods, believing they would catch up with the esquire brothers long before they reached Laval, let alone Rennes.

★

That evening, farmer Defray's wife prepared a substantial meal for the esquire brothers, even wrapping up some food in kitchen cloths for them to take with them on their onward journey. Farm work having early morning starts, Farmer Defray bade goodnight to his guests before nine o'clock, saying that they would be provided with a good breakfast before their departure.

After the farmer left the barn, the esquire brothers made up beds of straw and covered themselves with their monk's cloaks as bedclothes. Though they were tired, the brothers felt they needed to air the differences that were growing between them for the sake of their survival in this foreign land as well as their family harmony. The pitch darkness of the barn emboldened them to speak honestly. John began by saying that he was sorry for the way he had behaved over the past days and that in future, he would desist from saying anything that would create conflict with them. Robert rebuked John, stating that he would rather hear hard truths than soft words. William begged his brothers not to pursue their discussion as he believed it could lead nowhere good.

"Then, brother, answer me this: what can we debate if we cannot discuss that which gives cause to divide us? What then shall we talk about, eh, brothers?" asked Robert in a sarcastic voice. As no answer came, Robert continued. "Then let me suggest a topic for discussion, a topic that causes constant disturbances between us. It seems to me that a good many of our disputes stem from religion and the depth of our piety. So let that be the topic of our discussion. Let us talk about God, and the Church… and how it cares more for cosying up to the rich than caring for the bodies and souls of the poor and the needy. I freely admit that my religious devotion has never been as great or as strong as either of yours, but that is because I see little good in the Church, brothers, little good!"

"Please, Robert, do not attack the Church again, I beg you."

"Why not? Why not, big brother, why can I not attack the Church? I am sure that the Church is big enough to take care of itself and does not need you to defend it, so why cannot I criticise it, for criticism it deserves… and more besides!"

"If we do indeed hold this discussion tonight, then you must promise that we will never again talk of it."

"I cannot make you such a promise, brother, for the more I learn of the wicked ways of the Church, the more I feel compelled to speak out against it."

"Only speak? Not act, little brother? Have you not acted against the Church already?"

"What does John mean, brother Robert?"

"Very well, William, as you have asked, so I will tell you." Robert paused to gather himself before continuing. "There were those in the Holy Order of Knights who were strongly opposed to the Church. They believed the Church to be familiars of the aristocracy, helping them to subjugate the ordinary people and thereby attain secular power. Even worse, according to some knights, the Church—"

"Cease, brother! Cease! No more! Speak no more talk against the Church!"

"No, brother, I will never yield in my condemnation of the Church… never!"

"Let him continue, brother William. Let us see who we ride with."

"In the darkness of this barn, Satan has taken hold of my brother's tongue."

"You are wrong, William, you are wrong! I am no servant of Satan and, in all honesty, I truly believe that neither Satan nor God exists."

"From where do you get these distorted thoughts?"

"You call them distorted, I call them enlightened. There are… there were those in the Holy Order of Knights who taught of the heavens and the stars in the sky; the grandeur of nature, alchemy and experiments into transmutation, the construction of devices and so on, and in doing so attracted the wrath of the Church. Why does the Church act in such a way? Why does it suppress human endeavour in the way it does? Why does it not allow study into things that they should hold no sway over?"

"But little brother, the Church does much good; does it not, William?"

"It does indeed, John. Robert, tell me true. Did Thomas also hold such views as you?"

"He did. Together we attended those classes taught by the knights the Church branded as heretics. Tell me, brothers, how is it heresy to investigate sciences or natural philosophy, or even practise it? Where is the harm? The Church has denied mankind the right to progress as it should for hundreds of years. It holds all of mankind back to suit its own purposes so that men do not see the Church or creation for what they are."

"And what is creation, dear brother? Tell me… tell us both, what is creation, oh enlightened one?" mocked John.

"If you ask me the question in that way you are not fit in your mind to receive the truth of the answer."

"Hmmm, that sounds like a religious argument to me," laughed John.

Furious with his brother's mocking of him, Robert grunted, "Good night," turned his back on his brothers and all struggled to find sleep.

When the farmer entered the barn to begin his daily chores, the brothers were still asleep. *They're not farmers, after all,* he thought, and let them continue their slumbers. *For a couple more hours.*

★

The pursuing King's Knights, however, did not have a lie-in that morning and were fast closing in on the esquire brothers. Following the horses' tracks in the frost hardened earth was not easy, but what was clear to the knights was that they were not far behind their quarry. They were under orders to bring whoever they found, whether they be knight, soldier or serf, to the abbey at Orléans to receive the King's justice, where their punishments would follow the methods handed down, in writing, by King Philip himself.

★

At eight o'clock, Farmer Defray made sufficient noise in the barn to wake the esquire brothers from their black dreamless sleep. As promised, he provided them a hearty breakfast and while they ate, Farmer Defray checked over their horses to make sure they were sound in constitution. During their farewell conversation with Farmer Defray, the esquire brothers mentioned the rumours they'd heard of outlaws roaming on the road between Angers and Rennes and so they thought that they might take the Laval road. From this, Farmer Defray deduced that the brothers were probably making for either Saint-Brieuc, Brest, St Malo or the Cherbourg Peninsula. He replied that there were indeed, as far as he knew, "outlaws marauding on the Rennes road, but as they are against the King, and so likely to be for the Holy Order of Knights, they might afford you safe passage, or, most likely at least, leave you unmolested to go about your business… probably." This equivocal reply left the esquire brothers uncertain as to which of the roads they should take. During their ride to the city gate at Rennes,

Robert suggested they toss a coin for which road to take to St Malo. John commented that Robert's method was in keeping with his anti-Church, non-Christian beliefs. William intervened to prevent another argument and determined, as the eldest brother, that they should take the direct route to St Malo; they would therefore travel via the Rennes road and miss the Laval detour. Passing into the city of Angers, the brothers rode in single-file silence through its streets, trying hard to blend in and not attract the least bit of attention.

ROADS TO RENNES

During the mid-afternoon, the King's Knights arrived at the farm where the esquire brothers had stayed the previous night. They were closing in on their quarry.

Farmer Defray was away working in his fields when, lifting his head, he spied the knights trotting down the dirt track leading to the farmhouse. Sensing danger from the knights' arrival only a few hours after the departure of the esquire brothers, Farmer Defray made his way as speedily as he could to intercept the knights before they dismounted. Arriving in the small courtyard between the farmhouse and the barn, he found the knights alighted from their mounts and speaking with his wife. She had already told them of their guests from the previous day but pleaded ignorance as to where they were journeying to. The knights didn't believe her and told her so. Farmer Defray told the knights that it was he, and only he, who had had dealings with the strangers because he didn't trust them.

"I didn't introduce the men to my wife and children for fear of them committing some wrong against my dear family," stuttered Farmer Defray.

"But you trusted these men enough to give up your barn to them."

"Aye, my Lord Knight, I did, and I would do it again for what they paid me." Farmer Defray showed the knights the money the esquire brothers had paid him.

"Is that money stolen from the abbey?" asked Sir Gifford le Grande.

"I care not about a pittance of money, Sir Gifford. We are not here to persecute peasant farmers; we are charged by the King to locate those that perpetrated the slaughter at Poitiers Castle and take them to the abbey at Orléans to receive His Majesty's justice." Farmer Defray paled at hearing news of a slaughter at Poitiers Castle but doubted the esquire brothers could've had anything to do with it as they were un-warrior like, in his opinion. "You have heard then of the slaughter of the Holy Order of Knights at Poitiers Castle, farmer?" enquired Sir Aldred Benz, to trick Farmer Defray into admitting he knew more than he was saying.

"No, my Lord Knight, not until you mentioned it just now."

"Then know this, farmer, the men who you gave shelter to last night were party to the slaughter of the Holy Order of Knights and many more besides. They drugged their victims' wine and slit their throats while they were unconscious. Over a hundred throats did they slit in all, famer." Farmer Defray was of a mind that the esquire brothers didn't have anything to do with any slaughter, but his wife pleaded with him to tell the King's Knights all that he knew of the murderous esquire brothers so they could capture them and drag them kicking and screaming for God's mercy to the abbey at Orléans to receive the King's justice.

"I will tell you all I know, my Lord Knight, though it is not much because they were cautious men and told me but nearly naught of their intentions and plans."

"Before you speak, farmer, I warn you that if you deceive me I will return and put you and your family to the sword and raze your farm to dust. Now speak and be of truthful mind when recounting your tale, knowing that God will never forgive you if your testimony protects those who the King has branded plunderers, murderers and sodomites." At this declaration, the farmer's wife covered her children's ears and dragged them into the sanctuary of the farmhouse. *More of the King's lies*, thought Farmer Defray.

"The men told me that they were servants of the Holy Order of Knights and – forgive me in this, my Lord Knight –as many in these parts, including myself, having no quarrel with the Order I decided to give the men shelter for the night in my barn. I cannot lie, the money was a big inducement as the land yields little enough to support a family. They said little during their stay and we only really spoke this morning, just before they left."

"And at what time did they leave?"

"It was light an hour and some, so I would say three hours before midday, my Lord Knight."

"Carry on with your tale."

"They asked me about rumours concerning marauding outlaws infesting the road between Angers and Rennes. I told them that I had heard such rumours and believed them to be true. They considered the Laval road, which led me to believe they are heading beyond Rennes for either Saint-Brieuc, Brest, St Malo or the Cherbourg Peninsula."

"What makes you believe they are travelling beyond Rennes?" asked Sir Aldred Benz, leader of this company of King's Knights, though he believed he already knew the esquire brothers' destination was St Malo from the innkeeper; though after listening to Farmer Defray, Sir Aldred had doubts about the information he'd received. *These men might be leading everybody a merry dance about where they're headed to,* he thought.

"Well, my Lord Knight, I actually don't know, now that you mention it. I just got the feeling that they were heading beyond Rennes; they never said as much; it was just a feeling I had at the time. I don't want to incur your wrath, my Lord, but that was the feeling I had and so I mention it lest you later believe I deceived you."

"Show me where they slept," demanded Sir Aldred. Farmer Defray took the knight into the barn and pointed to the spot where the esquire brothers had slept the previous evening.

Sir Aldred searched the area but found nothing useful to him in his pursuit of the fugitives. The King's Knights, eager to be on their way to close the distance between them and their quarry, left Farmer Defray's farm at a gallop.

Arriving at the gate of Angers, Sir Aldred asked the gate-keeper if he'd seen any strangers entering the town that morning. Not being a lackey or a kingsman, he replied that it was possible, as 'many strangers come and go through this gate at almost every hour of every day and night, my Lord Knight.' Sir Aldred wanted to run the insolent dog through but, aware of the presence of archers on the ramparts, he brushed the gate-keeper aside with his horse and entered the town, ignoring the gate-keeper's angry shouts for payment of a gold piece for mounted entry.

★

Just beyond the reaches of Angers' northern perimeter walls, the esquire brothers took the Rennes road. John Clay asked his older brother if he was sure about what he was doing in taking the outlaw-infested road. He replied that he was not at all sure about the road they were about to embark on but one thing he was certain of was that they, in all likelihood, were probably being pursued and should pick up the pace to gain Rennes as quickly as possible.

★

The passage of the King's Knights through Angers was halted time and time again by carts spilling over, massive groups of children playing in the foul-smelling streets, soldiers and guards of the city carrying out manoeuvres, processions of priests, congregations marching in slow time, practising for saints' days, funerals, local dignitaries offering their hospitality, and even a troupe of travelling entertainers in the city centre stalled the knights' progress. The King's Knights were perpetually on the brink of using their mounts to dash down everything in their path, but their passage through the city was being shadowed along the roof tops by scores of archers and in their wake followed dozens of local knights armed with lances. Being so outnumbered, the King's Knights bore the delays with tooth-grinding patience. The delays cost the knights more than half a day.

Just beyond the reaches of Angers' northern perimeter walls, the King's Knights stopped and pondered the winding Laval road. Sir Gifford le Grande asked Sir Aldred Benz if he believed what the farmer had told them about their quarries' plans and suggested that they check both the Laval and the Rennes road for tracks. Sir Aldred looked at the knight and asked him, "Pray, Sir Gifford, how would we discern between the tracks on the road? They are many and our quarry only three." Tracking the esquire brothers to Angers had been relatively straightforward but due to the huge volume of horse traffic between Angers and Rennes, tracking their quarry became impossible. The King's Knights had little choice but to trust in what the farmer had told them and so took the Laval road.

★

With the King's Knights having taken the Laval road, the esquire brothers put greater and greater distance between them and their pursuers. The road between Angers and Rennes was one hundred and ten Roman miles and the esquire brothers hoped to complete the journey in three days. During the first day of their journey, the esquire brothers encountered other intrepid souls who, like them, were willing to risk the Rennes road rather than traverse two sides of a triangle by taking the Laval road. During conversations with drivers of slow carts, the esquire brothers learned of the likely spots they'd encounter marauding outlaws and of their demands for tribute in gold for permitting travellers to pass unmolested. Being without gold, or even any good amount of silver, the esquire brothers pondered how they would best deal with the outlaws as they huddled together for warmth during their camp that night.

After a meagre breakfast on the morning of the third day, the esquire brothers mounted their horses and prepared themselves for the likelihood of being taken prisoner by the outlaws and probably held to ransom. It wasn't long before they came across five mounted men blocking the road ahead. They sensed there were more men hiding in the undergrowth. When the esquire brothers got close to the men, their leader raised an open-palmed hand to signal them to stop. William and John Clay obeyed the command but Robert rode on to within a sword's length of the men and introduced himself. The men laughed, saying that Robert was perhaps too brave for his own good, as a dozen men emerged, swords drawn, from the undergrowth. Robert asked if the men would kindly introduce themselves, which they did, and in return Robert introduced his brothers, adding that they were esquires to the Holy Order of Knights. The leader of the outlaws asked Robert if he had mentioned the Holy Order of Knights hoping to gain some advantage, to which he replied that he hoped he would as neither he nor his brothers had gold with which to pay for the privilege of travelling the Rennes road unmolested. The leader of the outlaws regarded Robert with some humour for his sheer cheek.

"Where do you come from?"
"From Angers."

"Do not play games with me, boy, you know well what I mean."

"We are middle England men from near Leamington."

"Try again, boy, and this is your last chance for a straight answer. Where do you come from to be here at this time of year? There is no fair about and the Holy Order of Knights passed south some days ago."

"We come to be here from Poitiers Castle, where the Holy Order of Knights were summoned by King Philip to attend a feast in honour of the engagement of his daughter to King Edward the Second of England."

"You were at Poitiers Castle?" gasped Silas Creek, leader of the outlaws. "Bring Howard Manton forward," he demanded. An unkempt, scruffy cripple was pushed to the front of the knot of outlaws facing off against the esquire brothers. "Tell this Robert Clay what the messenger pigeon carried to Rennes."

"The bird carried a note inside a silver thimble attached to its leg with the King's crest emblazoned on it. I heard from the sheriff's daughter that the note was read by the captain of the King's Guard and then conveyed to his associates in Rennes prison. One of these associates being the Sheriff of Rennes…"

"Get on with it, Manton, or I swear to God in the heavens that I will cut your tongue from your mouth and feed it to you." Howard Manton was unmoved by Silas' threat, knowing that his crippled condition protected him. He continued in the same vein.

"According to the sherriff's daughter, the note told that the Holy Order of Knights was murdered to a man at Poitiers Castle… bar a certain Sir Michael de Gel and some men of the entourage. The note calls for the apprehension of Sir Michael de Gel, soldiers of the Order's guard – about three in number, a serf and three knight's esquires. The note states that King's Knights have set off in pursuit of the fugitives and on their capture they are to be taken to the abbey at Orléans to receive the King's justice in the bishop's court situated there. Of those—"

"So much news... Tell me, Howard Manton, how big was this thimble?" asked Robert, to the amusement of the outlaws and especially so their leader. Howard Manton cast Robert a scowl then returned to the back of the knot of outlaws.

"What have you to say of the happenings at Poitiers Castle, Robert Clay?"

"Being the eldest brother, it is for me to answer your questions, Sir," interjected William Clay.

"Stay your place, William Clay," commanded Silas of the eldest brother. "Robert here has done well so far and I have a liking for him. So I ask you again, Robert Clay, what say you of these deeds at Poitiers Castle?"

"We three brothers are loyal and obedient servants of the Holy Order of Knights and have been so for more than four years. We would no more do them harm than our own mother. The message the bird carried is a lie. The King was behind the slaughter of the Knights of the Holy Order."

Robert recounted the tale of that night in Poitiers Castle to Silas Creek and his men, the tale ending with the murder of his little brother, Thomas, his perfect little brother, who everybody adored and loved. Tears flooded from Robert's eyes at the telling of the tale. His brothers came to his side and held him close, and they sobbed together at their loss. Silas, much moved at this display of raw unmanly emotion, ordered his men to return the men their swords. By this display of collective grief, the esquire brothers rediscovered the love that they felt for one another; a love that lay deep in their souls.

"What are your plans, Clay brothers?"

"We are on the run from the King's justice so we must flee France for our home in England, where we will tell our mother of the loss of the most dear of her sons." Robert flinched at those words being spoken.

"A grim task and one I will not keep you from, but you might consider remaining here with us to enact revenge upon the King's men. It is not an easy life but it is a good life, and far enough away not to be sought by king or sheriff."

"How long do you think that will last?" interrupted Robert. "Once it is known we came this way, you can be sure that the King will mount an assault. I doubt there will be any sanctuary for you and your men in the forests of Rennes. I am sorry if we have ruined your paradise…" All knew Robert's words to be true.

The outlaws and the esquire brothers formed up together and rode to the outlaw encampment.

★

While the esquire brothers were in the company of the outlaws, the King's Knights were making rapid progress along the road to Laval. Throughout the day they passed merchants, pilgrims, lone riders and groups travelling in train. Interrogating each of them, none had any news of the whereabouts of the esquire brothers. Notwithstanding the delay forced on them at Angers, the King's Knights were of a mind that they should have caught up with their quarry by now. When they made camp that evening, Sir Marten Fitzwilliam sought consent to ride on ahead to see if he could overtake the esquire brothers during the night. Sir Aldred asked him why he thought that necessary. Sir Marten replied that if by morning he hadn't overtaken the fugitives, then they must have taken the Rennes road.

Sir Aldred considered that possibility for a moment before replying, "Sir Knight, had we gone by the Rennes road we would have, no doubt, come to engage in battle with the outlaws who occupy the forest through which the Rennes road passes. If indeed the esquires have gone by that road, they will have to overcome those same outlaws and, there being only three of them, I give little for their chances." Sir Marten was about to interrupt Sir Aldred but he held up an open hand to prevent him from doing so. "Their only hope will be that as they are servants of the Holy Order of Knights, they might be allowed to pass on to Rennes without coming to harm. Those same outlaws, however, are sworn enemies of the King and would do battle with us even upon payment of a toll in gold. No, Sir Knight, we must continue on the road to Laval and thence to Rennes." Sir Marten saw the sense in Sir Aldred's answer and swore that he would seek an audience with the King at the earliest opportunity to recommend he send an army to clear the Rennes road of outlaws. In that pledge, the outlaws' days were numbered.

While waiting for sleep to overtake him, Sir Aldred Benz lay pondering Sir Marten's proposal of petitioning the King to clear the Rennes road of outlaws, and believing it would create a good impression on His Majesty, he adopted the scheme as his own. Sir Aldred would do everything in his power to keep Sir Marten from achieving an audience with his King, and would even put him in danger of his life to ensure he never met King Philip again.

★

As the group arrived at the outlaw camp, a young man approached Silas Creek and whispered a message into his ear. Silas looked quizzically at the messenger and asked him if he was sure of his information. The young man nodded. Silas called a council of his outlaw band and invited the esquire brothers to join them because what he had to say concerned them.

"William, John, Robert… I have just been informed that five knights have been set on your trail and are pursuing you."

"How have you come by this information? Who is your informant?" asked William Clay, eager to promote himself as the brother with whom to discuss such matters, rather than his brother Robert.

"Come forward, Lorence Blackstone," ordered Silas, beckoning the informant to join the outlaw council. The young man sat down at the edge of the meeting. "Masters Clay, this is Lorence Blackstone. He is my chief spy in the city of Rennes." This title made Howard Manton sneer with jealousy. How he despised the young man with the body of a god, while he had a body like crooked sticks. "Master Blackstone, tell the council what you discovered in Rennes."

Lorence Blackstone stood to make his statement. He was tall, lean, blonde and muscular with a light beard and uncommonly dark blue eyes. It was easy to understand why somebody like Howard Manton, despite his vastly superior intelligence, would envy somebody like Lorence Blackstone, to whom everything came so easily.

"Certainly," spoke Lorence Blackstone, bowing toward Silas. *How casual he is with our leader, bastard son of a Dane*, thought Howard Manton, grinding his teeth in furious indignation. "Since the arrival of the messenger pigeon concerning the slaughter of the Holy Order of Knights at Poitiers Castle, I have been keeping close to the daughter of the sheriff of Rennes." Lorence gave the council a knowing look, at which they responded with raucous laughter, sexual gestures and jeers. It was clear to all that it was in fact Lorence who'd obtained the information about the slaughter at Poitiers Castle and not Howard Manton. "Several birds have arrived since with messages concerning the fugitives… the latest informing the captain of the King's Guard that three or four of them are making their way to the northern coast and will likely pass through Rennes. He is ordered to double the guard on the city's walls and to stop all travellers who enter Rennes to question them about the fugitives. One bird arrived advising the captain that a band of King's Knights were on the trail of the fugitives and were making their way to Rennes via the Laval road to avoid the 'bandits' who lay in wait for unwary travellers." At this, the outlaw council again dissolved into raucous laughter, pointing at one another and making mock gestures of robbery and surrender of goods. "The captain of the King's Guard at Rennes is ordered that should he apprehend the fugitives, he is to hand them over to the leader of the King's Knights… our old friend, Sir Aldred Benz." At the mention of that name, the outlaw council raised themselves to their feet and rampaged around the campsite waving their swords, threatening death to Sir Aldred and all who rode with him. After the council returned to take their places, Lorence Blackstone ended his report. "A bird arrived this morning with a message saying a corps of knights are making for Rennes from the northwest to cut off any hope the fugitives might have of escape." Lorence Blackstone ended by bowing comedically to the assembly.

"Is that all from you, Lorence?" asked Silas Creek of his chief spy.

"For the report, yes. For the daughter of the sheriff of Rennes? No! I return there tonight to continue my interrogations of her!" Once again raucous laughter and jeering erupted from the outlaw council.

The esquire brothers could not help but notice a strong similarity in manner and appearance between Lorence Blackstone and Thomas. They were two peas from the same pod as far as the brothers could see. The resemblance between the two bold young men brought on remembrances of their perfect little brother, which made them happy and sad at the same time.

Silas adjourned the council of outlaws to speak privately with the esquire brothers. He said that as the captain of the King's Guard at Rennes was alerted to look out for them and reinforcements were arriving from the northwest, and with the certain knowledge that

Sir Aldred Benz and four King's Knights were bearing down on Rennes, there was nothing else for it but for the esquire brothers to remain with him and his outlaws in the forest. He said he would make outlaws of them or not at their choosing. William asked Silas for a moment to speak on the matter with his brothers.

"I am not for remaining with these outlaws," whispered William. "To keep ahead of the news of the happenings at Poitiers Castle, we made our decision to race for St Malo, but we didn't count on messenger pigeons. Curse those winged devils! They have wrecked our plan." William stopped for a moment to consider their position before continuing. "But nobody will know what has transpired between us and the outlaws… everybody will most likely think that we have been taken to be their prisoners; surely we can use this to our advantage while we remain true to our mission to return to England with all haste to inform our mother of Thomas' death."

"Aye, I agree, but we must never tell her of the manner of Thomas' passing; it is too terrible, she will not be able to stand it."

"I'm for staying here," said Robert. "You two can return to England but I am for staying here. But you must tell our mother of the manner of Thomas' passing… she deserves to be told all concerning her youngest's murder." William and John nodded in silent agreement with Robert.

"But Robert, why do you wish to remain here? Your place is at our side. Please, brother, do not stay in this company… I have a deep foreboding of its doom."

"I have a desire to stay and to get to know Lorence Blackstone. He is a man after my own liking and I see Thomas in him."

"As we all do, brother, we all do, but that is no reason to give up your sworn quest."

"Think of our poor mother, Robert, think of her and not of yourself. When she hears the news of Thomas' passing she will want all her sons at her side. If you are not there she will never forgive us, or you." William's words wracked Robert with feelings of guilt.

"You blackmail me, brother? You blackmail me!"

"I speak what the truth is."

"Alright... I will ride with you but as soon as the message is delivered to our mother, I will return here to this band of outlaws."

"You must do as your heart and mind direct."

William placed a big-brotherly hand on Robert's shoulder to comfort him but he pushed it away and went off to talk with Lorence Blackstone. The two young men hit it off straightaway and were soon laughing, carousing and cajoling with one another. Realising Robert's grief at the loss of his brother, and with himself bearing such a likeness in mind and spirit to Thomas, Lorence formed an immediate and strong bond with Robert.

While Robert and Lorence were talking together like kindred spirits, William and John went to tell Silas of their decision to return to England with all haste, saying that they would not be turned from their path. Silas accepted what the brothers said but cautioned them that some plan would be needed to get them through Rennes, as to gain the St Malo road by any other route would mean a long diversion and, most likely, their capture.

After devising a plan to get the esquire brothers through Rennes and onto the St Malo road, Silas reconvened the council of outlaws. Silas announced the intention of the esquire brothers to return to England with all possible haste to carry the news of Thomas' death to their mother, adding that he believed it was their duty to do so. The outlaw leader chose his words carefully so as not to incite revolt within the outlaw council ranks, but each of them, with thoughts of their own mothers in mind, could only think of the esquire brothers having to stand in front of their poor mother and explain what had happened to her youngest son, and so they agreed with Silas that the esquire brothers should be allowed to go freely about their business. The outlaws were told of the plan to get the esquire brothers through Rennes and thence onto the St Malo road. Silas said the plan was simple yet daring, and that a large part of it relied on Lorence Blackstone's ability to inflame the passions of the city guards. Lorence's ears pricked up, eager to learn how his part in the scheme was going to save the day. *It always seems to be me that has to save the day*, thought Lorence, with smug, self-satisfied thoughts of glory-to-come written all over his face. His look was easily interpreted by Howard Manton, who rarely took his eyes off his object of hate, loathing and jealousy. Manton's mind turned to scheming on how he could get rid of Lorence Blackstone once and for all. He knew that if anything happened to Master Blackstone, the outlaws, especially Silas, would suspect his hand in it and then that would be the end of him, unless he had the perfect alibi.

Needing to be within Rennes' city walls well ahead of his outlaw brothers, Lorence Blackstone presented himself to the soldiers guarding the gate on the Angers to Rennes road. He was surprised to find that even in the short time since his departure to meet with the band of outlaws, the guard had increased considerably and was being very thorough in its examination of everybody entering the city, even with those known to it personally. Lorence waited in line for his turn to be admitted. When he got to the front of the queue he was asked where he'd been and what his business was in Rennes. Lorence replied, in his usual off-hand, casual way, that he'd been off visiting farmers to secure work for the spring and that his business in Rennes was to serve wine to patrons at the tavern belonging to the sheriff. One of the guards whispered something into the ear of the soldier dealing with Lorence, at which both men smiled, and Lorence's hand was marked with a red dye to show he'd been properly admitted into the city.

Once inside Rennes, Lorence entered the nearest guard tower and stole up a flight of stone stairs to the battlements atop the city walls to look for a suitable place to hide until his outlaw brothers showed up. As he exited out of the door beside the defensive crenulations, Lorence bundled into a guard, knocking him over. The guard was at first surprised and then angry until he saw who it was that had run into him.

"You hiding from somebody, young Lorence?"

"Aye, I am that, brother, please do not give me away."

"Who are you hiding from then?" asked the guard with a smile.

"Oh, you know…" replied Lorence with a cheeky grin.

"Got yourself into some trouble, I dare say. Woman trouble if I know you, young sir," laughed the guard. "Don't worry, she won't hear anything from my lips. I'll be at the tavern later tonight so perhaps you can show me your gratitude with a generous measure of wine?"

"Certainly, good soldier… you shall receive double what you pay for and cheese and bread for your silence." The guard, being pleased with the bargain he'd struck, helped Lorence hide away until the 'danger' had passed.

One hour after the light of day had vanished, the soldiers on guard duty atop the battlements over the city gate on the Angers to Rennes road noticed some lights emerging from the woods, about half a Roman mile from the city's walls. They looked like those of a merchant caravan, causing the guards on the battlements to shout down to those at the gate to prepare to receive a contingent of visitors. On hearing this, Lorence emerged from his hiding place and asked what was going on. The guard pointed toward the lights, saying he thought they were from a caravan of merchants. Lorence peered into the darkness and said that they looked like fireflies flitting in and out of the woods and asked the guard why he thought the lights weren't on the road itself. The guard said that he did not know why the lights weren't on the road itself, to which Lorence suggested that the lights might not be the lights of a caravan of merchants at all, and that the soldiers should be on their guard. The guard shouted to his comrades on the battlements and to those guarding the gate that the lights might not be the lights of a merchant caravan and so they should all be on their guard.

The walking line of fiery lights stopped one hundred paces from Rennes' city walls and in their light the soldiers could see wood being brought forward and neatly stacked in a conical pile. Once complete, the pile was set alight and the soldiers guarding the battlements could see that the caravan was not of merchants but of shabbily dressed vagabonds. Cries came from the soldiers for the vagabonds to disperse as they wouldn't be allowed into the city during the hours of darkness. At the sounding of a horn, the vagabonds turned their backs on the city walls, raised their tunics, bared their backsides and shouted to the soldiers that they should come with their tongues to lick their arses. The soldiers were furious at this barefaced disregard for them and their authority and in return shouted lewd remarks at the vagabonds. This shouting match between the vagabonds and the soldiers continued for several minutes. At a second horn sound, the vagabonds removed their tunics altogether and, turning to face the soldiers, waved their penises at them. The infuriated soldiers doubled the volume and quantity of their abuse at the vagabonds. The vagabonds then made hip-thrusting gestures toward the soldiers while yelling that this was the way they enjoyed their wives, sisters and mothers while they were on duty. At that provocation, Lorence stood atop the crenulations of the battlements urging the soldiers to pursue and cut down the vagabonds for the insults they had made at their loved ones.

"You cannot permit these vagabonds to go unpunished for the words and gestures they have made toward the good, virtuous sisters and mothers of Rennes." The soldiers, at first, were reluctant to leave their posts until one of them saw a vagabond holding an effigy of a woman, which looked remarkably like his sister and who appeared to be giving him pleasure with her mouth. The city gate flew open and the soldiers guarding it made to chase down the naked vagabonds but, there being few of them, they stopped short, stood their ground and shouted insults at the vagabonds about their mothers. This situation being insufficient for the outlaws' plans to succeed, Lorence urged the soldiers on the battlements to run the vagabonds down, promising that he himself, personally, would guard the city gate and admit nobody until they returned with the vagabonds in chains.

A contingent of sword-wielding soldiers swarmed out of the city gate and onto the Angers to Rennes road, took up position opposite the vagabonds and made ready in battle formation to attack them. Meanwhile, Lorence beckoned three shadows wearing monks' cowls and riding scabby but sturdy ponies to enter through the city gate. Lorence was curious to know what had happened to the esquire brothers' fine knights' steeds. William replied that it was all part of Silas' plan. He had convinced the esquire brothers that they could not travel in monks' cowls while riding such fine steeds and so 'swapped' them for three more suitable mounts. Lorence shook his head, laughed and told the esquire brothers to hold out their hands, which he daubed with red dye. "Now you will be able to pass safely through Rennes unmolested. Take the road through the centre of the city and keep going until you reach the St Malo gate. Once arrived, show the guards there your red hands and they will let you pass. They may ask you to remain until daylight, but tell them that you have a painful duty to perform and it cannot wait. Tell them that the fourth cowl belonged to one of your brothers who fell at the hands of a Godless traitor, and news of his passing must reach St Malo before the week is out." The esquire brothers knew they could be convincing in the telling of this tale, there being some truth in their deception.

As the soldiers formed up to attack the vagabonds, from the woods emerged a cavalry charge of mounted outlaws, swords pointed in their direction. The soldiers, being poorly paid and cowardly, ran back to the city gate to taunting and jeering from the vagabonds. In their hurry to reach safety, many of the soldiers dropped their weapons and were ordered to retrieve them by the captain of the King's Guard. The cowardly soldiers took blazing torches when retrieving their weapons as though to ward off the evil spirits of the woods, claiming their rapid retreat was due to ghost riders rather than the outlaws they knew the horsemen to be. While the soldiers were retrieving their weapons, the captain of the King's Guard thanked Lorence Blackstone for manning the city gate alone, saying it was a pity that there weren't more men like him around. This praise was spoken within earshot of the esquire brothers, who again thought of the likeness in character between Lorence Blackstone and Thomas.

After receiving the gratitude of the captain of the King's Guard, Lorence excused himself from his company, saying that duty called him to attend the tavern owned by the sheriff of Rennes, where he would serve food and wine to road-worn weary travellers and comfort their chaste daughters. The captain of the King's Guard smiled after Lorence, saying that he wished he had a son like him. The esquire brothers could not believe what they were hearing, except perhaps Robert, who recognised Thomas in Lorence's manner.

Lorence Blackstone beckoned the esquire brothers to follow him. Once out of earshot of the captain of the King's Guard, Lorence wished them all good luck then stepped to one side with Robert Clay to have a few final words with him.

"I call you brother, Robert Clay."

"And I you, Lorence Blackstone. May we meet again in this life."

"I swear it shall be so, brother."

"And I also, brother."

"I bid you safe journey."

"God speed you, brother." The two men hugged and then Lorence watched as his brother's back disappeared into the flickering lamp-lit shadows of Rennes' rough streets.

★

As Lorence made his way to his job at the tavern he spied Howard Manton's form foot-dragging its way a short distance ahead of him. He spied the cripple entering a house he knew to be that of an informant to the captain of the King's Guard and emerge minutes later with a pouch in his hand. Lorence instantly recognised the signs that treachery must have gone on in the house and understood that his time in Rennes had come to an end. He was sad at that thought but happy thinking of the new adventures that no doubt lay in the future path of his charmed life.

Lorence Blackstone stalked Howard Manton beyond the city gate, catching him up as he entered the forest. Manton was surprised to see Lorence and asked him why he wasn't at his work in the tavern. Lorence replied that the sheriff's daughter, being visited by the curse of Eve, was of no use to him that night and so he had taken it into his head to reward himself for his earlier bravery with a night off from his duties at the tavern of the sheriff of Rennes. Howard Manton was no fool and quickly guessed that his treachery was somehow exposed. He then made pleasant – suspiciously pleasant – conversation with Lorence as they walked along together under the cover of the trees in the darkness of the forest. Slowly, very slowly and very carefully, Manton gripped his right hand tight around the handle of the dagger hidden beneath his tunic. With one swift movement he thrust the dagger at Lorence Blackstone's heart, but Lorence was prepared for this move and blocked Manton's thrust with an iron-studded leather armguard. Manton, knowing he was no match in a fight with physically perfect Blackstone, threw himself to the frozen floor of the forest, begging Lorence for mercy. He claimed that he was being blackmailed and that his mother and sister were under threat of death if he refused to spy on the outlaws and report on them to the captain of the King's Guard. Lorence stooped, put a brotherly arm around Howard Manton's shoulders and raised him to his feet. Manton thanked Lorence for his godly mercy and for his kindness and understanding of a wretched sinner. As the final word left Manton's lips, Lorence, pulling him close, stabbed him through his heart while whispering into his ear, "Liar... Judas... Traitor! Die!"

★

The esquire brothers rode through Rennes until they came to the St Malo gate. As they approached it a guard challenged them in a brusque manner, for which, upon noticing the monks' cowls of the riders, he immediately begged their forgiveness, claiming that he hadn't recognised the holy brothers' garb. William admonished the soldier, telling him that he should not care about the garb of people in his dealings with them and, while quoting from memory an appropriate passage from the Bible, made the sign of the cross over the soldier, who then crossed himself and ordered those manning the gate to open it for the holy brothers to pass through. On passing through the St Malo gate, the guards wished the brothers well on their journey. Robert turned in his saddle and made the sign of the cross over the guards, who thanked him for his blessing. Taking to the St Malo road, the last leg of the brothers' journey through France, Robert thought, *The power God's representatives have over the ordinary people is truly remarkable. I wonder, though, if it is borne out of love of Him, or fear?*

"Brother, did you just commit a sin back there?" asked Robert of William. John, seeing the jest, joined in.

"I believe he did, brother Robert, I do believe he did. Though I am sure the Lord will forgive him this one time as he sinned out of necessity."

"I do not believe any sin was committed, though I am pleased to know that you are guarding my eternal—"

"Really, brother? You really believe you did not commit the sin of lying, as well as that of impersonating a member of the clergy, at the walls of Rennes?"

"I'm not sure that impersonating a member of the clergy is a sin, exactly, as it's not one of the commandments; nor, unless I'm mistaken, is it mentioned anywhere in the Bible… but William's the expert, so he should know. If it is indeed a sin then we are all guilty."

"If it's not there then it is an error of omission. How shocking to impersonate a member of the clergy and, if that wasn't bad enough, then to go about blessing people and… and… accepting their cowering and grovelling in return. I shudder to wonder what our mother would think of it all."

"I believe that you too impersonated a member of the clergy, Robert!" spoke John, feigning shock.

"I did not. I was merely wearing a cowl in the style of a clergyman."

"But Robert, dear brother," said John mockingly, "you yourself stole the cowls from an abbey, so it's not merely wearing a cowl in the style of a clergyman if it was formerly a clergyman's cowl; therefore you were, to all intents and purposes, impersonating a member of the clergy… just as was our brother William here." John and Robert laughed loud at their game but William was not amused.

"You behave in jest of what we have done? In fighting for our liberty… our lives… we have had to stoop low, and I for one will be begging for the Lord God's forgiveness for the rest of my life."

"William, dear brother, if that is the worst thing you do in your life then your admission through St Peter's gates is assured when your time comes." John and Robert laughed again and whistled to chase the Devil from their road north.

★

As the esquire brothers were making good ground on the fifty Roman miles to St Malo, the King's Knights were nearing Rennes. Their westerly passage had been dogged by one incident after another, the most recent being a fall suffered by Sir Henry Fitzherbert in which he broke an arm so badly that all thought he would lose it. Binding the broken arm in a crude splint, Sir Aldred spurred his remaining party onward after charging Sir Robinet de Guillen with the responsibility of accompanying Sir Henry to Rennes. Sir Robinet was happy to escort Sir Henry on a slow ride to Rennes as he had a certain feeling that Sir Aldred would not succeed in his quest to capture the esquire brothers, and he didn't want to be tainted by failure.

It was mid-afternoon before Sir Aldred and his remaining knights reached Rennes. On arrival they sought out the captain of the King's Guard. Still reeling from the discovery that Lorence Blackstone was an outlaw, the captain of the King's Guard hoped Sir Aldred would quickly pass through Rennes without discovering the sorry tale of the previous day's debacle. But Sir Aldred had his own people inside the city's walls and they informed him of the diversion put on by the outlaws of Rennes Forest, through which, it was rumoured, was gained the passage of the very people the captain of the King's Guard was charged with looking out for. Sir Aldred immediately convened a court of inquiry to establish whether the esquire brothers had passed through Rennes and, if so, what head start they had on the road to St Malo.

The court of inquiry provided Sir Aldred with information concerning the outlaws of Rennes Forest, among them Lorence Blackstone and a cripple called Howard Manton, but nothing of the passage of the esquire brothers through the city. It was testified by many citizens of Rennes that they'd long had their suspicions about the handsome young Lorence Blackstone, which they had not; they simply wanted the opportunity of replacing the captain of the King's Guard after he, inevitably, must be jailed for failing in his duty to his King. When Henry Manton's dead body was brought into the yard outside the court of inquiry it became clear to Sir Aldred that he was dealing with people every bit as ruthless and merciless as himself.

Weeping in a dank cell, the captain of the King's Guard sat contemplating his fate. He envisioned his own execution and it made him retch. People he had thought of as being loyal to him had embellished the 'facts' of the Angers road debacle in order to sink him and win favour with Sir Aldred. When his cell door was flung open, the captain was surprised to see Sir Aldred Benz filling its frame instead of the executioner, Reynard Abel. "Come, follow me," ordered Sir Aldred, who led the captain to his old quarters.

"Sit!" ordered the knight, pointing to an uncomfortable hall seat designed so sitters knew they wouldn't be sat for very long, "What shall I do with you?"

"Please, Sir Knight, have mercy on me. I was foolish to trust others to do their duty. I should have—"

"Silence!" screamed Sir Aldred, spraying spittle over the captain. "Tell me, Monsieur Daniel le Roche, Captain of the King's Guard, how can you expect to run a city the size of Rennes if you do everything yourself?"

"My Lord Knight, it is impossible to do all such work by one's own hand alone."

"Yes, Monsieur le Roche, it is impossible," agreed Sir Aldred. "That is why we must have others do our work for us. Their failings are our failings and they must be punished for their failings, as must you… but tell me, Monsieur le Roche, what did you think of the way they turned on you like a pack of dogs?"

"I was… shocked, my Lord Knight. I have always been good and fair in all of my dealings with them."

"You might believe yourself to be a good and fair captain… you might want your people to love you as a good and fair captain… but that is not what they expect from a man in your position. People despise goodness in their leaders, likening such to that of a weakling, and people despise weak leaders. Do you see your mistake?"

"I do, my Lord Knight, I truly do."

"Good. Then what are you going to do about it?"

"My Lord Knight?"

"Monsieur le Roche, I have a question for you: is it better to be loved or feared?"

"Until today I would have replied that it is better to be loved than feared, Sir Knight, but now I am not so sure…"

"You know the truth of the answer… reach inside yourself to find it."

"Please, my Lord Knight, put me out of my misery, tell me what I must do to be right in my thoughts."

"Let me ask you, Monsieur le Roche, am I loved or am I feared? You must answer truthfully or you will die." Taking his courage in both hands, the captain of the King's guard answered the Knight's question truthfully.

"In truth, Sir Knight, you are a man to be feared… indeed you are greatly feared."

"Is fear alone sufficient to hold men, to control their hearts, thoughts and deeds, and to keep them as loyal to you as your favourite dog who lays nightly at your feet and would sacrifice himself to save your life?"

"Yes... no... the answer is no, my Lord Knight, the answer I give you is no; fear alone is not enough to keep men loyal."

"Why, Captain of the King's Guard?"

"Because, Sir Knight, with fear comes hatred and if men hate you they will not fight for you... they might even fight against you."

"So, Monsieur le Roche, what is the answer? If men don't fear you they will perceive you as a weakling and betray you for lack of fear. How can you strike fear into hearts and yet have men remain loyal to you on surrender of their lives?"

"I know not the answer to that puzzle, Sir Knight."

"The answer, Monsieur le Roche, is love... your men must love you. Too much love and they will think you weak... as you witnessed in the inquiry... none stood by your side. Too much fear and they will hate you and will take any opportunity to overthrow you. Men must feel that you have love for them and go about their duties in that certain knowledge."

"Sir Knight, how can I strike a balance between fear, hate, love and loyalty?"

"Monsieur le Roche, what shall I now do with you?"

"My Lord Knight, I am your loyal servant and you would do no better than to let me prove it to you."

"How so?"

"By giving me another chance, Sir Knight, by giving me a chance so I can prove to you that I can be your man in Rennes."

"I have many men in Rennes, so what do I need you for? If I gave you another chance would you think me weak?"

"No, my Lord Knight, I would think you strong. Only somebody strong could show such mercy by giving somebody like me another chance."

"But to go against the will of the people will cause them to hate me, will it not?"

"No, Sir Knight, no it will not. Let me show you, Sir Knight, let me prove it to you."

"How will you show me, Monsieur le Roche? Tell me clearly, how will you prove it to me?"

"I will hold an inquiry and root out those who failed to execute their duties. I will find them guilty and I will punish them severely. This will make the people fear me. I will reward by promotion those who did not fail in their duties and they will love me. Those who fear me will also want my love and they will do their duties well in the future."

"Good, Monsieur le Roche, very good, you have taken the lesson well. But understand this also, Captain of the King's Guard: you owe me your life and you owe me your devotion and your love. If I find you lacking in either of these, I will take the life that you owe me from you. I will have you hung by your neck at the end of a rope… you will be cut down before you draw your last breath for your belly to be slit open and your entrails burned before your eyes… you will be quartered, having your legs and arms tied to four horses and then stampeded. Your four parts will be fed over four days to the pigs in the streets of Rennes so all can bear witness to my wrath." The captain of the King's guard visibly paled over the fate that could await him.

"Sir Knight, I am ready to be the most loyal and most devoted of your servants."

"What of the outlaw who tricked you? This Lorence Blackstock?"

"Blackstone, my Lord Knight, Lorence Blackstone." Being corrected in this way irritated Sir Aldred, which Daniel le Roche took note of, never to repeat.

"He made a fool of you and you rewarded him. You must bring him to justice without delay so all can witness the price to be paid for being an outlaw. The people of Rennes will love you for this."

"I will take it as my mission, my Lord Knight."

"If you fail in your mission, it will mean that your life will be forfeit for lack of devotion and love for me," said Sir Aldred, smiling.

"I will not fail you, my Lord Knight."

"It is not I who you will be failing, Monsieur le Roche… it is your family that you will be failing."

This threat was absorbed with as little fear painted on the face of the captain of the King's Guard as he could muster. '*You must never show fear even though you might feel it right to the depths of your soul,*' the Captain recalled his father once saying to him.

"You are hereby reinstated to the post of captain of the King's Guard. In your inquiry, be ruthless in your vengeance of those who betrayed you and be generous in your rewards to those you seek the loyalty of. There is only one more matter to discuss. The men I seek, the plunderers, murders and sodomites… it is unclear what has become of them. I am certain that they did not travel the Laval road, therefore they must have travelled by the Angers road. I believe they passed through the Angers gate in the confusion created by the outlaws. Why else would they do as they did?"

"How might this be checked, my Lord?"

"There's no point in checking, Monsieur le Roche; if they'd have been observed inside Rennes' walls we would've known it by now, would we not? No, we must assume they passed through Rennes unnoticed… but if not, then the perimeter roads around Rennes must be searched for signs of their passage. They are riding fine knights' steeds, so the marks of their tracks should be clear to even a blind man. If your men come across anything, you and you alone will decide the quality of what they discover, and if you believe the marks were left by the men I seek, you are to do two things: send riders to alert me of your find, and secondly, have your men follow the tracks to their end. Inform them that those I seek must be taken alive for me to bring them to receive the King's justice in the bishop's court in the abbey at Orléans."

"Bless you for your trust in me, my Lord Knight. My men will find those you seek and will bring them alive for you to take to the bishop's court at Orléans." Daniel le Roche bowed low and kissed the back of Sir Aldred's gloved hand.

Sir Aldred well understood that if the esquire brothers had passed through Rennes the previous day, they would now be far ahead of him on the road to St Malo. He cursed the outlaws of Rennes Forest for the detour he'd been forced to take and repeated Sir Marten's oath by again swearing vengeance on them. He was about to order his knights to mount up and be prepared for a hard ride when snowflakes began falling from a grey sky heavy with much more snow to come. At this turn in the weather, Sir Aldred screamed aloud and slashed with his sword at a hay bale like a man possessed. Daniel le Roche came running to ask Sir Aldred what had fired his rage. Ignoring le Roche's question, Sir Aldred asked him how quickly riders mounted on knights' steeds might reach St Malo. He replied that they could make the journey in forty hours with rests, and a day and a night without. Sir Aldred looked in anger at the captain, yelling that the fugitives he was pursuing had most likely already reached St Malo and would soon, no doubt, be aboard some boat bound for English shores. Daniel le Roche told the knight that he had some fifty messenger pigeons in a nearby loft, by which he could send a message to the captain of the King's Guard at St Malo, ordering him to search for the fugitives and capture and detain them. Sir Aldred asked Daniel le Roche how long it would take a messenger pigeon to reach St Malo.

"An hour… an hour and a half at the most, my Lord Knight." This news brought a huge smile to Sir Aldred's face. He ordered Daniel le Roche to bring him four messenger pigeons, saying that he himself would write the message to the captain of the King's Guard at St Malo, ordering him to search for and detain the men he was pursuing. Daniel le Roche, pleased with himself for being of assistance to his sponsor, bowed low and went with all haste to the lofts and retrieved four St Malo messenger pigeons.

"Daniel le Roche is truly mine," muttered Sir Aldred. "He came forward as he did because he loves me and he will always be loyal to me because he fears me. Perfect."

THE WISE OLD WOMAN
OF THE WOODS

The road from the northern gate of Rennes' city walls to St Malo was good and straight for most of its fifty-something Roman miles. It was widely regarded as one of the best and fastest roads in all of France, so it was said. The esquire brothers, concerned at being pursued by so notorious a knight as Sir Aldred Benz, resolved to complete their journey to St Malo without stopping to make camp. They hoped they might complete their passage in thirty hours of steady riding. With the ponies' gait being so much shorter than the stride of their former mounts, the brothers acknowledged that their journey was not going to be comfortable or speedy.

One Roman mile from Rennes' city walls, disaster struck when one of the ponies broke its leg by slipping on the soft mossy margin between the forest and the road. William Clay cursed their bad luck and, removing his sword from its scabbard, put the pony out of its misery. As the eldest esquire brother was of stouter build than either of the others, it was agreed that he would ride the smaller of the remaining ponies while John and Robert would double up on the larger.

Progress on the journey to St Malo slowed as the brothers constantly checked to see if they were being pursued as they knew they could not outrun knights' steeds and so must be prepared to stop and fight. The first snowflakes appeared a few hours into their journey and with heavy grey skies promising much more snow to come, the brothers needed to devise another plan, as to keep to the one they had meant they'd most likely be overtaken by the pursuing knights well before they reached St Malo.

"What do you say of the road we should take?" asked John of William, putting the burden of decision on the shoulders of the eldest brother. "What shall we do now, brother?"

"I say we keep to the road and look out for some place to wait out the coming snowstorm," suggested Robert.

"Let us hear what William has to say," insisted John.

"What is wrong with my idea?" retorted Robert angrily.

"Dear Robert... dear John... it is clear that you are still in conflict with one another... disunity will destroy us. More than ever, we must remain in harmony in thought and deed; if we argue among ourselves then we are doomed to capture. I know what troubles you both because it troubles me also. The closer we are to England, the closer we are to the ordeal of telling our mother of Thomas' death..."

"His murder, brother, his murder; call it what it is, brother William... his murder," demanded Robert.

"I venture that the look carried by Lorence Blackstone revived thoughts of remembrance of Thomas, and in doing so increased the depth of our loss, making our burden harder for us to bear." John nodded his agreement. "But I beg both of you... put Thomas out of your hearts, put him out of your thoughts, put him out of your prayers, until we reach England. Then... then, my brothers, we will hold a service of remembrance such as will befit him. If we do not reach England we will have failed Thomas, we will have failed our dear mother and we will have failed the Holy Order of

Knights, for it is we who must tell the tale of their slaughter at Poitiers Castle, lest others make lies about it."

"Shall we include in our tale the part the Crow Priest played in the treachery?"

"I will make no mention of it, but you must do as you see fit, Robert."

"I am for telling all, dear William… nothing hidden, brother… nothing hidden. Nowhere for the guilty to hide."

"So be it, Robert. But for now put all such thoughts from your head. The only thoughts we can entertain are thoughts of reaching St Malo and from thence to England's shores."

"So, brother, how shall we now proceed to St Malo?"

"As we were not recognised at Rennes, nobody will know that we travel not by knights' great steeds but by scabby ponies. They will be looking for signs of three large horses travelling the St Malo road."

"But, brother, will not the snow cover all tracks?"

"It will if it continues to fall, but otherwise the tracks we leave will lead our pursuers directly to us. Our ponies are slow and small and scabby, but they are tough and well used to travelling across country as well on roads. We shall therefore make our way off the road while keeping parallel to it. Any tracks we leave will not be visible from the road and we will remain undetected on our journey to St Malo."

"That seems a good plan, brother. My question is, if we travel in this way, how long will it take us before we reach St Malo?"

"In all truth, brother, I do not know. It depends on the terrain and the amount of snow that falls on us and on our path, but it is unlikely to be more than three days… four, perhaps."

"What? No! That is too long! I am still for racing ahead of the news of our flight and—"

"Racing ahead of the news, brother? Racing ahead of the news! Were you not listening at the outlaw camp? We were undone by messenger pigeons and will be so again. News of our flight is well known by now. Our only hope is that our pursuers are unsure of our destination…"

"But what if they have sure knowledge of it, brother?"

"Then to remain free, we may have to reconsider St Malo as our destination."

"If not St Malo, brother, then where? Where shall we go? Which way shall we go?"

"For the sake of our quest, for the sake of our mother and for the sake of all those who have fallen, commit yourselves into my hands. If we should fail then it will be because I failed and not because of anything you have done. I am prepared to accept the burden of this responsibility."

"Let it be so then, brother. Henceforth, you are our dictator and we your uncomplaining, obedient slaves," mocked Robert, laughing.

The esquire brothers pushed their ponies on through the bushes at the roadside and travelled into the forest until they were sure that they could not be easily seen from the road, but not so far that they couldn't keep a watch out for pursuers.

★

With snow now falling ever more heavily and with Daniel le Roche's men out looking for the tracks of three knights' steeds on the city's perimeter roads, and with four messenger pigeons on their way to St Malo and further pairs on their way to Saint Brieuc, Brest and Saint Lô, Sir Aldred was in no hurry to depart the comforts of Rennes. He would now leave it to others to capture the esquire brothers and return them to Rennes so that he might steal the glory of their capture. He had even ordered Daniel le Roche to send riders along the St Malo road instead of making the pursuit that way himself.

The notes Sir Aldred placed in the silver thimbles attached to the pigeons' legs were detailed in their instructions about the pursuit, capture and the return to Rennes of the fugitive esquire brothers. The captains of the King's Guard at all the places the messenger pigeons were sent to were ordered to ride out with all their men to search far and wide for the esquire brothers. Sir Aldred wrote that they would be easily spotted as they were English, well dressed and riding knights' steeds. Whoever found the fugitives must bring them to him personally at Rennes on payment of a substantial reward, which he intended to make by a promissory note and then renege on it. *Who would dare challenge my word of honour and hope to live?* Sir Aldred thought as he basked in warm thoughts of glory and rewards to come, doled out to him by King Philip himself. In order that Daniel le Roche might not be distracted, Sir Aldred rescinded his order for him to apprehend Lorence Blackstone. The outlaw could wait as far as the knight was concerned. *He's not going anywhere so there's no rush to bring him to justice. There are more important things for you to concern yourself with.*

It was the following day before Sir Henry Fitzherbert and Sir Robinet de Guillen rode into Rennes with their horses at a walk. Both were shocked and surprised to be brought before Sir Aldred, who was sitting in front of a roaring fire in the ceremonial chambers of the sheriff of Rennes. They had both expected him to be well on his way to wherever the pursuit of the esquire brothers had taken him. He asked them why their journey to Rennes had taken them so long. He wanted to know what it was, exactly, that had detained them.

"My Lord, was it not you yourself who placed Sir Henry into my care? And, not wanting to be negligent, I was bound in honour to ensure his safe passage. Believe me, my Lord, when I say that we made all the haste that it was possible to make, under the circumstances, to reach Rennes. Sir Henry, please tell our Lord Knight that it is so."

"My Lord, Sir Robinet speaks the truth. Look you… see… he even changed the splint on my arm as riding with the other splint caused me further injury." Sir Henry proffered up his new splint for inspection but Sir Aldred pushed it away. The story the knights told was a lie. The original splint had been changed by a so-called healer; a 'wise woman of the forest' is what the locals called her. Some said she was a witch. They claimed none could approach her with malice in mind, stating it was as though she could read the thoughts of people and would lay in wait to ambush those with dark deeds against her in mind. It was said she could make people disappear at will, leaving nothing but a smudge on the ground where they last stood. Some claimed to have witnessed the disappearances. They stated there was a bright flash and the person would be gone. What could not be denied was that the healing in Sir Henry's arm was nothing short of miraculous. With his new splint, he could even hold a lance without discomfort. Not wanting to be remotely associated with any possible form of witchcraft, the knights thought it best to conjure up an untruth rather than tell what happened and risk being bound over for inquisition.

"This splint that caused you discomfort, are you referring to the splint that I constructed for you, Sir Henry?"

"No, my Lord, no, of course not. I forgot to mention that the splint you made for me was… was…"

"My Lord, I cannot allow Sir Henry to bear the responsibility of what happened to the splint you applied to his arm with such supreme skill. It was while assisting him in dismounting his horse that I accidentally broke the splint by grabbing at it in a vain attempt to prevent him from falling from his saddle. In so doing, the splint shattered, and because it was fabricated so perfectly, I, with my limited ability, was unable to reconstruct it. I beg your forgiveness, my Lord Aldred, for my ham-fistedness."

What a cunning, resourceful and skilful liar Sir Robinet is… typical Belgian. I might yet find good use for him, thought the knight.

"What a most unfortunate occurrence, Sir Knights. Do you concede that the splint of my creation was far superior to that of this pale imitation?" While saying this, Sir Aldred examined the strange-looking splint and marvelled at what substance it was crafted from.

"Of course, my Lord, that goes without saying... I would tear off this arm-debris in an instant had I—"

"No! Leave it be. It is of no significance to our business in apprehending the fugitives."

"How goes the hunt, my Lord?"

"It goes well." The knights looked at one another, wondering what Sir Aldred meant by 'it goes well' as he was sitting in Rennes without his quarry.

"My Lord?"

"They will be delivered to me here in Rennes by those now searching for them from the towns of St Malo, Saint Brieuc, Brest and Saint Lô. I see you are perplexed." The knights made no response. "I will explain. As the snow began to fall heavily I had an inspiration. *Why?* I asked myself. *Why should I go running about the countryside when there are others who can do it for me?* So, I sent messenger pigeons to all the towns in the region ordering their captains of the King's Guard to mount a search for the fugitives. I gave them a description of the felons with strict orders that they are not to be harmed and that they are to be brought forthwith to me here in Rennes, on promise of a reward. I expect them to be delivered before the week is out." The knights again looked at one another and wondered why Sir Aldred hadn't done that in the first place, but were not prepared to ask the question for obvious reasons.

"How dazzlingly brilliant are your schemes, my Lord." This blatant piece of toadying didn't go unnoticed, or unappreciated, by Sir Aldred.

"Thank you, Sir Henry. I'm sure you appreciate it is vitally important that men in the field have somebody they can look to for leadership. Such a man is you, Sir Henry. You and Sir Robinet collect your rations, choose fresh mounts from the stables and ride to join the captain of the King's Guard's men on the St Malo road. I charge you both personally with the responsibility for ensuring that the fugitives are brought before me unharmed." Sir Henry and Sir Robinet both gave a swift, short bow and left to go on their mission. Saddling their horses, they each cursed Sir Aldred.

★

The esquire brothers resolved to rest only out of fatigue or the need for food or toilet. Walking with their ponies through the woods while remaining as close as they dared to the St Malo road was proving trying. Robert Clay suggested they abandon their ponies as the animals were hindering their progress and they could make better headway without them. William and John Clay agreed with Robert's suggestion and, taking as many supplies as they could carry, they freed their mounts. The ponies weren't at all pleased at being freed and kept on behind the brothers despite them trying their hardest to chase them away.

Just before dawn, the brothers made camp as they could go no further without at least a little rest. On setting up to eat a cold repast, for they could not risk making a fire, the ponies came close and nuzzled Robert's neck, and would not depart despite his flailing arms. Suddenly, the smaller pony gave a snort of fear and reared up as the larger one turned around and stumbled in his attempt to make away from the area. Looking beyond the panicking ponies, Robert saw a large, dark shape moving at speed through the deep snow toward the camp. "Bear! Bear!" he yelled.

At Robert's warning shout, William and John Clay drew their swords and in an eye-blink a massive bear was upon them. Had they made a fire the animal might not have approached, but that thought swiftly left Robert's head as he was smashed to the ground with the bear on top of him, mauling his body with its mighty claws. With the bear's back presented to them, William and John wasted no time in plunging their swords deep into the great beast, time and time again until it fell lifeless upon the snowy ground. When they dragged the bear's carcass off Robert, they saw he was very badly injured. In just a few seconds, the bear's claws had torn deep into his body, bearing testimony to the power and ferocity of the attack. Robert said he could still go on but how they imagined they would treat his wounds, none could say.

Just at that moment the brothers became aware of the smell of smoke. There being no wind, they wondered from where it had travelled. William ordered John to remain at the campsite to look after Robert while he went to find the source of the smoke. In the meantime the ponies returned to the camp, which John thought fortuitous because they would probably need them to transport Robert. Within a few minutes William returned to the campsite saying he'd come across an old cottage just over the hill beyond. He told John that he'd entered the cottage but nobody was there and, there being no fire in the hearth, the smell of smoke couldn't have originated from the cottage. He said the cottage had the appearance of having been abandoned years previously. John said they should not care so long as they could get Robert under cover to tend to his wounds.

When the brothers reached the top of the hill they saw thin wisps of grey smoke emitting from the chimney of the cottage. John asked William if it was the same cottage he'd visited just a few minutes earlier. William looked baffled and held up his hand to prevent John from going any further while he went to investigate. On entering the cottage William saw an old woman there, sitting on a rough-hewn bodged chair in front of a roaring fire. So close to it, in fact, that William couldn't understand how she could stand the heat. The old woman sat there wafting smoke toward herself, taking in deep breaths and belching out clouds of blue smoke. She turned to William and beckoned him to take the seat next to her. "Come, Willian Clay, sit yourself down next to me." William felt compelled to sit beside the old woman. What seemed like minutes later, he looked up to see John sitting in the old woman's chair while she attended to Robert's wounds as he lay on a bed. William couldn't explain what was happening and so took it that they were in the lair of some forest witch. Neither of the brothers recognised the potions the old woman was applying to Robert's wounds or the bindings she dressed them in.

The next thing the esquire brothers were aware of was sitting at a table while the old woman served them up bowls of steaming hot stew. William thought the meat in the stew was rabbit but, there being so much of it, he doubted it could have been. The old woman looked at William and said, "Bear," as though she'd read his thoughts. After their meal the brothers laid down to sleep under a bear skin, which they each assumed had formerly belonged to Robert's attacker. When they woke the brothers felt as though they were stirring from a sleep of the dead. How refreshed they felt. There were leftovers of the stew from the evening before sitting in a cauldron on the table but they couldn't eat it as it was dry, rank and mouldy. With no fire burning in the hearth, the cottage was dark and cold. As the brothers shivered, they called out for the old woman to thank her for her hospitality and to say that they must be on their way, but she was nowhere to be found.

Stepping through the cottage door into the deep snow, the brothers found their ponies waiting for them untethered. They looked fed and fat. Again they called out for the old woman to thank her before they left as they didn't want to appear ungrateful by simply disappearing after she'd been so kind to them. They called and called again but the old woman didn't show. Making their way away from the cottage, the esquire brothers turned to take one last look around. They saw smoke billowing from the cottage's chimney and there, in the aperture of the door, stood the old woman. She waved a slow wave as a voice called out, "Keep to your true path and you shall be rewarded in this life." William scolded himself and his brothers, saying they had been ungracious guests in not thanking the old woman before they'd left the cottage, but each somehow knew it was too late to go back. They walked on as in a dream, physically unable to return to the cottage. John asked Robert if he would prefer to ride one of the ponies as he was recovering from the bear attack. He replied that his wounds were not troubling him, and on inspection they looked almost healed.

★

After six days hunting for the esquire brothers, the various search parties returned in dribs and drabs to Rennes and made their reports. Sir Aldred was furious that none of them had located the fugitives and so convened an inquest to establish why they had failed, then to lay blame and punish those who, with the benefit of hindsight, had not performed their duties diligently.

First called to the inquiry by Sir Aldred was the captain of the King's Guard, Daniel le Roche. Before le Roche answered questions, he informed Sir Aldred of the latest news from each of the places he'd sent messenger pigeons to. The messages reported the efforts made to locate the esquire brothers; all strangers had been rounded up and interrogated, which everybody took to mean tortured, but it appeared as though the esquire brothers had disappeared into thin air. All seemed confident that they hadn't left France and some believed them to be dead. Le Roche conjectured that, being Englishmen, they might be more cunning and sly than was supposed, and perhaps they had doubled back to seek sanctuary with the outlaws of Rennes Forest rather than be hunted down and captured.

"They must know that they could never reach the coast without being overtaken by your—"

"Are you saying that I made an error of judgement, Captain of the King's Guard?" spat Sir Aldred.

"No, my Lord Knight, I am merely saying that… that those seeking the fugitives most likely somehow made their pursuit known to them and they… being crafty Englishmen… they doubled back to confuse those fools who were searching for them." Sir Aldred liked the way his protégé shifted blame onto others so that they might be held accountable and punished.

"You may be right, Monsieur le Roche, you may well be right. But how to be certain?"

"Give me a day to interrogate those who've returned to see how thorough they've been… Also, I'll request reinforcements from the captains of the King's Guard at Saint Brieuc, Brest, Saint Lô and Caen to mount an attack on the outlaws of Rennes Forest, to seek the fugitives or information concerning their whereabouts. Things would go better if I used the authority of your name when requesting such reinforcements, my Lord Knight," grovelled Daniel le Roche.

"I don't really think that necessary. Surely a man of your stature and reputation can convince others to support your actions. Yes?"

"Yes, of course, my Lord Knight," replied the captain of the King's Guard, believing that such requests would not be fulfilled without brokering disadvantageous deals.

Captain Le Roche had to work out how he could get other captains of the King's Guard to do his bidding without putting himself in their debt. He had a few favours he could call in and if that didn't work he'd use threats under the name of Sir Aldred Benz, and lie if he got caught out by the terrifying knight.

★

The esquire brothers made slow progress over the snowy terrain. Looking around them, much to their relief, they didn't see any sign of pursuers. As the weather brightened, Robert commented on the beauty of virgin white snow laid against a blue sky.

"At least the snow is no longer falling but it must have snowed a great deal during the night, going by its depth. If we continue as we are though, we won't ever make it to St Malo."

"That is a ridiculous thing to say, brother. Every step we take forward brings us closer to our journey's end."

"I understand what Robert is saying, William. We travel too slowly and will inevitably be overtaken and captured. We should look to the St Malo road for signs of tracks and if there are none, we should take to it for speed's sake. Perhaps our pursuers have been held back by the snow and the road is safe for us to use."

"How will travelling by road be any different? It too will be covered to the same depth of snow."

"But it is more practical to travel… there are no trees or bushes, nor has it has any rabbit holes!" said John, tripping over a snow-covered rabbit hole.

"Please brother, let us investigate the St Malo road and if it is free of signs of pursuit, I say we must take it." Then something occurred to Robert. "Brothers, we have no food. Where is our food? What happened to our food?"

"The old woman must've taken it," snapped John.

"No, surely not. She has no need to take it. We should go back to the cottage and look for our food."

"In which direction does the cottage lie?" With their tracks covered by snow, the brothers couldn't agree on which direction to take to return to the cottage.

"Our heads are confused. I say there is some fel magic at play here. We are all turned around in our idea of which direction the cottage lay in."

"Brothers, I will climb yonder hill and from it I will be able to see the cottage or the smoke issuing from its chimney." Robert climbed the hill but returned having to admit he saw sign of neither the cottage nor smoke.

"I tell to you, brothers, there is some dark magic at play here. The old woman is a witch. Look at Robert's chest... the bear ripped it open but after the old woman applied her potions, it is all but healed in a single night."

"Are you certain it was just one night, brother?"

"What do you mean?"

"We seem uncommonly rested and our ponies are fat and fed; a lot achieved in a single night's stay, wouldn't you say?"

"Aye brother, and now I think I recollect it... I am certain that we were there for two nights... perhaps three... unless I was in a dream."

"Cease John, you are playing your games with us. We were at the cottage for one night only... no more, no less."

"But William, you accused the old woman of being a witch and if she is so, then surely she could've cast a spell over us that—"

"Aye brother, I do say the old woman is a witch... if she is not, why then can we not find our way back to her cottage? It can only be but just a little way back but we cannot find it."

"I am tired of this word play; it achieves nothing. We are well and we are free and we should make our way to St Malo with all haste. Let us check the road." After looking around to get his bearings, Robert said, "In which direction is the road, would you say?" in mock of William. John appreciated the joke but William knitted his eyebrows in a scowl and walked in a huff in the direction of the St Malo road by keeping the sun at his face.

"Let us play follow our leader," joked John.

"Are you certain that is the correct way, brother?" asked Robert. William refused to answer. "You never know, oh big brother, the old woman could've cast a spell over the sun and it might now rise out of the west."

The esquire brothers were only half a mile from the St Malo

road and were heading straight for it. During their walk, Robert teased William over his claim that the old woman was a witch. The longer it went on, the more infuriated William became. "And what of the bear?" he shouted at Robert, "It should be hibernating! It was black magic that brought that beast upon us!" John and Robert ignored William's remark and kept on trudging through the snow. On reaching the St Malo road, the brothers stopped dead in their tracks in astonishment at the sight that greeted them. At the point where they joined the St Malo road there was virtually no snow, but to their right the snow was almost impassable and to their left, as though having been under the action of strong winds, the snow was banked up on one side of the road, leaving the other side clear. William stared at his brothers in justification of his claims of the witchcraft of the old woman.

John Clay climbed on top of the snowdrift to check for sign of their pursuers but there were none; in fact, there were no tracks or marks or signs in the snow whatsoever. Without saying a word, William Clay mounted his pony and headed north to St Malo. John and Robert Clay mounted the other pony and followed along behind their eldest brother in astonished silence.

Within a surprisingly short time, the esquire brothers arrived at the outskirts of St Malo. They were astonished at how close they were to it but said nothing lest it reignite discussion of witches and witchcraft. William rode on ahead of John and Robert wearing a smug expression on his face that seemed permanently etched. As the brothers entered St Malo they dismounted from their ponies and led them along with their heads bowed inside their monks' cowls, looking for all the world as though they were on a pilgrimage. Before making their way to the port to hire a captain and boat, the brothers stopped off at an inn to eat and gather what intelligence there might be concerning their flight from Rennes.

Entering the inn, William discreetly made the sign of the Holy Order of Knights to check for the presence of any devotees. Looking around the room, he counted eight responses to his sign. Moving close to one of those who'd returned his sign, William asked her for any word of the Order. She looked at him and reported that news had arrived in the city some several days earlier about a slaughter of the Order at Poitiers Castle, claiming that they had all been murdered and that eight men were sought by the King's Knights as being those responsible. She said it was also claimed that those same eight men had killed a large number of the King's Guard, adding that she didn't believe either the rumour of the slaughter of the Order or of the large number of King's guards slain.

"Not under any circumstances, Madame?"

"Of what circumstances do you speak, monk?"

William took up his courage and put the brothers' fate in the woman's hands.

"What if the knights of the Holy Order had drunk drugged wine and were slaughtered by mercenaries while they were unconscious? Then what if those murderers drank the same drugged wine in celebration and anticipation of promised riches?"

"It is true then? The Holy Order of Knights is no more?"

"No, Madame, not entirely. One of their number escaped together with me, my brothers, several soldiers and a serf. The knight is journeying to the Low Countries to check on the fate of his brother knights."

"Why was the Order murdered? Who would direct such a thing on them?"

"I am bound to say, Madame, that your King, being in much debt to the Holy Order, commanded that they be slaughtered. It was only by the merest chance that we escaped with our lives…

though our youngest brother did not, and now we must bear news of his death to our mother." The woman was visibly moved and asked the innkeeper to grant her a room so that she and other devotees of the Holy Order of Knights could hear the esquire brothers' tale in private.

After hearing the telling of the brothers' tale, the devotees sat in stunned silence. It was even as though the esquire brothers themselves were hearing the story for the first time after all they'd gone through. It was like a tale that had been told them about heroes of old.

"What is next for you and your brothers?" asked the woman.

"We must flee France for England without delay. If we are taken by those pursuing us, we will not live to tell our tale to others."

"Friends, stay here among us in St Malo. We will hide you until the hunt is called off. You'll be safe here... you are among devotees of the Holy Order of Knights and we will not betray you." So spoke the eldest of the group.

"We would not but others will. I daresay news of the arrival of strangers has already reached the ears of the captain of the King's Guard. He will take you into custody and transport you to Rennes, where you will be handed over to a Knight named Aldred. There is a big reward on offer."

"Then we must waste no more time. Is there any boat captain who would take us to England?"

"There are many but who to trust?"

"What about Captain Bellamy? He is no friend of the King's rule."

"Is he a devotee of the Order?"

"Who knows with him... he is so taciturn it is hard to know what he is."

"I will approach him on your behalf," said the woman, "and test his willingness to undertake a journey to England with a cargo that must travel undetected."

The woman left the brothers in the company of her comrades while she sought out Captain Bellamy. She was resolved not to lie to the Captain about his passengers as to do so would put them all in danger.

★

The promise of reward, the realisation of ambition and the pursuit of power are potent drivers and people will do whatever they need to do to achieve them, individually or collectively. To be in a positon to get all three by one action is the answer to a prayer for some, and just such a person was at the inn when the esquire brothers entered it. He wasn't sure at first whether these were the same men he'd been ordered to search for by the captain of the King's Guard but they deserved closer inspection. Manuel Abel, brother of the executioner at Rennes, should've gone to the captain of the King's Guard and alerted him to the arrival of the strangers, but since he'd been forced into searching for the fugitives against his will, he decided to take matters, his fate and his fortune, into his own hands. Manuel convincing himself of being forced into searching for the esquire brothers against his will was a complete fabrication; it was just a convenience that allowed him to act for himself to claim the entire reward. If he was right about the strangers, he knew he'd be unpopular with everybody who'd been out in the cold and the snow searching for them, but his little self-deception cleared the way for his self-centred actions.

After noticing a signal pass between the strangers and some of the inn's patrons, Manuel's suspicions were further aroused when four known devotees of the Holy Order of Knights took them into a private room. Afterwards, he went to the keeper of the pigeon lofts and sent a message about the strangers to Sir Aldred at Rennes, requesting instructions on how he should proceed. This is a perfect example of how ambition gets the better of good sense. What

Manuel did not appreciate was that there is a natural order of things and that order must be preserved, respected and followed. He did not foresee Sir Aldred's utter fury on receiving the note after it was eventually handed to him some hours after the pigeon had arrived at the Rennes lofts. Sir Aldred ordered Daniel le Roche to send messenger pigeons to the captain of the King's Guard at the port of St Malo informing him of the arrival of the fugitives there and ordering that he was to detain them immediately and bring them to Rennes without delay. Monsieur le Roche hesitated before giving Sir Aldred news that he knew the knight would not like to hear.

"My Lord, it being late in the day, the pigeon keeper will, most likely, be away from his loft and the message might not be received until the morning... there could be even further delay if he doesn't notice the arrival of the bird, or he has some other duties to—" Sir Aldred dashed ornaments, plates, books and whatever else wasn't fixed down onto the stone floor and proceeded to jump up and down on them until they were completely unrecognisable from their original form. He looked so ridiculous that a couple of men at arms had to stifle their laughter. The knight cast them a look neither of them would ever forget, sufficient to bring them to sensible order. Captain le Roche held himself from further speech. Eventually, Sir Aldred broke the silence with words spoken through clenched teeth.

"Tell me, Captain of the Kings' Guard, when did the bird arrive and how long has it been in the loft?"

"In all honesty, my Lord, it cannot be said as the loft keeper was ill in his bed and—"

"He has no deputy?"

"No, my Lord... I... it..."

"Your tongue seems tied, Captain of the King's Guard," spat Sir Aldred. Kneeling to the knight, Captain le Roche thought it best to throw himself on what mercy he might have in him.

"My Lord, my tongue is tied because you have been let down by the people of Rennes. They have placed your venture into jeopardy and I and the whole town wish to make amends…"

"Indeed, Monsieur le Roche, indeed… and what do you propose you do to resolve the situation?"

"I, my Lord?"

"Yes, you, Captain of the King's Guard… you! Tell me now what it is that you propose to do to remedy the situation." It is better never to try to placate a tyrant because the outcome can be unpredictable and make your own situation worse.

"My Lord, I will immediately convene a council of inquiry to establish the facts and punish the guilty…"

"Yes, good, see to it straightaway. And while you're about it, make sure the one who sent the message from St Malo is severely punished for circumventing the authority of the captain of the King's Guard there… how dare he! If those plunderers, murderers and sodomites escape, it will be on his head!"

"Yes, my Lord."

"Send Pigeons straightaway to St Malo and perhaps luck will be on our side for once."

Daniel le Roche raced to the pigeon loft and selected two fine birds to carry the message about the esquire brothers to the captain of the King's Guard at St Malo. The message being read in time to prevent the fugitives from escaping was in the lap of the gods.

★

The woman returned to the inn, bringing Captain Bellamy with her. He wanted to meet the men he'd be risking his life for and to ensure the woman wasn't taxing his payment. By this time, Manuel Abel had returned to the inn and was pointed out as a King's-man by Captain Bellamy. The devotees of the Holy Order of Knights thought not to cut Abel's throat but to keep watch over him instead for what they might learn in future.

The group retired to the meeting room to discuss terms. It was a short meeting and one that the esquire brothers thought would not end well when they couldn't meet the boat captain's price. But he said that they, looking like honest men and being devotees of the Holy Order of Knights, could pay him once he landed them in England. When the esquire brothers asked when they would be departing, the boat captain replied, "Immediately, it's best that we leave under cover of darkness."

Manuel Abel returned to the pigeon loft to send a report on the events at the inn to Sir Aldred, but as it was all shut up he resolved to return early the next day. Making his way back to the inn, Abel drifted off into wild imaginings of the rewards coming his way and decided to celebrate with a bottle of wine. He woke late the next morning and ran to the pigeon loft lest his message to Sir Aldred be delayed. When he arrived at the loft he found the captain of the King's Guard reading a note. Abel made to push past the captain, claiming he was on urgent business. Before Abel made three steps he was hauled back by his collar and thrown to the ground. The next words he heard were, "Take him away to the dungeons for him to await the judgement of Sir Aldred Benz."

★

Daniel le Roche's council of inquiry found Manuel Abel guilty of treason and he was hung then cut down before he was dead, disembowelled and quartered; the penalty stipulated under the law of the land. Sir Aldred demanded Manuel Abel's brother, Reynard, being Rennes' executioner, perform the deed under threat of forfeiture of his own life and those of his wife and children. The execution was so terrible that it passed into folklore as a tale to frighten folk to keep them obedient. When performing on witching nights, minstrels sang supernatural ballads of Manuel Abel's tormented spirit roaming the forests around Rennes and waylaying unwary travellers, who were never to be seen again.

As soon as it became apparent that the esquire brothers had escaped France, Daniel le Roche sent messenger pigeons to Saint Lô with instructions to the captain of the King's Guard there to disperse all the soldiers under his command along the Cherbourg Peninsula to watch out for Captain Bellamy's boat and waylay it. He further sent messages to the King's Guard captains of the major islands along the coast, ordering them to have boats constantly in the water searching for the fugitives. When Sir Aldred heard of Monsieur le Roche's scheme, he arranged a ceremony to publicly reward him with gold... which the knight retained for safekeeping, lest it be stolen by the still-at-large outlaws of Rennes Forest, telling the Monsieur le Roche that the gold would remain in his care while the outlaws remained at liberty.

Should the esquire brothers make it back to England's shores, Sir Aldred determined that would not be the end of the matter. He resolved in that case to use his ecclesiastical familiars to hunt them down and persecute them. What he most dreaded, should the esquire brothers reach England, was the loss of favour with King Philip. If this circumstance ever came about, he swore that he would revenge himself on the entire Clay family.

THE VOYAGE TO ENGLAND

Captain Bellamy's boat, the *Marie*, was really only an inshore craft and not entirely suited for the purposes of a voyage to England, but he reasoned that the distance between St Malo and Plymouth was not so great as to be regarded as open-water sailing. He claimed to have sailed the *Marie* to Plymouth on several occasions previously, making the journey in as little as two days depending on the winds, which at the time of their setting off were extremely favourable. The captain said they would make the crossing more or less direct, citing the obvious advantage of remaining hidden from sight of land along the coast of the Cherbourg Peninsula and the islands off its shores. The esquire brothers said that they would commit their trust to the captain's wisdom and experience, by the sign of his rough seaman's hands.

Before they had sailed the *Marie* a dozen leagues, the wind changed to an unfavourable quarter, the sky grew dark and grim, winter storms blew up on the horizon and made their way rapidly toward them. For a moment, Captain Bellamy seemed unsure as to what to do for best, as he remarked that his boat would not fare well in a storm such as was heading their way. He looked behind to where they had come from and shook his head. He knew there was no going back as news of the escape of the esquire brothers on his boat would be well known by those who, no doubt, would now be hunting them. He was, for the time being at least, as much a fugitive as the esquire brothers themselves were.

Taking a good swig from his jug of Calvados, Captain Bellamy announced a change of course and plan, both in reality being one and the same thing. He confided to the esquire brothers that with the wind being in the quarter it was now in, they would to sail to Portsmouth instead of Plymouth, and doing so would mean them sailing between the two largest of the islands off the coast of the Cherbourg Peninsula before heading northeast toward the Isle of Wight.

"We'll change our course to make the most of the wind and try to stay ahead of the worst of the coming storm. There'll be a fair bit of tacking to do but the *Marie* is swift and flighty in choppy waters and light to handle, so it'll be no hardship."

"How long will it be before we are back on English soil?"

"Well, the actual sailing is a bit more than to Plymouth, and with the wind set as she is I think it'll be three days… maybe four. If the storm blows out and we get a fresh southwesterly, we could make it in less than two more days. That's the beauty of sailing," laughed Captain Bellamy.

"You admitted that an advantage of sailing to Portsmouth was that we could not be seen from French soil along our escape route."

"Aye, that I did, but that didn't take account of French warships on the lookout for contra-banders in the waters between here and there. But fear not, good brothers, the gap between the two largest of the islands is four leagues or more, so there's little chance of a boat the size of the *Marie* being seen, especially in the choppy waters of a swell such as we have." The brothers cast a look of losing confidence, if not losing faith, in Captain Bellamy.

Being on the final leg of their journey home, the esquire brothers' minds were beset with the taste of freedom and so they set to work tacking at Captain Bellamy's orders, which seemed every few minutes with the wind set as it was.

★

The following day, news of the escape of the esquire brothers and the details of those involved in arranging it were sent by messenger pigeon to Sir Aldred at Rennes. Unable to travel to St Malo to vent his wrath due to the depth of snow, the King's knight rampaged about the ceremonial halls of the city's sheriff, slashing randomly at things with his sword while cursing his luck, the treachery and the incompetence of those around him and God also; he several times shook a clenched fist toward heaven. Those who bore witness to his blaspheming shut their ears to it and emptied their minds of it lest, they be called as witnesses at some future time. They had seen what happened to people who the knight bore malice toward and did not wish to share their fates.

"Where do you think the fugitives will head for? Which direction will they take?"

"That all depends on the direction of the winds, my Lord, but…" Daniel le Roche quickly reeled in his tongue as he knew to continue would land him in hot water with Sir Aldred in the mood he was in.

"Are you a sailing man, Captain of the King's Guard at Rennes?" slurred Sir Aldred, grinding his teeth in fury.

"No, my Lord Knight, I spoke only to rouse some debate… to bring suggestions forward… to awaken thoughts, ideas. I apologise for my words, which were without substance."

"Bring me somebody who knows the waters the fugitives have fled upon!" Captain le Roche sped away from the halls before Sir Aldred changed his mind about releasing him from his company. He returned some twenty minutes later with one of the guildsmen known as Allain de Quincey, a cousin of one of the knights of the Holy Order... a fact known to Sir Aldred.

"My Lord Knight, I bring Monsieur Allain de Quincey. He is a—"

"Can the monsieur speak for himself, Captain of the King's Guard?"

"Of course he can, my Lord Knight," muttered Daniel le Roche from a grovellingly low bow.

"Sir Knight, my name is Allain de Quincey, cousin to Sir Estienne de Quincey of the Holy Order of Knights."

"Did you tell me your pedigree to impress your family connections upon me, Monsieur de Quincey?"

"No, my Lord Knight," replied Allain de Quincey in a voice free from fear of Sir Aldred's reputation. "I spoke of my family connection openly so that no aspersions might be cast on any knowledge I might provide you with." Allain de Quincey bowed slightly in deference to Sir Aldred's position.

"Very well. What credentials do you have with regard to sailing the seas?"

"I am a guildsman here in Rennes, dealing in all manner of precious materials. My transactions are primarily with the kingdoms that trade with France. During these past ten years I have often had occasion to travel the waters around France as a ship's captain and navigator."

"Good enough, Monsieur de Quincey. Tell me, Sir, which route would you take if you were to sail to England from the port of St Malo?" The guildsman gave the knight a quizzical look, to which the knight returned a challenging stare.

"My Lord Knight, that question has so many variables that I cannot..."

"What do you require in order to provide me an answer to my question, Monsieur?"

"The first thing is knowledge of the type of vessel..."

"It is named the *Marie* and is a small boat. There are four men

on board, only one of whom is a sailor… a Captain Bellamy."
Allain de Quincey knew of Captain Bellamy's reputation but
made no reference to it.

"A small boat is likely to be a coastal vessel and will, in all
probability, sail on its route to England along the coast of the
Cherbourg Peninsula to reach its furthermost northern point, from
where it will sail straight across the open water to land in England…
probably somewhere between Langton and Osmington."

"What if the fugitives want to avoid being seen from the
coast?"

"In that case, my Lord Knight, the route is nor'west to
nor'nor'west to make land in Wessex… which involves a journey
of over forty leagues in open water, where they might come across
French ships. If however they follow the peninsula, once having left
its shelter, depending on winds, they might take a nor'nor'easterly
course to make for Sussex. Neither of these routes I would want to
venture in a small boat at this time of year"

"This time of year?"

"Yes, my Lord Knight. The winds are not favourable to make
such a journey at this time of year… ferocious northwesterly
winter storms might capsize a small boat."

"Then, Sir, you are saying that the fugitives will follow the
shelter of the coast along the Cherbourg Peninsula?"

"In no way, my Lord Knight, I am simply answering your
questions with the benefit of my experience, but who can say what
a boat Captain will do? Especially one fleeing France with fugitives
on board." Sir Aldred remained relatively calm in the face of not
getting what he wanted.

"If you were me, what would you do to apprehend these men?"

"I would send out pigeons carrying orders to the captains of
the King's Guards at…"

"That is already done!" screamed Sir Aldred, the fury in his
voice rebounding off the walls of the Guildhall. "Have you no
other advice for me, sailor?"

"Send out boats upon the two supposed routes to search for the fugitives, and trust that you overtake them before they make land in England." Sir Aldred dismissed Allain de Quincey from his sight with the merest flick of the back of his hand.

★

Despite the rising misgivings the esquire brothers were having about Captain Bellamy, he knew the coastal waters well and just before nightfall the little *Marie* passed between the islands off the Cherbourg Peninsula, dissecting them perfectly. They saw lights flickering on the islands but no boats ventured out to seek them. It now being night, Captain Bellamy hauled in all sails and let the wind play on the hull of the boat to keep it ahead of the waves. This caused the *Marie* to roll violently and the brothers to vomit copiously.

By first light of morning the storm had increased in its fury. Captain Bellamy shouted above the noise of the wind that they needed to head for the cover of a small cove he knew at the tip of the peninsula as "to continue on our course would be deadly folly". Manoeuvring such a small boat in such big winds and waves is no easy task, but Captain Bellamy got the *Marie*'s bow headed in toward the cove. Dropping all sails and taking to the oars, the four men rowed for all they were worth to gain the mouth of the cove. A few strokes from safety, the strength of the esquire brothers began to fail them. The power of the wind and the rush of the waves breaking on the sharp rocks caused fear to rise in their throats. Captain Bellamy expected this and screamed at them to keep up their stroke. "Keep rowing all the way to the shore, otherwise we're doomed."

When the *Marie* reached the shelter of a triangle of rocks, Captain Bellamy jumped into the water with an anchor rope tied across his chest. He knew the depth of the water and that he could wade in it chest deep to secure the *Marie*. It was at this point that the gods of the sea turned against the crew of the *Marie* and a gigantic seventh wave crashed into the bay, its power dashing Captain Bellamy against the rocks. The Captain's body went limp as the anchor rope went slack. In an instant, Robert Clay launched himself headfirst into the pounding surf and, grabbing both the Captain and the anchor rope, he tied the *Marie* to one of the rocks.

Beyond the triangle of rocks Robert spied a small cave and, pointing to it, he screamed that they were to make their way into it. John refused to leave the *Marie* as he wasn't a swimmer but William, grabbing him by his monk's cowl, took them both into the water. William carried his brother against the mighty beating of the waves to the safety of the cave. A minute later they were joined by Robert carrying Captain Bellamy slumped across his shoulder. William took hold of the brave captain from his brother, placing him gently on the floor of the cave. It was then that the brothers saw just how bad the captain's injuries were from the beating he'd received from the gods of the sea. Captain Bellamy hovered between life and death for four hours before passing from this world. There being nowhere on the rocky cove to bury the captain, Robert picked up the poor man and carried him as far as he could into the bay, where he released him to let the waves take him where they may. William and John bowed their heads in silent prayer, crossing themselves when they were done. Robert took no part in any religious act, service or sign; instead he singlehandedly pulled the *Marie* up inside the cave lest it be dashed on the rocks as her captain had been.

As the esquire brothers sat wet and shivering on the cave floor, the intensity of the storm increased still further. Waves were now washing into the cave, causing the brothers great alarm. William knelt and prayed for deliverance from their predicament, beckoning his brothers to do likewise. John joined William in prayer but Robert walked to the waterlogged entrance of the cave and let out a loud torrent of blasphemous abuse against the Creator, citing all of God's inconsistencies, faults and follies he could bring to mind.

"Dear brother, why do you speak so against the Lord our God? Come, join us in prayer. It will bring quieting calm to you and your soul."

"Pray, brother? Pray? Me? To who? To who should I pray, brother? What good does it do to pray? What good ever comes from it? We, each of us, has prayed and prayed and prayed all our lives but to what end, brother? To what result? Unless fate draws us a good hand we are destined to die in a watery cave on a lonely shore in a foreign land. Are we or are we not? Will we or will we not? Praying will not help decide either way, brother. How can it? Has the storm quieted? No, it has not! In fact it is now worse than ever. What good has praying done for us in our flight from Poitiers? None. No good whatsoever. By praying, brother, we consider ourselves good men, humble men, righteous men, yet we have been undone by cruel men, cowardly men, deceitful men, and yet, no doubt, they too pray, because not to pray is to be singled out by the Church as unchristian, and being so brings expulsion from society…"

"Robert," interrupted William with a voice full of authority to silence him, "can you not see God's hand in everything that has happened to us along our road? It was He who delivered us from the slaughter at Poitiers Castle, it was He who gave us food and shelter when we most needed it, it was He who afforded us the protection of the outlaws of Rennes Forest while the knights pursuing us had to go a longer road, it was His hand that guided us through the snowstorm and delivered us safely to the port of St Malo, it was He who provided us a boat captain to sail us to England…"

"Listen to yourself, brother, just you listen to your own words! They make no sense! It was by the merest good fortune that we escaped the massacre at Poitiers. Hear the word, brother, understand the word and what it means. Massacre. There was a massacre at Poitiers Castle, a massacre, brother. Would a benevolent and loving God permit such an atrocity to be carried out on His humble servants? To what end? To what purpose did He permit such an act? Through our own instincts and wits did we accomplish the journey to Rennes. And what of the old woman in the forest? The one you call a witch. Was she not an angel, brother, if there even be such things? It was she who tended to my wounds, it was she who gave us shelter, it was she who gave us food, it was she who—"

"Aye, brother," interrupted William again, this time full of fury, "and it was she who packed the snow hard against our pursuers and lifted it for us to pass swiftly to St Malo. Do you not see witchcraft at play in everything she did, brother? One minute she was there and the next she was gone… there was smoke from the chimney and then no smoke… food from one night became rank the next day, if it were indeed even the next day. She is a witch, brother, and should suffer a witch's fate."

"William, I love you as much as any brother can love his brother, but I cannot agree with you. I will say now as I have thought for a long time that there is no God… there is no heaven and there is no hell."

"If there is no God, no heaven, no hell, then tell me, brother, what is there?"

"What is there? Look around you, brother, this is what there is."

"And you say this was created without His divine hand?"

"I do, brother, that I do. I do not know what created all this and neither do you, but show me proof that there is a God, brother, and I will recant my words, repent all my sins and throw myself on His divine mercy to beg His forgiveness," spat Robert, emitting a little laugh.

"I, brother, have faith, and with faith I have no doubt that…"

"Very convenient, isn't it, brother, this thing you call faith. With faith you simply accept things as God's work. Faith in God requires no proofs but proofs are required for everything else… and people need to have faith that the proofs are not genuine and not fabricated."

"Are you saying," interjected John, "that if there are proofs that God does not exist, then people would need to have faith that the proofs are genuine?"

Robert ignored John's question. "If there is a God, then why are we here in this cave and not at our home enjoying its comforts with our mother and the rest of our family? Whenever things go well we all thank the Lord for His divine blessings but when they go ill we say it is His will or He is testing us. But the reason for the test is never made clear. Let us say, just for a moment, that there is no God and everything is either chance or what we make of matters, or a combination of the two. Then, when events such as the slaughter at Poitiers Castle take place, those involved must be players caught up in a game of chance, otherwise God would surely punish the guilty."

"God does not interfere in the ways of man, brother, He leaves us to our devices until the day of judgement when He weighs the balance and—"

"If that is so, brother, why do you thank Him when things go well and pray to Him especially hard when things go badly? To no effect, I say. You kneeled and prayed and bled over Thomas' grave and yet here we are, barely alive, sitting cowering in a cave to wait out a storm and then attempt to sail a boat home to England when not one of us knows how."

"Have faith, brother, have faith. Leave matters in His hands and He will look after us and guide us home… you'll see… just have faith."

The argument continued for hours until it was brought to a temporary halt by John pointing to the sky outside the cave and shouting, "Look! Look, brothers, cease your arguing; the storm is dying." But he was mistaken; it was a mere lull, and after four more days of howling winter storms the brothers were still imprisoned in their cave, now starving and thirsty. Of the two privations, thirst was the worst as it drove the minds of the brothers mad when looking at the water surrounding them. In the occasional respites between arguments, Robert's conscience pricked him for his thoughts about Thomas and the jealousy they invoked in him. He cursed himself for having wished his little brother ill. Arguments with William and John brought Robert some sort of solace so he provoked them more and more to ease his mind.

On the fifth morning of the brothers' confinement in the cave, the storm was still blowing hard and was showing no sign of abating. They were slowly starving to death and knew they could wait no longer to attempt the last leg of their journey home. And so, driven on by thirst and starvation, the esquire brothers took the *Marie* to the water, clambered aboard her, cut the anchor rope, grabbed the oars and rowed for all they were worth to take the small boat out of the bay. After fifteen minutes of hard rowing, the esquire brothers were exhausted, but they'd done just enough to put the *Marie* into open water. Their lives were now in the hands of the gods of the sea once more. Robert used the mainsail to cover himself and his brothers from the worst of the storm as they struggled to keep the *Marie* ahead of the wind and the waves.

★

The storm carried the esquire brothers far beyond their hoped-for landing place. By dawn the following day, the winds had blown themselves out and the little *Marie* was bobbing gently on the water, wrapped around her exhausted cargo as she beached in a broad shallow bay sheltered by low cliffs. Anybody peering at the scene from the cliffs above would have seen nothing to make them think there was life on board the small boat. Robert was the first to wake, though how any of the esquire brothers slept through the storm was a mystery. When they woke they felt just as they had following their night's stay in the old woman's cottage in the woods. This recollection disturbed William but not so John or Robert, the latter paying it no heed whatsoever. The esquire brothers pushed the mainsail from on top of them onto the sand at the margin where the water lapped the shore. The sail eventually drifted away on the tide as it moved slowly out to sea. The question was, where were they? Where had they landed? Were they home? Were they in England? If so, where in England were they? They did not recognise the landscape.

"William, do you recognise the country? I do not," remarked John.

"No, brother, I don't, though it seems to me we are not any longer in France."

"What makes you say so?"

"The smell. It's the smell. This place does not smell like France." Robert laughed a scoffing laugh at William's reasoning.

"Well, all I can smell is the sea… I smell the sea, that's what I smell, and the sea's the sea and smells no different no matter where you be," grunted Robert in rhyme.

"Why are you behaving in so contrary a way, brother?" asked John.

"Let him to his own devices, John, he will come round soon… soon enough when he realises he is no longer in danger of his life. We are none of us in our normal mind."

"Make no excuses for me, brother, I am in a fine state of mind. My mind and me have never been finer," replied Robert, marching away from the *Marie* and making his way to the lowest of the cliffs.

William and John watched Robert as he made his way from them, shaking his head and cursing. Looking beyond him they saw a man peering at them from the top of the cliff. William was caught in two minds as to what to do for the best. If they were in England, the only thing they need be in fear of was being mistaken for smugglers or being held for ransom by some local outlaw band. If they were in France, they'd better hope the watcher was a devotee of the Holy Order of Knights. If they had landed in the Low Countries then they might seek out Sir Michael de Gel and find out if his search for his brother knights had borne fruit... those and like thoughts rebounded around inside William's head.

Without considering the situation they might find themselves in if they were not in England, John shouted, "Good day to you, good sir," to the stranger, who answered, "And to you too, good sir." Robert, being closest to the stranger, entered into conversation with him and established that they were in fact not far from the estate of a distant relative of the Clay family. *At last,* he thought, *things are turning our way.*

The man descended the cliff and introduced himself as Nicholas Yoxhall, a family name the esquire brothers recognised as originally heralding from the Middle Lands of England. Nicholas could see the esquire brothers were in bad shape and so told them to remain where they were until he could return with a cart to carry them to the estate of Squire Spenser, on whose land Yoxall worked. Believing it all too good to be true, the esquire brothers waited on tenterhooks to see if Yoxall was all he made himself out to be. Two hours later, the esquire brothers heard a great commotion and on raising their heads from the sand they saw a huge crowd heading their way bearing all manner of farming implements; some were waving swords above their heads, their blades reflecting the light of the morning sun. Dread set into the brothers' hearts, but recognising the shouts were of Englishmen, they put their faces in their hands and sobbed tears of relief and joy that they were finally safe. Their ordeal was at an end.

★

The esquire brothers recuperated at the home of Squire Spenser for four days to regain their strength. In that time they recounted the whole of the terrible tale of the slaughter of the Holy Order of Knights at Poitiers Castle and their trials and adventures during their flight from France to England. On their departure, Squire Spenser provided the esquire brothers with horses, money and supplies of food and water for their journey home. One of the things they discussed as they began their homeward journey was the tragic death of Captain Bellamy. William avowed that when they returned to France to bring home Thomas' body, they would visit the good Captain's wife, who would now probably be destitute, and give her suitable compensation for the loss of her husband.

The final part of their journey home was undertaken at a slow pace as none of the brothers wanted to break the news of Thomas' death to their mother, but when the esquire brothers saw familiar landmarks a countdown began in their heads; a countdown to the dread moment when they would face their mother and tell her that her youngest and most beloved son was lying in a rocks-and-stones grave in France, murdered by an assassin whose right to justice he was defending. William spoke first.

"It won't be long now ere we are at our home," spoke William.

"Aye, brother, not long now," muttered Robert.

"Will you tell our mother of Thomas' passing?" John asked William.

"His passing, brother, his passing! His murder, you mean! Call it what it is… his murder!" screamed Robert, his voice cracking under the strain.

"Robert, you are my dear brother, but I swear that if you say or do even the littlest thing to make our mother's coming sadness greater or more unbearable, I will cut out your tongue and spike your eyes," spoke William without raising his voice or changing his manner in the slightest. The last time he had acted so was when he slew the assassin who'd murdered Thomas. Robert did not doubt his eldest brother's resolve in carrying out the threat. William continued speaking as calmly as before. "After we are home there will be no mention of the crow priest or the part he might have played in the slaughter at the castle, nor will there be any blasphemous talk of the existence of God, which might bring our mother further torment. I will not allow that to happen." Back on English soil, the eldest brother reverted to his dominant position in the family by demanding obedience in everything.

"Certainly, brother, it will be your way until I quit our home and then I will be forever my own man. In any event, I would never do anything that would bring grief or sadness to our mother or our sisters."

"You say that, brother, yet you aim to quit our house to be your own man, which I take to mean that you will speak and act as you wish, without care or consideration of others. This I cannot give sanction to. First and foremost, brother Robert, you are a Clay… you are a Clay wherever you be, and forget that fact at your peril." Robert bit his tongue and wished his eldest brother dead for speaking to him so. John Clay checked how Robert had received William's words and from the expression on his younger brother's face, he knew a storm was coming.

"William, will it be you that tells our mother of Thomas'… passing?" John asked for a second time. Avoiding the word 'murder' aggravated Robert, though that was not John's intention.

"I will indeed, good John. It is my position as head of the family to carry out such matters, it is for me alone to tell our mother of Thomas' passing…"

Robert had heard enough of his brother's pomposity. He turned his horse around and headed for the nearest town. In anger, William snatched his horse's reins and made to go after Robert but John prevented him from doing so, saying for him to leave Robert be and that he'd come round in his own time. William screamed curses at Robert's back, which he ignored as his thoughts were fixed on wishes for misfortunes to be visited on William.

Not wanting his mother to suffer more than she was about to, Robert relented and re-joined his brothers. Silence passed between them for the last few miles of their journey. Their thoughts were their only company, and they were bad company.

★

The Clay estate wasn't a particularly vast estate as far as estates went. It consisted of a dozen tied farms, each with its own farmhouse and barns and anywhere from a few to forty acres of land, depending on the type of farming being carried on there. The main farm, Manor Farm, was the Clays' family home, with all the children, their spouses and offspring living under one roof. The Clay estate provided the Clay family with a living that most would be happy with. They were good citizens, always paid their taxes and looked after their tenant farmers in times of need. The Clays were well known in the parish, having lived there for eight generations or more. They were regular churchgoers and devout Christians, as well as being considered pillars of the local community. Bad news seldom came the Clays' way, but all that was about to change.

★

As William, John and Robert slow-trotted up the lane on the final furlong to their family home, they spied their mother hopping from one foot to the other, moving this way and that, looking left and looking right, trying to catch a glimpse of them all... trying

121

to see if they were all okay. They'd been away a long time, over two years. They knew she would be looking out for Thomas in particular; her lovely, adorable Thomas, spoiled by mother and sisters alike, the apple seed of all their eyes. As the brothers drew close, their mother came toward them.

"Where's my little 'un then, eh?" whooped Elizabeth Clay, matriarch of the Clay clan. "Where's he to then, eh? Is he coming on later or is he still in France?" The brothers discerned a slight change in the tone of their mother's voice; it became more solemn with every word. "Got hi'self a woman there if I knows him," spoke Elizabeth, her speech slowing. "Got hi'self a woman in trouble there if I knows him." Elizabeth attempted a brave little laugh but she could tell by the expressions on her sons' faces that her youngest and most dear child wasn't coming along later, nor was he detained by his customary woman troubles. She'd have been grateful if that had been the case this time. Elizabeth Clay collapsed to her knees onto the dirt road and howled the mournful howl of a mother whose heart has been stricken by sudden and terrible grief.

After receiving confirmation of her worst fears from William, Elizabeth Clay was never the same again, retreating further and further from family life, wasting away until she died, many said of a broken heart, before the year was out.

THE CROW PRIEST AND
THE PARISH COMMISSIONERS

1307 was a difficult year for England. Edward I, a very great and much loved king, died in July that year. His son and heir, Edward II, was a mere shirt button in comparison with his father. From the very beginning of his reign, the son did nothing to defend or protect his subjects from the rapaciousness of aristocrats, nor from the persecutions of their chief familiars, the Church. It was to be Edward's lack of love for his subjects that fostered the birth of the Brotherhood.

Whereas Edward I was a staunch supporter of the Holy Order of Knights, his son had no love for them or their causes. He was, however, eager to learn whether stories of the Order being infested by sodomites were true. Had this been the case he might've given it protection against those that sought to destroy it, but finding no evidence of sodomy among the Order's ranks, he turned his back on it to concentrate on his proposed marriage to Isabella, the pre-teen daughter of King Philip IV of France.

★

After burying their mother in the November, the esquire brothers made plans to return to France to bring Thomas' remains home to England, exactly as they had promised to do at his graveside. They resolved to start their journey following William's wedding to his childhood sweetheart. While the esquire brothers were away serving the Holy Order of Knights, many of the family's tenant farmers had ceased paying their rents and the husbands of the Clay daughters had failed to act to prevent them from doing so. The situation around the family finances was a disaster wanting to become a catastrophe. But catastrophe in another form was not long in visiting the Clays. Their living hell began four weeks prior to the brothers' planned date of departure to France when a council of parish commissioners led by a crow priest arrived at the Clay family estate. They set up their Office of Inquisition in the main hall of the house and first called William before them, demanding he furnish them with forty gold crowns for 'services to be rendered'. The Church did not operate its accounts in arrears.

"You are William Clay of this very parish?"

"I am, Father."

"You should address me as 'Your Grace'. Now, William Clay, do you know why we are here, what our business is with you and your family?"

"I do not, Your Grace."

"As servants of the Holy Order of Knights, themselves condemned by His Holiness Pope Clement as plunderers, murderers and sodomites, you stand accused, along with your brothers John, Robert and Thomas Clay, of committing many heinous crimes and sins against the laws of God and man; thereto treachery, murder, robbery and impersonating members of the clergy. You and your brothers are likewise alleged to be sodomites, having lain with men on the written account of several witnesses. What plead you to the charges, William Clay?" William was in shock at hearing the charges and was stunned into tongue-tied silence. "Have you no answer to these serious charges against the natural laws of God and man?"

"Your Grace... Firstly, I would tell you that Thomas is dead. He died at the hands of an assassin in Poitiers Castle." The crow priest offered no condolences to William on the death of young Thomas Clay. "Secondly, these charges are fabrications... falsehoods... lies made against me and my family for profit or revenge. They are not charges that will bear up to scrutiny. I say now before you, and with God as my witness, that I have never committed any act of crime against man, nor any sin against God or His laws."

"One witness bears testimony that you..." spoke the Crow Priest while referring to his documents; reading from one of them, he continued, "that you took up a sword in the great banqueting hall at Poitiers Castle and slew an innocent man, him being senseless from partaking of wine that you and your brothers supplied to the festivities arranged thereto for the celebration of the engagement of Isabella to our own King Edward. Do you deny this? Do you say that this freely given statement is a falsehood, William Clay?" William felt unsure how to answer the question without sounding guilty of what he was being accused of.

"It is true in part, Your Grace... It is true that I took up a sword and struck down a man but he was not an innocent man; he was an assassin responsible for the murder of many knights of the Holy Order and also that of my brother, Thomas, who was trying to protect him from others in our company who wanted to take his life. He cowardly stabbed Thomas in the back and while I was taken by the rage of revenge, I—"

"You say the man you killed was not an innocent man, William Clay? Do you sit in judgement of men to decide who is innocent and who is not?" With the utterance of these weasel words, William fully realised the trouble he and his brothers were in. They were damned no matter what they said in their defence about the events that had taken place in France.

"Your Grace, I did as any brother would have done in witnessing the slaying of his little brother... his innocent little brother, Your Grace, by the hand of—"

"Innocent little brother you say, William Clay? Innocent? Really? Do you speak of the same Thomas Clay who stole Church money to spend with prostitutes? Innocent? I do not think so, William Clay. Thomas Clay was a godless sinner of the very lowest order, fit only to spend eternity in the fires of hell for stealing money from the Church for the pursuit of earthly pleasures to satisfy his base desires." The crow priest held William in an icy glare before continuing. "Have you nothing else to say in defence of your 'innocent' little brother, William Clay?"

"Your Grace… I… I…" William could not reply, feeling a deep sense of shame and guilt over Thomas' conduct. The same conduct that he and his brothers had laughed and made light of during their remembrances of him while they were in France.

"I thought not. What is there to say when the evidence is so clear, William Clay?"

"Your Grace, it is true that Thomas was not without sin but there was much good in him. He did many good deeds for the poor, the sick and the unfortunate of the parish." *Deeds that the Church should've undertaken*, spoke a silent voice inside William's head. "He dedicated much of his time and life to the glory of God, our Sovereign King and the Holy Order of Knights, whom he served to the cost of his life. Surely, Your Grace, that has to weigh in the balance on the day of judgement? A life without sin is a life—"

"A life without sin is the path through life we must all seek and adhere to. Do you not agree, William Clay?" All William could do was nod in agreement.

During their interrogations, William, John and Robert Clay defended the family and their reputations as best they could against the many accusations raining down on them from the Crow Priest and his Council of Parish Commissioners. Ultimately William capitulated, accepting the Church's case against him and his brothers by agreeing that they had indeed committed many sins during their escape from France. Deep inside of him, William simply could not bring himself to argue against the keepers of God's given laws, and so conceded every point of sin to the Crow Priest. William begged for forgiveness without further thought or word against the treatment or the torments they were being subjected to in God's name. He hoped that by confessing all to the Crow Priest , the Clay family might be handed some penance to perform and thereafter be left alone to continue with their lives as before. Robert, on the other hand, was defiant in his attitude and manner and defended the family's honour, piety and integrity throughout his questioning. John took the middle path, deflecting both confrontation and capitulation in his answers to all the accusations being made. The crow priest took special note of John's ability to weave weasel words into a plausible defence.

Inquiries concerning improprieties and loose morals conducted on the Clay daughters were hard for them to hear as they were innocent in mind and deed and completely without worldly knowledge. Ignorant of all matters, the mouths of the daughters of Elizabeth Clay – Mary, Margaret and Marion – refused to open to speak in defence against the shocking allegations made by their inquisitors. Robert noticed how the Crow Priest hid his hands inside his robes when he questioned his sisters, then demanded complete privacy so he could contemplate and reflect on the answers they had provided to his questions.

The Crow Priest and his Council of Parish Commissioners continued their inquisition of the Clay family for four days and nights, demanding food, drink and accommodation for them and their servants during the period of their stay, though they were content that the servants slept outside or in a barn. Before the unwelcome visitors left, they charged the Clays an additional forty gold crowns as advance payment for the next stage of the inquisition. This meant the esquire brothers no longer had sufficient funds to journey to France to return Thomas to England.

As soon as the Crow Priest and his Council of Parish Commissioners were out of sight of the Clay family home, Robert launched a vicious attack on William, berating him for collaborating with their inquisitors and for his unwavering trust and faith in God and the Church. William was shocked by the ferocity of the attack on him in front of the entire family.

"Robert, my dear brother, I know that you have faith inside of you. I can feel it. You are angry now but that will soon pass," was all William could find to say in the face of Robert's attack on him.

"Brother! Who do you think set the Crow Priest and his tick men on us? Do you think they turned up here by chance? No! We are still being pursued by France." Robert perceived the Crow Priest's inquisition as a cosy arrangement between the aristocracy and their chief familiars, the Church, against the very people they should be protecting from the harms of the world.

"Your fantasies become too much, brother," spoke John, sucking up, as usual, to William.

"Brothers, look at what is happening, see what they are doing to us… see things for what they are… look at what your Church is doing to us… I sense the hand of the French King in all this, or at least that of his servant, Sir Aldred Benz. France is set on wiping out the memory of the Holy Order of Knights and are at us for escaping their clutches, and they will not stop until we are ruined, dead or both."

★

News of the inquisition being carried out by the Council of Parish Commissioners against the Clays quickly spread throughout the six parishes. Rumours abounded about the charges levelled at the family. It was not long before details were leaked. The Clay brothers were accused of being plunderers, murderers and sodomites, and that during their time in France they had stolen from an abbey, willingly fell in with outlaws and passed themselves off as members of the clergy. It was said that no charges, as yet, were being laid against the Clay daughters, but they were forbidden to travel outside their parish except under command from the head of the Council of Parish Commissioners, who had generously agreed to take them under his holy protection for the sake of their immortal souls. It was rumoured that the husbands of two of the Clay daughters had left their family homes on the Clay estate, taking their children with them.

The bad news kept on rolling as far as William Clay was concerned. On hearing of the charges laid at his feet, William's childhood sweetheart declared their engagement off. William received a note from her father stating that under pain of death should he dare venture close to his former fiancée. As if to punish William further, she married John Belcher, detested neighbour of the Clays, who had recently, though some thought suspiciously, had become a widower.

The visits made by the Council of Parish Commissioners on the Clay family continued for over a year, during which time they became more protracted and consequently more costly. The Clays having sold off most of the tied farms that the Clays' ancestors had worked so hard to acquire to pay the fees of the inquisition, and possessing no more gold, the Council of Parish Commissioners suddenly ceased their investigations of the Clays, declaring the charges 'unproven', which is to say they were not declared innocent and their inquisition could be reopened at any time. The Clays might've then expected that some form of neighbourly relations be reopened, but rumours of the Clay brothers being sodomites persisted and were added to by rumours of exclusion or even excommunication by the Church. The Clays' miseries were continuously stoked by the Council of Parish Commissioners, designed to keep them isolated from the community and at the mercy of the Church , and the Clay sisters were to be received by the crow priest in his private rooms for confession. Who could blame the people of the six parishes for their lack of humanity or Christian goodness, when to be even remotely associated with sodomy could lead them to a fiery death at the stake? A form of living death, excommunication, was to be avoided at all costs; the threat of which the Church played on in their dealings with the aristocracy and peasantry alike. The clergy well knew how to play the excommunication card in their power game, and who would dare to interfere with the machinations of the Church?

★

With the Clay family fortune taken by the Council of Parish Commissioners, the plans the esquire brothers had of returning to Poitiers to recover the remains of their youngest brother to English soil were in pieces. Even then William refused to criticise or attack the Church. He would only repeat to his brothers that they had indeed committed sins and they should pay for doing so. William's stance enraged Robert and divided the brothers even further.

A family meeting was held to decide how to best proceed with the family fortune gone. Their priority was to put the family estate, such as it now was, back on a solid footing. Once accomplished, the brothers would then honour their youngest brother's memory by bringing his remains back home to England as they'd promised. As the Clay family estate was reduced to four farms, it would be a comparatively easy task to prepare the fields for planting, which they would set about doing with the assistance of those tenant farmers who'd remained because they had nowhere else to go. It was at this meeting that Mary and her husband, Galen Spurling, came forward with gold that they had kept hidden from the Crow Priest. It was an amount sufficient for one of the brothers to journey to France and, once there, hire help to return Thomas to England. The other brothers would necessarily need to remain at home to work on the remaining farms of the estate. It was agreed that this was best course of action as the Clay family could not afford to have three men away from the estate at that time.

"Bless you, Mary... bless you, Galen. Without your pot of gold, God knows when we would've been able to make the journey to France."

"Surely, brother, if God does know, then why did you not ask him? Kneel to pray, brother... see what answer you get back," spoke Robert mocking William.

"What is this?" asked Mary, puzzled by her brother's words.

"Take no note, Mary, it is simply Robert's way of—"

"Do not answer for me, brother! Tell her... tell her what transpired between us on the road home to England."

"Robert, I warned you what I'd do to you if you mentioned your perverse views on our Lord God and His servants while you remain in this house!"

"What, brother, that you would cut out my tongue and spike my eyes? That is not such a Christian thing to do now, is it, brother? Are you quite sure you are a Christian? Or perhaps you're a lackey of the Crow Priest? As far as I could see, you seemed quick to confess to him. Tell me, brother, did you notice how the Crow Priest was with our sisters? How his hands would disappear inside his robes? What do you imagine he was doing with his hands while they were hidden from view? Praying? And how he always retired immediately afterwards to... what was it he said?... ah yes... 'to reflect and contemplate their answers'. Look inside yourself, brother, and you will know what he was doing in the privacy of his quarters, being hot inside himself after leching over the form of our sisters..."

William could not bear to hear anymore and lashed out at Robert with his fist, catching him flush on his jaw and sending him sprawling to the ground. He immediately regretted his actions.

"Robert… Robert… my dear brother. I am sorry… forgive me, brother, forgive me."

"Forgive you, brother? There is nothing to forgive you for. You did as you thought necessary to do for your God and His servants," Robert replied almost laughing. "Go, brother, go to France. Perhaps you'll find your salvation there because there is none here for you. You are a hypocrite and a sinner as much as me or the next man, but wrapping yourself in a shroud of piety, you believe yourself better than I or the next man. You are not, brother, you are not. You delude yourself, brother, and in your delusion you cannot see that which is right in front of you."

"And what is that, oh wise one?" mocked William of Robert.

"That the Church's only interest in God is in how much it can exploit His name for its own profit and purposes. It is an empire of evil, scheming purely to increase its temporal power through the possession of the souls of the very people they should be protecting from the harms of this world. Your Church is the hand in the glove of aristocrats and nobles, crushing ordinary people so they—"

"I've heard all this before from you, brother, is there is nothing new for me to hear? Have you nothing new to say on the subject?"

"You are a deluded fool, William. I can no longer bear the sight or sound of you. I will journey to France to bring Thomas back home for a proper burial and then I will leave this place, never to return to it while you live."

"*You* go to France? You? You! You do not, have never, and will not ever represent this family in any of its duties. It is for me, as the eldest son, and me alone, to take up the quest to journey to France and bring our brother home so he can be buried among his ancestors."

"Tell me, brother, can you really do that for the godless sinner you gave Thomas up to be to the Crow Priest?" William turned away in shame. Robert shouted at his retreating back. "Hypocrite! Traitor! Coward! Who gave you the right to speak—"

"Robert, please, my good brother, do not make any more of this than it need be. William is the eldest and so it falls on him to bring Thomas home," pleaded Mary, tears streaming down her cheeks. "I miss Thomas so every day. All I have of him are my memories and I will not have them tarnished by angry, misspoken words. I beg you, Robert, no more; promise me, no more." Robert placed his arm around Mary's shuddering shoulders to comfort his sister. They went and sat together in the solitude of the family burial place to commune with the spirits of their ancestors. "Do you hate him?" asked Mary.

"No, I only hate myself," replied Robert without explaining his meaning.

William Clay departed for France before first light the following morning. He didn't bother to say goodbye to anybody; he just took the gold that Mary and Galen had kept from the Crow Priest and left the house.

★

As time rolled by, neighbours came to assist the Clays with their farm labours as many of them too had suffered some form of persecution at one time or another. In fact, most families in the six parishes had suffered inquisition over the generations, but few were willing to cast aspersions on the Church, preferring to lay the blame for their woes at the feet of aristocrats. The Clays were humbled by just how many people came to help throughout the year, and had it not been so they would not have been able to bring the harvest in as two of their tenant farmers died during the summer and their families left the estate to live with relatives in distant villages. So many people were helping the Clays that Robert thought it suspicious and mentioned as much to John.

John reprimanded his little brother, telling him not to be so distrustful of the 'goodness of God's children', but Robert couldn't rid himself of the suspicions burning inside of him.

Soon after the harvest was stored away in the barns, the Council of Parish Commissioners reappeared with the Crow Priest at their head. He accused the Clays of being in league with the Devil as "how else can you explain the transformation of your fortunes?"

"It does not surprise me you do not understand how such a transformation could take place, good Father, because it was made by hard work and long hours toiling in the fields... something you are unfamiliar with," taunted Robert while casting a sly glance at John. He was determined not to inform the Council of Parish Commissioners of the help they'd received from their neighbours. But his silence on the matter was in vain.

"And what of the help you received in your working of the land? How did you pay those who came to work for you on the estate farms?"

"No payment was made, Your Grace, we had nothing with which to pay them," interjected John to stay his brother's mouth.

"Then why did these people toil in your fields as well as their own?" asked the Crow Priest.

"Again, good Father, it is something you and your council are not familiar with. Neighbours toiled in our fields to help us in our hour of need... as all good Christians should."

"You go too far, Robert Clay. However, to show you the depth of the Church's Christian compassion and charity, you will not be flogged or imprisoned; instead you will serve penance by building a wall around the field adjacent to your parish church."

"That is one of our fields," stated Robert in monotone.

"It is indeed, and it is to become the site of the six parishes' cemetery and therefore property of the Church." John grabbed Robert by the wrist to stay him from provoking the priest further.

"I see your brother has better sense than you, which is just as well. Now to taxing you for our visit here today. As you have no gold, we will take what is in your barns in compensation of our time."

"But how will we survive the coming winter, Your Grace, if you take all we have in our barns?"

"Well, we will then see just how Christian the souls of this parish are, John Clay… Will they share their stores of grain with you after we have taxed them? Will they give up any of the animals they have fattened for slaughter after we have taxed them? If they do, they will have to answer to me for helping a family set in exclusion by this very council… a family tainted by sodomy while in the service of the Unholy Order of Knights!" The change in title of the Holy Order of Knights did not go unnoticed and angered John and Robert.

"But, Your Grace, those of our parish who aided us should not be punished for their acts of kindness, they only sought to—"

"And what of the sudden deaths of the tenant farmers? It seems that after the planting was done, you had no further need of them… This will need to be investigated but as you have no coin for it, I shall set it aside until your fortunes change; otherwise it is not worth our while to convene the Council of Parish Commissioners for the purpose." After gathering up his documents, the crow priest continued speaking. "I must take my leave of you to see those who have taken part in the aiding of you Clays. My churchmen will be by before the day is out to empty your barns… but be warned, do not remove any of the grain therein on pain of a flogging and imprisonment."

The crow priest and the Council of Parish Commissioners left the Clays devastated at losing their grain stores, wondering how they would survive the winter, and pushing concerns they had over the time it was taking William to return from France with Thomas' remains to the back of their minds. As soon as the Council of Parish Commissioners was out of sight, Robert set horses in harness to two carts and proceeded to remove as much grain from the barns as would fit in them. John and the Clay sisters went to stop him but he refused to listen to them, saying that those coming to steal their grain could not possibly know how much was in the barns. Mulling over Robert's words, all conceded that he was probably right, and it being considered worth the risk, the whole family set about filling the carts with as much of the harvest as they could.

When the churchmen arrived to pick up the grain from the barns, their leader took John and Robert aside and begged them not to think badly of him and his men as they were under threat of punishment if they did not carry out the orders of the Council of Parish Commissioners. The brothers sympathised with the man, saying that they understood his predicament and that they did not hold him or his men to any blame in the matter. Looking from side to side with quick, searching eyes, the leader of the churchmen leaned forward and whispered to the brothers that he would leave two cartloads of the harvest in the second field along the lane for them to collect later.

"Thank you, brother. God bless and care for you in the carrying out of His work, and let His goodness shine through you and your men," spoke John in deep gratitude of the man's Christian kindness and the risk he was taking in leaving behind some of the grain. Robert held himself in check until the churchmen had departed before berating his brother. He asked him how it could be God's work or His will that they have their grain taken by the servants of His Church. Robert was outraged that John had passed God's blessings on the churchman, who left them only a small portion of it. John was unmoved and said it was by His divine will that the churchman had shown such Christian compassion.

"If seems that if things be good then it is by His good grace that it is so, and if things be bad He is testing us or punishing us for our sins... sins that none can recall or put words to. You are as much a fool in this as William. If He be real then why does He allow such bad things to happen to His flock?" John neither had nor gave any answer to Robert; he just turned his back and walked away from his faithless brother.

That night, after they'd recovered the grain left by the churchman, the Clay family sat nervously at home waiting for news of the privations their neighbours had suffered at the hands of the Council of Parish Commissioners. They were half expecting to be burned out of their home by an angry mob but the night passed without incident. As the Clays emerged into the lane the next morning, they spied a delegation from the village approaching them. At the head of the group was Crawdyke Simmons, a man of about forty years who'd harboured a grudge against Elizabeth and Edward Clay, the parents of the current generation. As they were now both deceased, John, Robert and their sisters wondered how this might affect matters between them. Crawdyke Simmons approached the Clays and hugged them close to him. He invited them to attend a village meeting to plan how they were going to survive the coming winter together. The effect of the actions of the Council of Parish Commissioners was that it brought the communities of the six parishes together like never before, forging a spirit of unity and comradery between families across generations.

★

It was coming up to one year since William Clay had set off to France to bring Thomas' remains back to England. The family, as well as the communities of the six parishes, were coming to believe that some terrible misfortune had befallen him. All wanted news of him as the not knowing was driving everybody to despair.

One Sunday morning, as the Clays were leaving their home to attend church services, they noticed a man sitting on a horse at the top of the lane. Behind him was a cart drawn by two horses. The man turned to speak to the driver of the cart before riding at walking pace toward the family. Staring at the man, John could not help but think that there was something familiar about him, something about his manner as he sat in the saddle. It was Robert who called out to the man, "Lorence Blackstone? Is that you, Lorence Blackstone?"

Replying that it was indeed he, the man spurred his horse to a fast trot to come to stand in front of the Clay family. A deep sense of foreboding descended on the whole family as Robert and John had told them stories of the outlaws of Rennes Forest, with special mention of Lorence Blackstone.

"It is good to see you, brother," spoke Robert to Lorence with trepidation in his voice.

"It is good to see you too, brother… though I would wish our meeting were under better circumstances." The Clay family looked beyond Lorence to the driver of the two-horse cart that was now making its way down the lane toward them. As the cart drew close, they could see it contained a single item bound in heavy cloth.

"What do you bring us, Master Blackstone?" asked Mary.

"I give you my answer without dressing it: I bring the remains of Thomas Clay, as I was sworn so to do in a pledge I made to William Clay."

"That was my brother's quest, Master Blackstone. Why is it that you are fulfilling it for him?" asked Margaret Clay, a recently made free woman of the parish.

"Alas, it falls on me to tell you that William Clay lies dead in France… but I will say no more of this until the ladies have removed themselves." The Clay sisters stood outraged at Lorence Blackstone's words but before they could unleash their collective fury on him, Robert intervened.

"Lorence, my outlaw brother, there is not one chance in a hundred that my sisters will withdraw from this scene until they are satisfied with your story of William's demise." Looking into the faces of the sisters, Lorence Blackstone did not doubt Robert's words and so requested they adjourn to the house as the telling of the tale would take some considerable time.

"No, not yet. We must first plant our beautiful little brother in our ancestral burial place, right next to mother and father as he and they would've wanted," insisted Mary. "His journey has been long and we have long missed him, and so want him at rest without further delay."

A neighbour passing by the lane called out to the Clays to hurry them to church. John replied to her that Thomas had been returned to them and they were burying him that very morning. On hearing the news of Thomas' return, the neighbour wept openly, remarking that it was a pity that Elizabeth was not alive to see her son returned home to her. The neighbour asked if they wanted her to give the news of Thomas' homecoming to the congregation. They said they did and asked her to beg their forgiveness for them not attending services that morning. Before the woman walked away John told her that they would hold a service of remembrance for Thomas' friends to attend the following Sunday. On that day, before the grave-hole was fully dug, a crowd of over two hundred people arrived in a sad silent procession onto the Clay estate. The presence of the strangers who'd brought Thomas home did not go unnoticed, especially by the females of the six parishes, both maidens and mothers alike.

★

It was late into the evening before the last of the mourners departed, leaving Lorence Blackstone in the company of the Clay family. He said the story he had to tell would be hard for them to hear and wondered if it might be put off until morning. Robert spoke for the family when he said Lorence should tell them the tale without further delay and leave nothing out. "The telling should take as long as it takes," added John Clay.

Lorence Blackstone's tale began with him meeting William Clay at an Inn in St Malo. William had grabbed Lorence by the shoulders, recognising him immediately despite his beard, unkempt hair and shabby town-clothes. Lorence told William the tale of soldiers clearing out the outlaws of Rennes Forest, Sir Aldred Benz at their head. Many of them had been taken alive and were tortured to tell what they knew of William and his brothers, which, of course, was very little. This angered Sir Aldred, who had all but six of them hung before being thrown alive onto fires, one at a time, each waiting their turn in a dreadful queue to witness their comrades going before them in screaming agony to meet their maker.

William had asked Lorence how then he came to be standing in front of him in St Malo. "Were you one of the six?" Lorence replied that he wasn't, but had the soldiers looked up they would've seen him with three others, including Silas Creek, hiding in the trees. He said it as though a spell had been cast over them that the soldiers' vision could not penetrate. Lorence asked William what he was doing in St Malo. He replied that he had been to pay a debt of honour to the wife of a boat captain who'd given his life in the esquire brothers' escape from France. Lorence asked how it went. William replied that as the woman had taken up with the boat captain's brother and appeared to be doing very nicely, he didn't pay the debt as there seemed no longer any honour in it.

Over a bottle of wine, William had told Lorence of his quest to travel to Poitiers and exhume his brother's remains to return them to English soil. Lorence asked what he could do to help, to which William replied that he could help him recruit some men 'handy at sword' as his mission was likely to encounter some trouble along the way. "I have little coin, mind you, so not so many men and not so costly." Lorence asked William to make the sign of the Holy Order of Knights. As he did so, eight men, devotees of the Order, made themselves known to the pair and signed up for the quest on payment in wine and food. Their journey to Poitiers passed with singing and storytelling and without incident.

"It was coming onto darkness when we arrived at the gravesite in the wood just beyond Poitiers Castle. The grave looked intact, showing no signs of disturbance. William turned to us and begged he be allowed to approach the grave in solitude so that he might say a private prayer over his brother. After he returned he said that as night was drawing on, we should give Thomas one last night of rest in French soil before his long journey home. I and another went into Poitiers to replenish our supplies and took some rest there. We arrived back at the camp the following morning to find a scene of carnage. All but one of the men from St Malo was dead and there was no sign of William.

"I gave the dying man some sips of water. Before he passed from life he told me that the assassins seemed to know that William was amongst them as they separated him from the group before cutting them all to pieces. He mentioned hearing a knight tell four of his retinue to take William to the abbey at Orléans to receive the King's justice while he would hunt down the two unaccounted-for men and follow on afterwards.

"The horses had scattered in the melee and two soldiers were left behind to round them up. After they had done their work, I and another man, Charles Leclerc, the one who drove the cart, ambushed them and we took back our horses."

"What did you do with the soldiers?" asked Margaret. Lorence looked about his audience before answering. "I killed them both, good lady, as we were not in a position or of a mind to do otherwise."

"Did you beg God's forgiveness for breaking his holiest and most sacred commandment?"

"No, good lady, I did not, for to do so I would be a hypocrite for all the other sins I have committed without seeking His forgiveness."

"Then, Lorence Blackstone, you are no better than—"

"Margaret, dear sister, hold your tongue and judge not Lorence lest you too be judged."

"I had no choice in the matter, good lady; if they had remained alive they could've given us away. I hope you come to understand that one day." Master Blackstone paused to gather his thoughts before continuing. "We set off after the company of soldiers hoping to catch them unawares and… and do what, we did not exactly know. It is a long road from Poitiers to Orléans and we travelled more in hope than expectation of freeing William. After many days travel we drew close to Orléans. We resolved that we must make some attempt to free your brother. We were in sight of the walls of the city when two soldiers left the company to go on ahead, for what purpose we could not guess. We reckoned that as we had surprise on our side it was worth two or three soldiers, so we resolved to make our move to rescue William. Coming up behind the company, we were about to strike when trumpets sounded from within the city walls and a mighty cheer went up. All along the battlements, folk were mingling with soldiers to get a look at 'the leader of the men who slaughtered the soldiers at Poitiers Castle'. Shouts came from atop the walls and fingers pointed in our direction. All at once soldiers appeared and chased after Leclerc and me. They were on us before we could make any distance. We had no fight left in us and we were quickly taken prisoner.

"We heard later that William was taken straightaway to the bishop's court, where he was pronounced guilty of all charges. The abbott, it was said, not wanting to make a mistake with so sought-after a man, wrote to King Philip to learn his pleasure in dealing with the convicted man. In the meantime, Leclerc and I were imprisoned. With us being unknown in the district, and there being no real charges to face, we were set to work for the guild of stonemasons for one month as punishment for common vagrancy."

"You seem to lead a charmed life, Master Blackstone; too charmed, I would say. You hide in trees and become invisible to those surrounding you; you are taking rest in Poitiers when the camp is slaughtered; you are held in Orléans prison but face no charges. What next, Lorence Blackstone, what next will we learn about you? That you can fly?" spoke Margaret Clay in an accusatory tone.

"Good lady, what would you have happen to me? That I had died in Rennes Forest along with my brother outlaws? That I had been cut to pieces in Poitiers along with everybody else? That I was executed at Orléans? I make no apology, nor do I give excuse or reason, for the good fortune I have had."

"Margaret, dear sister, we could not have made our escape through Rennes without the diversions created by my outlaw brother here. He does indeed run a charmed life, that much is clear from his escapades. Pray, let Lorence continue his tale."

"I am not oblivious to how this must appear or sound to you, good lady, but it is nevertheless a true and accurate account." Lorence Blackstone paused to regain his composure before continuing. "While Leclerc and I were working in the stone quarry, rumours began to circulate that the King had put it upon the abbott how to execute William and had written down the manner of it for him to follow. As I do not know the truth of it, I will not repeat what I cannot be certain of for a fact."

★

King Philip was delighted at the news that one of the men responsible for killing so many of his hired assassins had been captured and was languishing in prison in Orléans awaiting his justice. He wrote to the abbott, congratulating him and ordering him to deal with the plunderer, murderer and sodomite personally. This sort of blood bond was one of the devices King Philip employed to instil blind obedience in those in his service. After committing one atrocity they were owned by the King, while subsequent atrocities were all the easier to perform at his command.

The letter sent to the abbott contained in it precise details of how William Clay was to die. Death would not come quick and it would not be easy to endure the giving or the receiving of the horrors on the list. The abbott, whose normal role was to merely administrate the bishop's court, had hoped to simply turn William over to the King's men but Philip's note was specific, demanding he do the deed himself. The abbott read the letter over and over again, trembling and weeping as he did so. He wrestled with his conscience and at one point resolved to let William go free and escape with him to England rather than commit this foul sin.

The abbott, however, had a couple of dark secrets. Not only had he fathered eleven children by local women, he was a sodomite boy-lover, responsible for seducing countless young male children over many years. He knew his secrets would come out as soon as he fled and so he prayed for divine guidance; not only did he not want to commit the sin of murder, but he strongly desired to keep himself, his secrets and his offspring safe. He read the note for an eighth time. Read one way, it appeared the King wanted the abbott to personally carry out the execution, but read another way… "the Devil's in the detail," as the abbott was oft wont to say.

After pondering his novel interpretation of the wording of the letter for over an hour, the abbott summoned six local peasants and ordered them to execute William. "The King of France commands you to execute the prisoner William Clay. Look! See! Here! It is a letter from King Philip ordering the execution of the plunderer, murderer and sodomite. Look, all of you! Our King has even set down how it must be done." The illiterate peasants were led to the vaults where, held in a dim shaft of light lent from an opening above, they could just about make out the shape of a chained-up man. Two of the peasants refused to have anything to do with this crime against God's laws in His house. The other four peasants looked uneasy. Seeing his scheme going up in smoke, the abbott promised to pay the remaining peasants a huge sum in gold to carry out the torture and execution. Walking away from the scene, the abbott muttered to himself that he would get all his gold back from the peasants in tax; if he even gave them anything at all, that is.

After almost two days the deed was done and William was dead. The abbott replied to King Philip, informing him that the execution of William Clay had been carried out exactly as he'd prescribed. The King now had an obedient servant for the remainder of his life.

The two peasants who'd refused to take part in the execution told their story to anybody who'd listen to it in the inns of Orléans and so the rumours of William Clay's inhuman suffering and death spread to reach the ears of Lorence Blackstone and Charles Leclerc.

★

The end of Lorence Blackstone's tale was not long in coming. He told his audience that the guild of stonemasons, being pleased with the work he Leclerc had done, took pity on them and paid them for their labour so they could no longer be detained as common vagrants. They had just enough money to return to Poitiers to exhume the body of Thomas Clay and return him to England. The family asked Lorence what happened to Charles Leclerc, to which he replied that he was the driver of the two-horse cart that had delivered Thomas' remains but had elected to keep incognito to see what type of reception Lorence received.

"Now that you have returned Thomas to us, and remain safe in our home, why has Leclerc not given up his incognito?"

"I know not, good lady. I will look for him in the morning if he remains out of our company past breakfast."

The four esquire brothers that had been were now two. Those that were the eldest and the youngest were dead and gone, replaced by a new eldest and new youngest, which was remarked to John and Robert Clay by Lorence Blackstone. John Clay began experiencing terrible pangs of guilt identical to those suffered by Robert after Thomas' death. He'd always wanted to be the eldest brother, the inheritor of the Clay estate, and now that he was, his guilt over his thoughts against the noble William and the cruel death he'd suffered ate into his soul. John Clay got not a minute's sleep that night for fear of dreaming of William.

The following morning, the cart and its two horses were found in the stables and Leclerc was away hunting in the woods. When he came by to breakfast at the Clays' house, he presented them with a brace of fine fat conies.

After discussing Lorence Blackstone's tale of William's death, John and Robert Clay, together with Galen Spurling, made ready to leave for France to take revenge on those responsible for his death, especially the abbott who sent him from this world in the most inhuman and unchristian of ways. The Clay sisters, Lorence Blackstone and Charles Leclerc convinced the three men that two deaths was more than enough for the Clay family to bear and to give up their blood revenge. And so, the esquire brothers remained in England as their hatred for the French King festered inside them, and hatred for the Church grew stronger and stronger inside Robert Clay.

THE RETURN OF THE ORDER

Over the following year and a half, the crow priest and his Council of Parish Commissioners fell upon the Clay family many times. They again took their harvest from them, as they did with many of the families of the six parishes, it being their payment to investigate crimes against God, man and the Church. Anticipating that their harvests would be snatched, families hid good portions of their crops from the Council of Parish Commissioners, who, with spoils being thin, departed to find richer pickings elsewhere. During this period, arguments raged between John and Robert Clay as to who and what lay behind the persecutions set upon them and their neighbours. John Clay blamed a vengeful aristocracy while Robert blamed a rapacious Church. Over time, Robert came to pretend to agree with John as he'd thought up schemes to secretly wage war on the Church while remaining close to his brother and family.

★

Following the death of William Clay, John Clay, then being the eldest son, inherited the family estate; such as it was after the crow priest and his Council of Parish Commissioners had plundered it. Inheriting the mantle of running the estate was not what John thought it would be, and as pressures piled up on him, John became more and more detached from reality. The root cause of John Clay's melancholy and his subsequent slow slide into madness was the burning guilt he felt inside of himself for wishing ill on William and for himself to inherit the family estate. Now that he had it, he wished he didn't. John's delusions became markedly more intense as his madness grew. He was convinced that his ill thoughts had somehow taken physical form and killed William. In an attempt to absolve himself of his guilt, John prayed ten or more times a day and made religious devotions, such that he had little time for anything else. Family members became concerned over John's erratic behaviour and the madness behind his eyes. They were frightened to be around him, scared of him and what he might do, what he might be capable of, and wondered if they should have him committed to an asylum for everybody's sake. Robert wouldn't entertain such ideas and chastised the family severely for even thinking of such a thing. In doing so, the family thought Robert showed good but misguided love for his brother. However, they weren't aware that he was conjuring schemes and planned to use John's position as head of the family for his own ends, and his being locked up in an asylum would not suit Robert's purposes.

In contrast to John Clay's melancholy and guilt over William's death, Robert Clay had reconciled with himself for having had unbrotherly thoughts about Thomas, which had included wishing him dead. His conscience was clear and untroubled. He now had clear focus on his scheme of bringing those responsible for Thomas' murder to justice; with those responsible being the Church. He was going to make war on the Church. It was not simply a matter of declaring war on the Church; if he were to do that, he would find himself at the end of a rope or lashed to a pole above his own funeral pyre. He would need to be cunning if he was to stay alive. His war would necessarily be carried out in the shadows. To progress his plans, Robert first needed to find people with beliefs akin to his own or, if not that, people he could control through blackmail such that their mutual destruction would be assured if they ever gave him up. However, fate was about to get in the way of Robert's scheming.

★

One day during the spring of 1311, John and Robert Clay were attending a village fair when a rabble rouser caught their attention. He was telling the gathered crowd of how the Holy Order of Knights had risen again and were looking for men of good standing to join their service in France. On hearing this news, a weight seemed to be lifted from John Clay; the madness in his eyes subsided and his careworn face took on a carefree look. He stood transfixed and listened to all the rabble rouser had to say.

The esquire brothers, needing no word of encouragement, raced back to the Clay estate and gave everybody the news that they were going to France to enter into the service of the resurrected Holy Order of Knights. They asked Lorence Blackstone to join them. He not only refused to go with them but was astonished that John and Robert were even considering such a move. No matter what anybody said to them or what objections were raised, the esquire brothers were determined to return to France and take up once again their service to the Holy Order of Knights. They said it was their calling to do so, to honour the fallen William and Thomas. The Clay sisters told them not to be so ridiculous as to assert such a calling but the esquire brothers refused to listen to them; their minds were made up.

Robert Clay, in particular, was surprised that Lorence Blackstone would not be journeying with him and his brother to France. He asked Lorence his reasons, to which he replied that the entire venture gave him a deep sense of foreboding and as he'd learned not to go against his instincts, he would not travel to France with him and his brother. Robert asked Lorence if there was any other cause as he was not convinced of the reasons he'd given. Lorence could no longer keep his feelings for Robert's sister, Margaret, a secret. He confessed that he was besotted in love with her and he believed, he hoped, she had grown to love him. Lorence had planned to ask John for Margaret's hand in marriage at the coming solstice celebrations but as he and Robert would be away before then, he saw no point in further delay and sought John out to tell him of his love for Margaret and to ask him for his blessing to marry her. The talk went well as John had noticed a change in the former philanderer and had wondered what lay behind it. John did not hesitate to give his permission for the marriage to go ahead. Margaret, on the other hand, was rather cool about the match and rather angry with Lorence that he'd gone to John before discussing marriage with her. Lorence begged Margaret's forgiveness, claiming he was following the only etiquette he knew. She forgave him his error of judgement and a date was set for their wedding. They were to be married on the day of the solstice, with many residents of the six parishes invited to attend the nuptials.

★

On their arrival in France, the esquire brothers sought information on the whereabouts of the Holy Order of Knights. They discovered that they were gathered at a number of encampments across France, with the closest of them being at Rouen. The esquire brothers, being familiar with the region, set off immediately.

Reaching Rouen some four days later, John and Robert Clay sought the sergeant-at-arms in charge of provisioning the camp for the Order and were directed to a man whose back was turned to them. When they approached the sergeant, he was already known to the brothers; it was none other than Samuel Black, the soldier who was first to strike down the assassins at Poitiers Castle.

Samuel greeted John and Robert in the manner of people who have come through some terrible ordeal together. It is a bond that lasts a lifetime. The esquire brothers told Samuel that news of the reforming of the Holy Order of Knights had reached them in England and they came straightaway to offer up their services. "Basically," they said, "we want our old jobs back." Samuel replied that with them already being known to the Order, they would be given their jobs back on approval of its leader, Sir Michael de Gel. John and Robert rejoiced at hearing that knight's name again and were taken to his encampment situated on the outskirts of Rouen.

When the esquire brothers reached Sir Michael's encampment they were taken by Samuel Black to meet him. When Sir Michael set eyes on the esquire brothers, he grabbed each of them by the shoulders, clasped them close and kissed them as tears of joy ran down his tired face. Looking around beyond John and Robert, the knight asked them for news of the eldest esquire brother, his old favourite, William. John told the Knight that he had a sad tale to tell and would tell it to the knight if he wished to hear it. Sir Michael ordered Samuel Black to remain for the esquire brothers to impart their tale to them both. When John Clay got to the part in the story about William's death at the hands of the abbott of Orléans, Robert cursed the Church for the part it had played in his torture and execution. Sir Michael, himself not as devout as previous leaders of the Holy Order of Knights, reprimanded Robert for his blasphemous talk, saying that the Church had to act, more so than ordinary citizens, under the orders of a sovereign who has the God-given right to rule his country and his people as he sees fit. Robert replied saying that he would hold his tongue until later on in his brother's account of events. When John Clay got to the part in the story where the crow priest and his Council of Parish Commissioners held inquisition over the Clay family, Robert again cursed the Church, branding the clergy as familiars of the aristocracy. On this point, Sir Michael was not quite so severe in his reprimand of Robert Clay but reminded him that the aristocracy are the familiars of the monarch and as such are bound to do his bidding, "and so it is passed down the line".

After John finished telling his tale, Sir Michael gave the esquire brothers an abridged account of his escape from those of the King's Knights who had pursued him and his attachment of soldiers into the Low Countries. Once he arrived there, Sir Michael discovered that most of the Holy Order of Knights had been slain but a good number had survived, thanks to the protection afforded them by several Counts opposed to King Philip. The King's Knights pursuing Sir Michael eventually surrendered, and then switched sides to aid the Holy Order of Knights' reform. John Clay asked Sir Michael if it was wise to bring such knights into the Order, to which he replied that they had been free to do as they wished and in that freedom they chose not to return to live under Sir Aldred Benz's tyranny. He added that having made their choice, the former King's Knights became the most trustworthy of men, unlike the vagabond knights Sir Michael had felt compelled to take into the Order to swell their numbers; though he implied he had a plan to deal with these second-rate knights by recruiting others of better standing to replace them.

After their talks with Sir Michael, Samuel Black took John and Robert Clay to the tent they'd be billeted in to meet some of those others in service to the Holy Order of Knights. The esquire brothers were introduced to their companions in service as senior valets to the Holy Order of Knights, with special attachment to its leader, Sir Michael de Gel. All the men in the tents and the surrounding area bowed to John and Robert, saying what an honour and a privilege it was to serve with them. "Under them," corrected Samuel Black in clipped concise tones, "under them." The men servants corrected themselves, saying to John and Robert what an honour and a privilege it was to serve under them, bowing lower this second time.

Despite their position as esquires at the bottom rung in the order of English nobility and having, since their youth, overseen tenant farmers on tied lands, neither John nor Robert Clay felt at ease being overseers, especially in this company, but their Englishness directed them to accept the position with apology.

Back in the old routine, the esquire brothers couldn't have been happier. There they were, back working in the company of the Holy Order of Knights. They had their old jobs back. They knew what to do and how it was to be done, and they were satisfied to such a degree that Robert swore he would serve the Order to the end of his days, turning his back on the past and even forgiving those who'd murdered his brothers and persecuted his family. For John's part, his insanity seemed to lessen with every passing minute.

"Are you sure about that, brother? You forgive those responsible for Thomas' death?"

"Aye, John, I am sure. Never have I felt so at peace with myself and the world. I harbour no grudges or ill will, even against crow priests and the aristocracy, whose interests they serve. They can all go and hang themselves for now I no longer care what they do."

"I am content that you are no longer set against the Church, though for my part I can never forgive those aristocrats who drive them to commit evil deeds at their behest."

"You cannot draw me into an argument, brother. Inside of me I know what the Church is, but I am no longer set against it. I just want to be left alone to get on with my life and I live in the hope that the Church will not persecute our family now that you and I are out the country. It is us they wanted and the crow priest and his Council of Parish Commissioners sought to divide our family and community, but it didn't work… and now, with us gone, it will never work, so I am content."

"That is quite a turnaround, brother… what next? Are you to become a knight of the Holy Order?" laughed John.

"And why not, dear brother, why not? You heard Sir Michael, did you not, when he said that many of the knights now in the service of the Holy Order are only what was available, not what he would've chosen. That is what he said. I will be a knight in the customs and manner of William Marshal, Lord Knight and Protector of the old ways."

"Be careful, brother, not to set yourself impossibly high standards," scoffed John Clay. "I think you might delude yourself, but request Sir Michael train you as it would be detrimental to your ambition not to ask."

Robert Clay sought an audience with Sir Michael de Gel to request he be schooled in the art, methods and behaviours of the brotherhood of knights. Sir Michael, though sceptical of Robert's pedigree to fulfil such a role, nevertheless agreed that he should be given as an apprentice to a knight. Samuel Black, though envious of Robert's assignment, offered to assist his knightly tutor in some of the military and fighting aspects of the novice's instruction. While all this was going on, John Clay wondered time and again if Robert really had renounced his old ways or was playing to the gallery. He'd keep a close watch on him, but he was happy that his little brother was happy.

The time of the solstice came and went but no news of Margaret Clay and Lorence Blackstone's nuptials reached John and Robert. They weren't too concerned, however, as Sir Michael's encampment had moved several times since their arrival and so, thought they, all home news would follow on. Besides, being the senior valets to the Knights of the Holy Order, responsible for overseeing all the camp's attendants, the esquire brothers were very busy men and had little time to ponder on matters or goings on in the middle lands of England.

The lives of both John and Robert Clay were complete bliss. They were truly happy and often thought of how William and Thomas would have enjoyed being a part of this new era of the Holy Order of Knights. John's duties were mostly taken up with organising the knight's attendants and the camp followers, while Robert was dedicating most of his time to becoming a knight and hoped one day that he would become a Sir Knight like many of those he had served before the slaughter at Poitiers Castle. The good works and deeds of the Holy Order of Knights once again became legendary throughout all the lands, which made the attendants very proud and privileged to be in the service of their masters. Samuel Black, for his part, had recruited some fine men; and when the whole column of knights, soldiers, valets, attendants and camp followers were on the march with their colourful banners blowing in the breeze, they looked a wonderful site, striking fear into the hearts of the wicked and hope into the hearts of the poor, the weak and the needy.

★

All the while the Holy Order of Knights was rebuilding, diplomatic works went on in the background to reconcile their old disputes and differences with the various monarchies of western Europe. Being monarchs, they wanted to be able to do as they pleased in their realms, but having to kowtow to the rules of and grovel to the whims of the Holy Order of Knights, not to mention be taxed by them, was too much for them to take and they wanted them gone... again. Monarchs had got used to a world without the meddling Holy Order of Knights and wanted rid of them more than they had before. Pope Clement V and his sidekick-lackey King Philip IV of France had more reason than all the others put together for wanting rid of, once and for all time, the Holy Order of Knights, who were prosecuting their claims for the debts owed to their Order by both the Pope and the French King.

King Philip sought an audience with Pope Clement to beg His Holiness, once again, to help rid him of the interfering and self-righteous Holy Order of Knights. Once again Pope Clement agreed to help the French King, but this time in payment of a tribute of fifty thousand gold crowns. King Philip had already splashed out twenty thousand gold crowns for the first attempt to eradicate the Order and with this additional, and not inconsiderable, sum, he wondered whether he would be better off paying off his debt to the Order and then backing them to overthrow Pope Clement. As King Philip left his audience with His Holiness, he had not settled on a resolution to his dilemma of whether to pay off the Holy Order of Knights versus paying tribute of fifty thousand gold crowns to Pope Clement. A week later, his decision was still in the balance.

★

During October of 1311 messages were received by each of the heads of the Holy Order of Knights, at their separate encampments, that Pope Clement V and King Philip IV of France had reached agreement with the Order's negotiators to pay them the sums each owed to it. In celebration of this settlement, a Holy Mass was to be held to sanctify the monetary settlement under Holy Treaty. And so all knights of the Holy Order were directed to attend a communion service where they would receive a blessing from Pope Clement, witnessed by King Philip, and at which time full payment would be made to the knights of the Holy Order. Sir Michael de Gel was, at first, dubious of this turnaround in relations but his brother knights urged him to forgive past misdeeds and trust to the goodness of the Church. On hearing of the arrangement, Samuel Black sought an audience with Sir Michael where he begged him not to go to the Holy Mass as he did not believe that people could so readily change their hearts and minds. Sir Michael thanked Samuel Black for showing such dedication and concern over his welfare and told him that he'd be on his guard to watch out for any foul play.

The expression 'history repeating itself' was as common in the early fourteenth century as it is in the twenty-first century and the knights of the Holy Order should've been more suspicious when surrendering their weapons as they entered the abbey at Rouen. The knights were assured that nobody was allowed weapons upon the reason given that Pope Clement and King Philip, fearing an outbreak of old hostilities, thought it preferable that all parties be unarmed. "None shall enter into the city so armed," said those guarding the city's gates.

The combined companies of the Holy Order of Knights was so large that the service had to be held in the abbey's grounds. There, stood under the massive entrance arch to the abbey, were Pope Clement V and King Philip IV of France side by side with one another. Noticeably, both bore swords, as did their guard, which numbered over twenty. The knights of the Holy Order were situated in the centre of the grounds while those guarding the proceedings took up the perimeter. Valets, attendants, serfs, camp followers and soldiers attached to the Holy Order of Knights were not invited to the ceremony as, it was claimed, there was not enough room to accommodate them.

At the direction of Pope Clement, the knights of the Holy Order knelt and bent their heads in prayer. This was the signal for hundreds of soldiers to burst upon the scene, each carrying two swords; one to use and one to pass to those soldiers supposedly guarding the blessing. Within a few minutes the entire Holy Order of Knights was slain, cut to pieces by those they'd sought to make peace with.

"What of those others who are presently at the encampment, Sire? Shall I take my soldiers there and finish the job?"

"No, Captain, no. Stand your men down as there is another way. Send messengers to the encampment to tell how the knights of the Holy Order turned to attack my person and that of Pope Clement and, in defence of us, good soldiers came to our aid and bravely fought the knights in battle… a battle which they lost. Tell them the knights fought to the last man and in their passing they took with them some hundreds of courageous soldiers, whose lives shall be commemorated in stone and their souls prayed for by a king and a pope."

A sizeable group of soldiers disguised as peasants was assembled and told what story to tell those at the camp of the now defunct Holy Order of Knights. There being such a large number of story-tellers, those in the camp would be convinced of the lie when told it by so many and, on returning to their homelands, they would tell the same story until it became folklore, with its account sung at every fair in every country throughout all lands. What a mistake it was to send such a large number to tell the lie. The Devil's in the detail, and so it was inevitable that the detail would not stand up to scrutiny being told by so, so many liars telling slightly different lies. "Keep hold of your tongues," was the order issued by Samuel Black to all at the camp. "Don't let slip that we do not believe a word of what they say." The entire camp understood the importance of appearing to swallow the lie and so played along with the deception.

After the tale was told and done, the valets, attendants, serfs, camp followers and soldiers were told that they were free to return to their homes unmolested or, at their wont, they could remain in France to enrol in the service of the captain of the King's Guard at Rouen. None took up the offer to remain in France. Samuel Black, a wanted man in most of England, asked if he might return to the middle lands with the esquire brothers but under an assumed identity. To keep matters simple, Samuel said he would change his name from Samuel Black to Samuel White. If he was ever asked his origins, he would claim to come from a tiny coastal village that had been raided by Corsairs, with all but himself carried off into slavery. The esquire brothers and Samuel White grasped each other's hands and swore to protect one another on their journey back to England.

The band were not far along the road on their journey when a familiar argument broke out between Robert and John.

"Tell me, brother, that this was not the work of the Church in the massacre of the Holy Order of Knights," spoke Robert to John in acid tone.

"Robert, dear brother, we have done with all this before. You are against the Church no matter what I or others say, so let it be and we shall leave it at that," replied an exasperated John.

"What is that you're saying?" asked Samuel White.

"I say that the Church was behind the slaughter at Poitiers Castle and it is behind this present massacre of the Holy Order of Knights... from which I have not a hope that a single one has survived."

"What nonsense you do speak, Robert Clay! It was the work of the French King and his land-owning cronies what did for the knights at Poitiers and at Rouen. You don't really believe that the Church was behind all this, do you?"

"Aye, Master White, I do. The Church... the aristocracy... feudal lords... nobility... royalty... they're all the same; they're all in it together."

"All in what together?" coughed Samuel White.

"The Church are familiars of aristocrats and their like, carrying out for them any request then turning to them to seek payment for their collusion. Payment in any form does for the Church... in gold, in kind, in land, including land promised through deed of will to ensure passage to heaven for the signing over of a man's worldly possessions to the Church. Some say that the Church owns over half the lands in England! Soon they will own all of the lands, unless some monarch comes along to put pay to them and deprive them of it."

"Nonsense! Where do you get these ideas, Master Robert?"

"Are you a devout man… a Christian man, Samuel White?"

"I am that. I am a true believer in all the teachings of the Holy Scriptures."

"So why then must you travel to England under the name of another? And what of your actions at Poitiers Castle, Samuel White, when you instigated the murdering of the King's soldiers? Is that the act of a Christian man? Is that not an act against God's holiest commandment?"

"I have never claimed I was a saint, Master Robert. I have done many things in this life for which I will have to answer to St Peter before I am accepted into the glory of His kingdom having passed from this life."

"After all you've done, you still believe in God? If there's a God then why did He turn you into a sinner… a murderer?" snorted Robert Clay in derision.

"It's no use, Samuel… Robert has a bee in his brain about the Church and how it acts for the aristocracy against ordinary people, and no matter what William said…" At the mention of their dead brother's name, John and Robert looked at one another and knew that the conversation was over for the time being.

Whereas the esquire brothers' previous passage through France had been fraught with danger and hardship, this journey went completely without incident. The three men passed through countryside and towns like phantoms blown on a breeze, not seen and leaving no trace behind. It was as though the whole country somehow knew what had happened at Rouen and wanted nothing more to trouble their souls; even crossing over the water to England was like a leisurely Sunday float on a mill pond.

All throughout France, the sea crossing to England and the leg of their journey to the middle lands, Robert Clay and Samuel White argued endlessly over all things concerning God and the erratic inconsistencies of His actions toward believers and non-believers alike. "They are treated the same, so where is the profit in believing in God?" Samuel told Robert that he should be careful who he shared his words with as they sounded like heresy and heresy got people burned alive at the stake. Robert asked Samuel if he would turn him in as a heretic. Samuel was unequivocal in his reply; calling him brother, he said he would never do any such thing. John tried his best to stay out of discussions concerning God and faith, believing them to be futile, but he was dragged into them time and again to the ruin of his mind; his melancholy and madness returning to him with every passing mile.

THE MIDDLE LANDS OF ENGLAND

The journey from Rouen to the Clay estate in the six parishes took the travellers four and a half weeks. The effort they put into their return took its toll on each of them physically, emotionally and spiritually, especially so with John. By the time they reached their home, John Clay was babbling incoherently as his guilt over William's death attached itself to him once more.

As the travellers turned into the lane leading to the house, they appeared for all the world as the three Clay brothers had looked when they returned home from Poitiers in 1308: dirty, dishevelled, travel-worn, hunch-shouldered and weary, and bearing the posture of those carrying some huge burden. Lawrence Blackstone and his wife Margaret were standing on the newly laid stone courtyard to the house and believed that it was indeed William who had returned with John and Robert and the stories of his death were false. "He lives!" they shouted. Just as Elizabeth Clay had, Margaret hopped from side to side to catch a look at the three horsemen. She could tell Robert straightaway; he looked more like Thomas than ever. It was as though their dead brother had entered Robert's body and reshaped it. As the riders came closer, Margaret spied John and pointed at him, waving and shouting his name; but the third rider, she concluded, was not William; there was to be no happy homecoming after all.

Margaret's shouts of greeting brought Marion, Mary and her husband Galen to the front of the house, with others following close behind them. By the time the three riders dismounted there were more than a dozen people there to greet them. Each wanted to know what had brought the brothers back so soon from France, and who the stranger was that accompanied them. John said all would be told in due course but he first wanted to look upon the swelling belly of his sister. Margaret blushed and, placing a hand on her bump, said she had no idea what had caused it. Robert laughed and, slapping Lorence on the back, said he hoped the wedding had taken place on the solstice and that he hadn't shamed his sister. Everybody fell silent and Margaret ran away crying. Robert ran after her. When he caught up with Margaret he grabbed her by the shoulders but she wouldn't look him in the eye.

"Sister, what is wrong? Was it something I said that brought about this reaction in you?" Though Robert asked the question, he could easily guess what had set his sister off.

"I don't want to speak about it. I only want to hear your news. What happened in France that returns you home after so short a time?"

"I don't want to speak about it," replied Robert, jokingly mocking his sister. She saw the jest and they both laughed and hugged one another. After Margaret had dried her eyes, she and Robert returned to the house just as John was telling the tale of the killing of the knights of the Holy Order while attending a service of blessing arranged by Pope Clement and King Philip at the abbey in Rouen.

"There you go, brother, there you go... just like William, calling what happened a killing! It was not a killing, nor was it a tragedy; it was not anything but murder! Slaughter! Call it what it was, brother... murder, a massacre conjured by a conspiracy made between Pope Clement and King Philip to rid themselves once and for all of the Holy Order of Knights… only this time they succeeded." The family were greatly surprised at Robert's outburst and put it down to fatigue brought on by the exertions of such a long journey in so short a time. But John was not going to remain silent.

"Our brother William told you what punishment you would suffer if you brought your wicked and ungodly notions into the family home, and I will tell you the same," spoke John with raging madness flashing in his eyes.

"What, brother, that you would cut out my tongue and spike my eyes?" Those listening to the argument, spoken with such venom, were shocked.

"John… Robert… please do not speak to one another so," urged Mary. "Whatever differences you have between you can be resolved without recourse to an argument that would cut a permanent rift in family relations."

"Tell me, Margaret… tell me, Lorence… what was it that prevented you from marrying on the solstice?" Neither would reply to Robert's question but the answer was obvious. "See, John, see what your Church… your God… does to ordinary people, good people! Good honest people trying to live a life, working hard day in day out for little enough and wanting to raise a family."

"The Council of Commissioners of the six parishes decreed us unfit to marry in church. The crow priest branded me a whore and Lorence an outlaw and a sheep-worrier." With the words out of Margaret's mouth there was no putting them back in again.

"The Church!" screamed Robert, spittle spraying from his mouth. "You see, do you, John? The Church branded our sister a whore… who are they to make so terrible an accusation on a good woman?"

"It was made at the behest of John Belcher," said Margaret in a whisper, wanting the whole conversation to go away.

"It's Sir John Belcher, now that he's caught the favour of the King," added Marion. "It was his vendetta that the crow priest was carrying out."

"It is as I have always said… the Church are the familiars of the aristocracy, always eager to do their dirty work on some payment of tribute. What do you suppose Belcher paid him?"

"Why did he do it?" asked John, unconcerned with Robert's tirade against the Church.

"Why? The only conclusion we can draw is that he hates us and we him, and it has always been so between us."

"Aye, and there are rumours that his bride wasn't pure when Belcher took her in the marriage bed," scoffed Lorence. "It seems William had his way with her after they were betrothed… so the rumours have it."

A change of subject is needed, thought John. "Well, there's a child on the way and I for one care not if my nephew is born out of wedlock…"

"Niece, you mean! See how high she's carrying!" shouted Mary, pointing at Margaret's fine bump, making everybody laugh.

"That's always been the way of it with the peasantry," added Lorence. "No church weddings for the likes of us. I have come to regard us as peasants, working our own fields as we do. So let us rejoice in the coming happy event."

"Aye, we will that, when the time comes," said Galen Spurling, "but carry on with your tale, John."

"Before my brother proceeds, tell me, is that Jethro Marley I see there, skulking in the shadows? What's he doing here?"

"I have returned to Marion. It was wrong of me to have left her. You see, Robert, I was scared for the children; you know what it's like when the Council of Parish Commissioners are around… there's no telling where it'll end. So I left. I ran away. I hope you can forgive me same as others have done?"

165

"Is that right?" asked Robert of the assembled group. "Have you forgiven Jethro for abandoning my sister, and his cowardice in the face of the Church Commissioners?" The question was asked in a voice both calm and cold.

"Leave it be, my outlaw brother," interjected Lorence Blackstone, tickling Robert around his waist. "There's much to tell you of the happenings since you left, but this is neither the time nor the place; besides, we all want to hear John's tale. So, on with your tale, Master Clay, and no stopping to take breath!" People were always taken with Lorence Blackstone's relaxed and casual manner and his way with words, and how well he used them when he wanted something.

John Clay's tale didn't last very much longer because in essence there wasn't much more to it. When he reached its end, an argument broke out between him and Robert as the former laid the blame for the deaths of the knights of the Holy Order at the feet of King Philip and his aristocrat cronies, whereas Robert argued that it was the Pope who was behind their murders as it could only be he who could sanction such an act of wanton slaughter in the grounds of an abbey. The esquire brothers faced off against one another and were about to come to blows when the Clay sisters intervened to calm the situation down. John and Robert were separated and made to sit as far away from one another as possible while the story of the events in the six parishes since the time of their leaving was told.

Lorence Blackstone was nominated to tell the tale of the Clay family's fortunes since John and Robert left home to journey to France to join the company of the Holy Order of Knights. With every sentence that he spoke, the blood of the esquire brothers became hotter and hotter. Lorence told how their neighbour, John Belcher, caught the favour of King Edward and was made Sir John Belcher and given feudal rights over large swathes of the middle lands. He told of Sir John's land grabs throughout the six parishes and beyond, growing his estate at the expense of others. He told of levies on land owners and peasants alike and how he directed the crow priest and the Council of Parish Commissioners to carry out persecutions on those who argued against the taxations he made. In the telling of the tale, John saw the evil hand of the aristocracy at play, while Robert saw guilt on the side of the crow priest, his Council of Parish Commissioners and the Church itself; but, for the time being, both brothers kept their own counsel on their different opinions.

In summing up, Lorence Blackstone listed each and every one of the ill deeds carried out by Sir John Belcher on bending his fingers, including their tied farms and the field originally taken from the family by the crow priest, thus leaving the Clay family with but a couple of fields and Manor Farm itself to make their living from. After a look from Margaret Clay, Lorence added that Belcher was also guilty of denying them a marriage in a Church under the eyes of God. At the mention of the word 'God' in all of this, Robert Clay gave a snort of derision, after which he was ordered to leave the house. The Clay sisters would not tolerate impiety under their roof. Before he left, Robert apologised to all, saying that it was not his intention to offend those he loved, and then announced he would take up accommodation in one of the barns. "Leclerc has taken residence in the barn by the stream. You and he will make good company for one another," spoke Mary Clay with a sly smile.

★

This was not the homecoming Robert had hoped for, wished for, or expected. Sitting alone in the barn by the stream, Robert summoned up to mind his old scheme of destroying the Church and all it stood for and began plotting his vengeance. Just then, John Clay entered the barn in the company of Lorence Blackstone and Charles Leclerc.

"Are you not concerned that merely being in my presence will taint you and that you too will be banished from the house by the women?" spoke Robert Clay.

"We swore us an oath together in Rennes Forest to be outlaw brothers, did we not, Robert Clay?" said Lorence Blackstone.

"Aye, we did that."

"I remain your outlaw brother as I am still an outlaw, as is Leclerc nowadays," Leclerc nodded. "I have much to tell you but you must learn to control your emotions… learn to keep them in check. If you blurt out things that are in your head or your heart we will all end up at the wrong end of a rope."

"I speak as I find!"

"I say to you again, you must learn to control your emotions; there's nothing to be gained in not doing so. There's no honour in a death that makes our enemies stronger."

"Speak plainly."

"I shall. With things going well there seemed no need to live outside the law but as soon as Sir John Belcher started his land grabs and began persecutions of innocent people, I formed an outlaw gang across all of the six parishes. We are eighteen in number, and with you and John that will make us twenty."

"But Lorence, my outlaw brother, it is plain to see that Margaret holds the whip hand. How does she sit with your banditry?" mocked Robert.

"To you it might appear that I am whipped but I am not as Margaret alibis me from arrest. She not only knows of my banditry but approves of it, and in fact, joins in it whenever she can do so in her condition." Robert was staggered at the thought of his prim and proper sister involved in banditry. "As we are commonly known hereabouts as a brotherhood, nobody suspects a woman of being involved."

"Are there other women involved?"

"Only Mary and Marion at the present time… but we're hopeful of others joining…"

"My sisters? But they are women! Women! Are you mad? Women cannot keep silent even for a minute and will give you all away in idle chatter."

"I wouldn't let your sisters hear you say that if I were you," retorted Leclerc. "You know how strong-willed they are and how easily they take offence. I speak from personal experience." Leclerc looked sheepish when making this admission.

"Don't you go worrying about your sisters, it is your nature that raises our concerns. You are too hot-headed and need to—"

"Yes, I need to control my emotions... so you keep saying."

"Yes, you need to control your emotions. If you cannot, then we might not admit you to our band of outlaws."

"Who is this 'we'? You make it sound like a committee. Have you not a leader?" asked Robert.

"Well, I suppose I am the leader, but the title doesn't sit well nor does it suit me. Not that there's been a vote or anything but people just seem to follow me, you know, like the outlaws of Rennes Forest did with Silas... he just sort of took up the job one day and nobody said otherwise."

"Well, I'm saying otherwise to you, Lorence Blackstone," spoke John Clay in a firm voice. "If I am to join this venture of yours, I, as the eldest son, will be leader. What say you, Lorence Blackstone? And you, Leclerc?" Both men looked at one another and shrugged their shoulders.

"I never wanted to be the leader so I have no objection to you being leader."

"Nor I," added Leclerc, disinterestedly digging dirt from beneath his fingernails.

"Then it is settled, is it not, brothers? I am the leader!"

"Aye, brother, it is settled... you are the leader of our gang," agreed Robert, smiling and seeing how this would play nicely to his scheme.

"You can be John's second in our gang, Robert," added Leclerc, trying to be his usual peacekeeping self.

"We are not a gang," John insisted. "A gang is common and sounds violent and we are not violent men; we are a… a society… a brotherhood."

"And what about the womenfolk? They're… women… can they be in a…" Leclerc's voice tailed off before he finished his sentence, "brotherhood?" The last word was spoken without much sound.

"I'm sure they will not mind us calling our society a brotherhood… besides, naming it so will keep them from suspicion and out of harm's way. I'm sure there are other benefits for the womenfolk of our brotherhood, which I am yet to bring to mind."

"Yes," nodded the others, "the women will be perfectly fine with us calling our society a brotherhood." And so, with those few words, the Brotherhood was born and commenced its first seven hundred years of existence.

"What bandits we'll make, what outlaws!"

"Bandits? Outlaws? Is that the extent of your ambition, Lorence Blackstone? Little wonder that you are no longer leader. We shall be something bigger… grander…"

"Bigger… grander? How?"

"People such as us are fed up with being put on by the aristocracy and so we will do away with them. We'll make a start in the six shires."

"Aye, and the Church too!" added Leclerc. After flashing a disapproving glance at Leclerc, John Clay continued, "Bringing down the aristocracy in the six shires is a big job, and I'm all for making a start with putting Sir John Belcher away into an early grave. How's that for a beginning? Grand enough?"

Robert Clay was delighted at how quickly things were developing. Having his crazy, deluded brother leading a gang of outlaws would leave him free to progress his scheming against the Church. He brought to mind the thoughts he'd had before leaving England for France to re-join the Holy Order of Knights. Thoughts of how he could find people with beliefs akin to his own or, if not that, people he could control through blackmail such that their mutual destruction would be assured if they ever gave him up. Now fate was turning in his favour. Robert could see the road ahead for his scheme and the Brotherhood was its key.

★

None of the original bandits recruited by Lorence Blackstone had any confidence in John Clay's leadership and so, one by one, they left the Brotherhood to take up separate careers in banditry. Within six months, the Brotherhood was reduced to a membership consisting of seven men: John and Robert Clay, Lorence Blackstone, Galen Spurling, Jethro Marley, Samuel White, Charles Leclerc, and three females: Mary Spurling, Margaret Clay and Marion Marley.

A NEW BEGINNING

Things soon went from bad to worse for the people of the middle lands and especially so for those residing within the boundaries of the six parishes as they were right on Sir John Belcher's doorstep, right under his acquisitive eyes. All in the six parishes hoped he would move to King Edward's court in London but Belcher, having found himself hopelessly out of his depth in all matters concerning the statecraft, stayed away from court as much as he possibly could.

With Belcher, it wasn't so much a matter of *if* he would steal your lands, but *when* he would steal them. Of course, according to the law of the land from the times of Magna Carta, he couldn't simply just throw people out of their homes. No, he had to follow due process, but being Chief Overseer of the Parish Councils for the middle lands, he was always able somehow or other to divert matters to his purposes; for example, compulsory land purchases based on untruths such as cutting culverts for the removal of non-existent excess water on pasture land. The price the Parish Councils paid for the land was but a fraction of its real worth. Afterwards, the land would be sold to Sir John at a modest profit. "Barely enough to make it worth our while," whinged the parish councillors, the majority of whom were clergymen. Never a thought did they give to the people they'd made homeless and taken their livelihood from.

Sir John Belcher's only real competition in land grabbing was the Church. Over the centuries, crow priests had made it their business to keep close to the dying to persuade them to leave, by deed of will, some or all of their lands and possessions to them to guarantee a sure passage into heaven. An uneasy alliance developed between Sir John and the Church in the middle lands, with each knowing that they couldn't push things too far with the other lest they ruin everything. Deals, in fact, were often made between the Church and the Sir John Belchers of this world to their mutual benefit. If one piece of land could be advantageous to the other party, some arrangement would be entered into to either sell the land or swap it for another parcel of land to, for example, increase the size of an estate.

★

Tired of waiting for the men to make a move, the Clay sisters put it to them that they needed to increase the membership of the Brotherhood if they were to put an end to Sir John Belcher and his like. With the men being short on ideas, Margaret Clay said, "You must get out and about and talk to people of the woes they've suffered at the hands of the aristocracy. Surely finding recruits will be like shelling peas if everybody is sick and tired of working night and day, as we do, only to pay levies and taxes to the Church and the gentry, leaving nothing for those who work the land." Lorence Blackstone, of course, agreed with Margaret and proposed that he and the other men looked for likely recruits from the ranks of those who'd been worst done by in the six shires.

Even recruiting among those who'd been treated badly by the likes of Sir John Belcher was no guarantee that they wouldn't go running to him, or the Church, and inform on the Brotherhood's recruiters in order to gain some favour. Such attempts to gain favour are invariably unsuccessful as the informants become despised by those they seek to serve. It's strange how when people go running like dogs to those who treat them badly, perhaps to demonstrate some perverse kind of loyalty, a loyalty that neither aristocrats nor the Church deserved, they regularly end up worse off.

"What we need is a plan to grow our numbers by recruiting more members," said John Clay, speaking identical words as his sister Margaret while trying to sound as though it was all his idea and he was in command, "but a plan that protects us from arrest while we are recruiting." It was a simple and a sensible idea but none of the men could come up with anything that would mitigate the risk involved in inciting people to act against the laws of the land. Being eager not to end up at the end of a rope for treason, it was suggested that anybody who went running to the sheriff would have to be killed.

John Clay was not in favour of this suggestion. "We must not go against our Lord God's commandments and so nobody is to be killed, even if they prove treacherous. After all," he added, "they did not ask to be recruited!" This non-lethal approach to dealing with traitors wasn't shared by Margaret Clay, nor her brother Robert or several others. When challenged about this non-lethal policy, John Clay said that they must all put their trust in God, His good grace, His wisdom and His kindness, and so they must not kill those who betrayed them and all would be fine in the eyes of Heaven.

Robert Clay responded with, "In that case we may as well make an appointment with the hangman now..." He added, "Tell me, brother, why would God be on our side and not on the side of those we are seeking to destroy? How does God choose sides? It makes not a bit of sense, no matter whichever way you look at it." For

174

his ungodly remarks, Robert Clay was cast out of the Brotherhood by John. Later, when he was alone, Robert approached Lorence Blackstone.

"Lorence, my dear outlaw brother," spoke Robert in a mocking tone, "pray, tell me, why do you play along with them? You no more believe in God than I do."

"It does no harm," Lorence replied with a shrug. "They have faith in God and if their faith gives them strength and belief in what they do, then where is the harm in playing along with them?"

"Where is the harm, you ask? People look up to you for guidance and leadership and you behaving this way plays them into the hands of the Church, where the God myth is fed to their gullible minds… and all for the Church's profit and power. We non-believers must stand together in denial of God's existence for the good of all mankind."

"But brother, I am not so sure in my beliefs as you are… or I'm backing both sides, just in case."

"Just in case of what?"

"Just in case there is a God and She—"

"She? She! Now you mock me, Master Blackstone? How can God be a She?"

"Of course God is a She. How can it be otherwise?"

"I am not convinced of your sincerity in this and so will not take further part in the debate."

"But outlaw brother, I am serious. Think back on the words you yourself have used. You have said, 'when things go well, then the Church claims that it is by His divine hand, but when things go badly, the Church says we are sinners and have made Him angry and so He is testing us or punishing us.' You then ask, 'Why would God seek to punish his own creation? It makes no sense that He would intervene on one side or the other at His whim. Are not all events then just the outcome of some fate or fortune or nature?' Have you yourself not used those very words?"

"Yes, I have used such similar words as you have spoken, but—"

"If through your own beliefs, as you say, whether matters go well or ill it is by fate or fortune or nature, then are these not the characteristics of the capricious female temperament?"

"Is that then your reckoning on the case for God being a woman? You say as women are capricious, so it follows that God, being capricious in His dealings with circumstance, must be a She?"

"Not only that, of course not… What of creation? You cannot doubt, surely, that there is creation at work all around us." Robert returned no reply to Lorence's assertion. "Do you consider men to be creators? We are not… men are destroyers… man creates nothing but war and destruction. Woman creates life… through the female, therefore, there is creation. Women risk death in childbirth to create life. Would any man do such? I do not say God exists, but if She does then God is surely a woman."

"If, as I believe, you are making some jest then tell the mask of your face that you are simply making fun of me and let us end this talk of God as Mother."

"God as Mother! There, you said it yourself! God as Mother… Don't those words make sense of it all?"

Weary of the conversation, Robert Clay changed tack. "While travelling with the knights of the Holy Order I met many learned men… men, mind you, not women… so how could a female be the Creator if all the learned are men?"

"Tell me, Robert, have you heard of the wise women? Commonly known as the wise women of the forests… You told me of one such you met in France; after the bear attacked, you said she used such art that you were cured in a trice. I recall you said William branded her a witch and you, to be contrary, argued for her as being an angel."

"Of course I've heard of wise women of the forest. Who has not?"

"So explain to me why they live in isolation... in some out-of-the-way wood or other."

"No doubt you have the answer?"

"As they aren't men, they're deemed by the Church as being possessed as witches and burnt at the stake for their art. If that was to be your fate, would you too not hide in the depths of a forest? Are not women, therefore, as wise as men? Wiser?" Robert ignored Lorence's argument and continued with his monologue.

"To continue... in speaking with men of both the natural and philosophical sciences, they observed that there is no proof of the existence of God, yet people believe in Him. They concluded, therefore, that faith in His existence requires no proofs; however, proofs, which are abundantly clear to all who perceive them, require faith to believe in them."

"An example?"

"Certainly. When divining the future from a chart of the firmament, many choose not to believe in the prophecies it gives up. They have proof of the reading but no faith in it. Yet stars are there for all to see. The reverse is true of God. There is nothing to see or hear or touch, yet the great mass of people have faith that He exists."

"She exists, Robert, She exists. You have a point?"

"The men of the science philosophies concluded, therefore, that faith is more powerful than proof... which is contradictory, is it not? What is better than proof of a matter?"

"I agree, faith is stronger than proof."

"But why so? I believe it is fear of punishment for lack of faith that drives people toward having faith?"

"Your philosophising will not win you any recruits."

"Perhaps not. The Brotherhood is set on striking a blow against the aristocracy when it should be striking a blow against the Church."

"It has already been said to you many times that attacking the aristocracy will win us favour, but attacking the Church will lead to certain doom."

"Then we must be cautious, my outlaw brother. Let us bury our enmity against the Church deep inside of us and only reveal it when we are sure of our ground."

"I think you misjudge me."

"I think not. I think you speak so because you are swayed by the skirts of my sister." Lorence smiled at the image Robert's words created in his mind.

"If your monologue is not yet ended, pray continue with it."

"Those learned men of which I spoke maintain that the Church does not want man to possess any knowledge that would diminish the Church's power, and so it outlaws practices that would otherwise advance mankind; investigation into and explanation of the firmament, for example. Those ignoring the Church's edicts on this matter suffer excommunication, inquisition and fiery death as a heretic. Some of these learned men believe that the Church, in holding the sciences in such contempt, has held back man's advancement by centuries, if not millennia."

"I will say this: approach me when you deem the time to be right to put your scheme into action, but in the meanwhile you must renounce your ungodly ways. You must undergo some transformation to allow you to return into the fold of the Brotherhood, otherwise all your plans and schemes will come to nothing."

"How can I bring this transformation about?"

"A divine miracle might be too much to ask, so how about a dream? A dream where you're visited by Gabriel and he commands you to do the Lord's work. That should do it," Lorence Blackstone said, laughing at the look on Robert's face. The two men shook hands and kissed to seal their contract of understanding.

★

Four days later, Robert Clay left the barn and entered the house, where he told all those there about a dream he'd had the previous four nights. In the dream the Archangel Gabriel had visited him to tell him that he was to do the Lord's work. When asked about this work, Robert answered, "That has yet to be revealed to me, but I believe I will find my way through prayer... Will you take this sinner to church on Sunday so that he might begin his long road back to the loving light of God's good grace?" The family swarmed around Robert, overjoyed to embrace him, while Lorence Blackstone looked on, admiring Robert's work.

During church that next Sunday, everybody was delighted to witness Robert's return to the fold. The congregation watched as he prayed so ardently that his brow gave the appearance of fever. They were gladdened by the serenity etched on his face and the demeanour of his manner when divining the Lord's works for all the congregation to understand. He even went into battle against those who saw no wonder in the Lord's works and criticised sinners for not obeying God's commandments. Lorence Blackstone looked on, proud of Robert's performance, as they each drank in the congregation's acceptance of Robert Clay's return to the Christian fold.

John Clay was not so easily convinced as others were of his brother's renunciation of his ungodly beliefs and so made no move to involve Robert in the Brotherhood's business. But Robert lay patient as a snake, knowing John's love for him would drive him to convince himself of his change of heart and mind. Robert was counting on John wanting to see the good in him and when so doing, talking himself into accepting his transformation. Slowly, slowly, John trusted Robert to carry out small tasks for the Brotherhood. Small tasks were all the Brotherhood seemed to do, according to the Clay sisters. In their opinion, progress was far too slow. They openly criticised the men for being too easily distracted by activities that did nothing to grow the membership or reputation of the Brotherhood.

★

Feeling himself under pressure from the Clay sisters, John Clay, self-appointed leader of the Brotherhood, called a meeting to discuss recruitment of new Brethren. Thus far, under John Clay's leadership, not a single person had been added to the ranks of the Brotherhood. Having diluted down the Brotherhood's principle aim of destroying the aristocracy to 'breaking the hold of the Aristocracy in the six parishes', John Clay claimed that twenty recruits was all that was now needed. Margaret Clay was not in favour of this change in policy but held her tongue. To keep the pressure on their leader, the Clay sisters declared that they were ready to step in and take over the Brotherhood if John failed to recruit at least twenty new members before the next solstice.

★

Hammering his fist on the dining room table, John Clay called the first full meeting of the Brotherhood to order. As he was about to speak, Margaret stood and demanded to know who appointed him as leader. He replied that he, as the eldest surviving son, was by right the leader of the Brotherhood. Margaret demanded a vote be held to officially appoint the leader of the Brotherhood; her call was backed by Lorence Blackstone and Robert. A show of hands had John Clay scraping in as leader by one vote… his own. Margaret then demanded that their cause should be voted on. "Were we not formed for the destruction of the aristocracy? Are we now merely to 'break the hold of the aristocracy in the six parishes'?" A second show of hands determined that the Brotherhood's aim was to simply break the hold of the aristocracy in the six parishes. "I don't even understand what that means!" she yelled. Margaret was furious at what she saw as a dilution of the Brotherhood's principles but she'd bide her time to get her way. *Things change… they always do*, she thought.

"If now we are not going to destroy the aristocracy, despite all the wicked things they've done to us and our kind, then why do we need to recruit members to our cause? Surely we here can break the grip of the aristocrats of the six parishes?" Margaret knew the answer to her own question. It was all just a matter of power as far as her brother, John Clay, was concerned. With his upbringing, he understood that the more people one has under one's control, the more powerful one is, and John Clay wanted a position of power within the community.

"Margaret, my very dear sister," began John Clay, with his sweetest snake smile adorning his mad visage, "the greater the number of people brought to the service of our cause, the quicker our goal will be achieved. Surely even you can see that?" John ended his little speech with a condescending snort of derision. Jethro Marley then spoke up.

"Y'know, John, Margaret's right in what she says, and besides, what's the hurry? There can't be more than a dozen of them aristocrats in the whole of the six parishes anyway, and if we pick off the weakest first we'll be able to take our time over the rest."

"Now Jethro, just consider for a moment, if you will," answered John Clay, maintaining his condescending tone, "do you want a quick end to this so we can all get on with our lives or do you want our quest dragging on for years and years? Bear in mind that as soon they get a whiff of what's going on, the aristocrats will retaliate and that'll make our job ten times harder. They'll be forewarned, and forewarned, as they say, is forearmed."

"I agree with John on this," interjected Robert, on John's side to everybody's surprise. "We should build up our numbers… it's better to have an army and not need one than to need an army and not have one."

"An army! Hah! We haven't even got the village fool to join our ranks, let alone the makings of an army. If we are indeed going to raise an army of the Brotherhood, where will we begin?"

"Like all good things," snapped John Clay, "we'll start at the village fete!" The assembled Brethren were unsure if John was serious but with the madness in his eyes none dared to ask the question.

After the meeting was over, Margaret wrote down a list of who she thought most likely to join their cause. John whittled it down to only two likely recruits. John and Robert Clay volunteered to be the recruiters and Lorence Blackstone said he'd 'look on', and at the first sign of treachery he'd act to prevent anybody running off to the sheriff… "or anybody else", he quickly added. Robert took inference that Lorence meant the Church. After perusing the list, Robert insisted they burn it, "Lest anybody learn of our intentions." This precaution wasn't really very necessary as most people could neither read nor write, but the Clays could and with the Clay sisters being great believers in literacy, they were holding classes for Lorence, Samuel, Charles and Jethro Marley; the latter being in his third year of learning his letters but still showing no sign of grasping the use of the strangely shaped symbols.

★

On the day of the village fete, one of those who was to be approached was away in his bed, lying at death's door from the sweating sickness. The other, a troublemaker named Duane Catchpole, was stomping around the stalls of the fete, making a nuisance of himself as usual. Robert suggested they approach Catchpole together but the older brother refused, saying that if things didn't go well then at least Robert wouldn't be implicated in something that may cost him his life. The real reason John wanted to approach Catchpole alone was that he wanted Duane to understand that he was the leader of the Brotherhood.

After following Duane Catchpole around the village fete for over twenty minutes, he turned to John Clay and asked him what he wanted.

"What is your business following me?"

"I…" John Clay hesitated but knew he had to continue, "I would like to speak with you on a delicate matter, Master Catchpole…"

"Master Catchpole?" he laughed, "Duane, call me Duane, everybody does… I don't possess no airs and graces, so no Master Catchpole for me." Even when speaking these few simple words, Duane Catchpole's voice was laced with menace.

"Duane… I have heard that you've lost several fields to compulsory purchase by the Parish Council—"

"Sir John the bastard Belcher, more like." *Perfect*, thought John Clay. "Everybody knows he's behind it all as the lands always seem to end up with him… or the Church… but I don't begrudge the Church nothing for all the good works that they do." *Even more perfect*, thought John Clay. "So what about it? What about me losing my fields? It's not as though I'm the only one." *More perfect still*, thought John Clay.

"How do you think about the injustices you've suffered?"

"What's it to a Clay? Why are you provoking me by stirring my memory in these matters?"

"I am merely seeking to understand to what degree you feel yourself wronged by the Parish Council and Sir John Belcher… Perhaps you feel provoked inside of you by the wrongs that you have suffered, and you might be willing to undertake certain actions to pile retribution upon those who—"

"Speak plainly, Clay, I have no patience with wordsmiths." The babbling John Clay now wished he'd accepted Robert's offer to join him.

"Then speak plainly I will. Duane Catchpole… will you join our Brotherhood to fight against those who've wronged you and all those like them in these six parishes?"

"Are you trying to set me up for them at the Parish Council to take the rest of my lands, John Clay?" If when speaking simple words Duane Catchpole's voice sounded menacing to John Clay's ears, it now sounded like imminent threat of death.

"No, Duane, no, of course not! You know well that we too have suffered greatly under Belcher's hand, as have many others here around , and we're ready to be rid of him and his antics…"

"Be rid of his antics? What do you mean by 'be rid of his antics'? Do you propose to kill him, then?"

"No, certainly not… The Brotherhood's aim is to break the hold he has over the parish councils of the six parishes. We do not condone murder as it is against God's commandments."

"What about beyond the six parishes? Belcher's reach extends across all of the middle lands."

"We should only concern ourselves with Belcher's activities within the boundaries of the six parishes."

"It seems to me that you lack ambition, John Clay. What says your brother over there?" asked Duane Catchpole, pointing at Robert. "And that fly husband of your fine sister Margaret?" he added, pointing at Lorence Blackstone. "What say they?" John was surprised at how observant Duane Catchpole was.

"As their leader, they bow to me on all such matters."

"Would I be bowing to you on matters if I should join your Brotherhood, John Clay?"

Not wanting to lose a potential recruit, John Clay fudged his reply. "Master Catchpole, it is clear to me that you are your own man, and our Brotherhood needs such men as you. Will you join us?"

"What would I be joining?"

"Let us away from here so that we might speak more freely."

"Will your brother and the fly husband be joining us in our discussion?"

As John Clay took Duane Catchpole by the arm, he signalled to Robert and Lorence Blackstone to follow them.

The four men filed away in a silent column to a quiet glade in the wood. They checked the area for eavesdroppers before beginning their talk. Duane Catchpole simply wanted to know what the Brotherhood stood for. John Clay explained that its purpose was to break the hold that the aristocratic landowners had in the six parishes so ordinary people, 'just like us', could have better lives. Duane Catchpole replied that it sounded like a good reason for him to join the Brotherhood and asked how matters had progressed thus far as he hadn't noticed anything going on. John Clay claimed that progress had been hampered due to the lack of numbers, hence they were recruiting new members. Duane asked how many recruits were needed. "Twenty... at least twenty," John replied with a gleam of empire in his eye. Duane thought for a moment before saying that he could get more than half that number signed up if Master Clay thought it useful. John Clay was so beside himself with excitement at the thought of gaining so many recruits that, without consulting his brother or Lorence Blackstone, he clasped Duane Catchpole's hand to strike the bargain with him. The approach of a group of merrymakers from the village fete stopped the men's discussions momentarily. After making passing acquaintance with those the men knew from the group, John Clay told Duane Catchpole to bring the new recruits with him to the next meeting of the Brotherhood, which was to be held at nine o'clock the following Wednesday night in the barn by the stream on what was left of the Clay estate.

The moment Duane Catchpole disappeared from sight, Robert Clay grabbed his brother by his shoulders, shook him, and asked him what he thought he was doing by allowing Duane Catchpole to recruit random volunteers into their secret society, the mere forming of which carried with it a death sentence. John Clay pushed Robert's hands away and made to leave the glade. Lorence Blackstone barred John's path and demanded he answer Robert's question. Defiantly, John Clay said he'd meet Catchpole and his band of recruits alone if necessary, in case he planned to betray the Brotherhood. Lorence Blackstone responded that they were in their Brotherhood together and it would be together that they'd face whatever came their way. Robert Clay slapped Lorence Blackstone on the back and kissed his cheek for his healing words before putting an arm around both men and declaring them each dearest to his heart. In Robert's mind, however, his hatching plot was in writhing form and nowit seemed to change direction; he wanted to make Master Catchpole leader of the Brotherhood. As soon as the thought entered Robert's head he instinctively knew it was the right path to follow for his ambitions of destroying the Church.

★

Just before the meeting of the Brotherhood the following Wednesday evening, the Clay clan, plus Lorence Blackstone, Charles Leclerc, Galen Spurling, Samuel White and Jethro Marley, made their way to the barn by the stream. On approaching the barn the group caught the glimmer of a light that suddenly became extinguished. Sensing some treachery was afoot, John Clay held up his hand in command for the group to stop as he made his way alone to the barn. Before he reached the barn, its door swung open and a voice he recognised greeted him, saying that, "With all the noise you and your kin are making, it is a wonder that the sheriff and his men aren't on top of us already." No matter what he said, Duane Catchpole's voice always sounded like some violence was imminent. John Clay beckoned his party forward to join him and Duane inside the barn. Once there, Margaret Clay lit a candle, which revealed the shadow shapes of a large group of men sitting on the floor beneath a low hayloft.

"Some Brotherhood this is," mocked Duane Catchpole. "A Brotherhood what admits women!" The recruits laughed but their laughter didn't last long.

"I've known you by name and reputation for years, Duane Catchpole," responded Margaret Clay, standing, "and I know the secrets of your bedchamber, so best you be careful what you mock lest your secrets be spoken out loud." At Margaret's words, total silence reigned inside the barn.

"So, John Clay, are you the leader of this Brotherhood or not?" Duane Catchpole eventually asked.

"He is," responded the Clay clan in unison.

"Then why does Margaret Clay, lovely fine woman that she is, speak harshly without rebuke from the leader?"

"Without my sanction, Master Catchpole, none of you would be drawing breath beyond this night," spoke Margaret Clay. John Clay became angry, wondering what had become of his policy of non-violence toward those the Brotherhood sought to recruit. *Perhaps it is some subterfuge by Margaret*, he thought, *to make the ruffian Catchpole think twice before stepping out of line?*

"How so, Mistress Clay?" asked one of the men from the shadows below the hayloft.

"We all know that membership of a group such as ours carries severe penalties so when Master Catchpole went off to recruit the men he'd promised he was followed, and those who he met with were followed, and one of those men, Robert Morris, was followed as he made his way to the sheriff but before he could turn us in, Master Morris was taken."

"Followed? By who?" asked Duane Catchpole, more concerned that he had not noticed he'd been followed than by the taking of Robert Morris.

"By my sisters and myself, Master Catchpole," answered Margaret Clay. "You didn't spy us, Master Catchpole, because men do not note women unless they are dressed as tavern whores do dress. Being modest women, we move as unseen spectres, not attracting the slightest attention. I say that you need to be more careful in future, Master Catchpole."

"And what of Robert Morris?" asked another of the men from the shadows.

"Master Morris will hold his tongue or he will find himself holding the eggs of his manhood in his hands," Margaret Clay spoke her words in such a way that nobody doubted she would carry out her threat.

"What next then?" asked Duane Catchpole. "Some sort of oath of allegiance, I suppose?" Up until then nobody had considered it necessary to have an oath of allegiance, but with their increased numbers John now believed it a good idea to have one. *They can swear their oath to the Brotherhood and to me!* was his thought. "To be taken with reciting of some sort of constitution to abide by, I should imagine. You know, with a hand on the Bible and all that." All nodded in agreement with Duane Catchpole's idea.

"Master Catchpole, as you know," began John Clay in an officious voice, "we are family and, to date, we have not required such affirmations, but you make a good point. As it is your suggestion, I would like you to create for us an oath of allegiance and a constitution for the Brotherhood to abide by. What do you say?"

"I say that I can neither read nor write, Master Clay, so I don't see how I can," admitted Duane Catchpole. Seeing the funny side, he laughed, which was an unusual thing for him to do. His recruits likewise laughed.

"In that case, Master Catchpole," spoke Margret Clay, "I will help you write an oath of allegiance and I will teach you to read and write so that you may script our constitution in the fullness of time. In the meantime, however, I ask all here to raise their right hands and place their left hands across their chests and repeat after me: 'I... say your name... declare my absolute loyalty to the Brotherhood and hereby renounce any and all allegiances or fidelity to any power, whether that power be mystical, sovereign, domestic or foreign, on pain of death, so help me God'. That will do for now. You'll all need to retake the oath after Duane and I have written it up properly." The uttering of the oath of allegiance by the assembled group was more of a hubbub rumble than anything anybody could attest to but it bound those present in the barn to the Brotherhood.

"What next then?" asked Duane Catchpole once again.

"I would like to officially welcome our newest members to the Brotherhood and wish us all every success in all our endeavours," announced John Clay.

"That's fine and all, but what next then? What are we actually going to do to break the hold old Belcher has over the parish councils so we can fight back and make everybody's life better?"

"It's the parish councils that are at the back of it all, if you ask me," shouted a voice from the shadows. "Belcher is a scoundrel and all, but the clergymen on the parish councils are just as bad."

"Friend," shouted John Clay, "this Brotherhood is a God-fearing institution and does not condone talk, nor any actions, against the Church or its servants, either here or anywhere beyond this place. Do I make myself clear?" The assembled group nodded their assent.

Robert Clay noted who it was who had spoken out against the Church and resolved to make contact with him immediately following the meeting. When the meeting was over, most of those leaving were sceptical that the Brotherhood would ever achieve much 'as long as that John Clay has anything to do with it', they grumbled. *This is perfect,* thought Robert. As the Brethren dispersed, Robert Clay shadowed the man who'd spoken out against the Church so that he might discuss his outburst with him further. Meanwhile, in the barn, John Clay pulled his sister Margaret's arm so hard it span her around. He asked his sister what she'd meant by the threats she'd made during the meeting about the taking of Duane Catchpole's life and the de-manning of Robert Morris.

Margaret wrested her arm from John's grasp and stepped away from him before turning back to face him again. Her demeanour was calm as she spoke to her brother, saying that she, her sisters and 'others' had discussed matters and taken Robert's orders to follow Duane Catchpole and his recruits, and that if they proved treacherous they should pay a price. Margaret held up her hand to prevent John from replying and made her way from the barn. John shouted to Margaret's disappearing back, asking her who, if not he, was leader of the Brotherhood. Receiving no reply, John shouted that he, as leader, had decided upon a course of non-violence as murder was against God's laws. Margaret shouted back, asking John what God had to say about de-manning Robert Morris. Receiving no reply, Margaret shouted again, saying that she wished now that she'd done it, and laughed. John Clay was furious at the arrogation of the Brotherhood's principles by his family but he would not allow his face to show the raging anger he felt inside. He'd bide his time. *Things change… they always do*, he thought. Foolish John; everybody was gone, nobody was around to see his face, and in any case, they could not have done so in the black darkness of the barn. Standing alone in the barn, John's eyes took on a familiar madness and the nerves surrounding them began to tick.

Out of earshot of John and Margaret's argument, Robert Clay caught up with the man who'd spoken out against the Church at the meeting. He was now walking by himself and whistling a tune to keep the Devil from taking him on his lonely road home. Robert asked the man his name and if he cared for company on his journey. The man nodded yes and said his name was Paul Martin. Master Martin's home was the furthest out in the fourth village of the six parishes, reached in a fast walk of over an hour and a half. For fear of being overheard, Robert kept his counsel, saying he would only speak after they'd reached Paul's home. So the men walked side by side, whistling tunes to ward off the Devil while kicking rocks into the bushes to scare away anything that might be lurking in them. The spirits of the trees didn't like the men kicking rocks at their foliate family cousins so they cracked their branches and creaked their boughs to frighten them, hurrying the men along on their journey.

When they arrived at the shambolic hut of Paul Martin, it lay silent and in complete darkness. Robert asked Paul whether it was normal that his hut was thus. Master Martin replied that everything was as it should be as he lived alone. Before they went inside the hut, Paul Martin asked Robert Clay what his purpose was in accompanying him to his home.

"In the barn tonight, you spoke out against the Church. I too have spoken against the Church and in doing so, a wedge has been driven between me and my family, but in you I believe I may have found an ally."

"Is that it? Is that all? You want to discuss my feelings about the Church with me? Nothing more?"

"No... nothing more. What else could there be? We have never met before tonight so..."

"You do not then remember me?"

"Remember you? How could I, we have only just met this night."

"True... true enough, we have indeed only met this night, but we travelled so far together in the service of the Holy Order of Knights." After pausing to see if Robert's eyes gave some sign of recognition, which they didn't, Paul Martin continued. "I thought you recognised me in the barn and believed you desired to lie with me in my bed." Robert was struck dumb by the words he'd heard spoken. "Serving the Holy Order of Knights as you and I did, I took you for a sodomite."

"Sir! I am no sodomite!"

"Come, come... do not be so shocked, handsome Robert Clay... unmarried Robert Clay. You must've known that many of the knights of the Holy Order took men to their beds? Why do you suppose there were so many camp followers?" Robert could not speak in reply. "I believed you to be a boy-lover too… but it seems I was mistaken."

"Sir! I am no boy-lover! This night you spoke out against the Church and I… tell me, Sir, why you are against the Church? Is it because you feel, as I do, that it was the Church who was behind the slaughter of the knights of the Holy Order?"

"Oh, I hadn't thought about it like that, but that gives me another reason to hate the Church and all those in it."

"Speak plainly; your purpose confuses me."

"There's not much to say. I hate the Church and all in it for what they did to me… what they made me." Robert immediately took Paul's meaning but gestured for him to continue with his tale. "The Abbott of our town demanded of each family that they give up one child to labour for the glory of God and the Church in the fields of the abbey to feed the clergy there. During our stay we were required to live in at the abbey. Some were chosen to be educated by the clergymen. We thought them lucky at first. It began in the fields, hidden among the long grasses… children, boys and girls, became the playthings of priests… They used to invite others from all over the middle lands and beyond… day and night, night and day. Some tried to escape and were beaten and chained in the cellar… Their situation seemed to incite the priests to greater depravities. We knew it was a sin but we could not do anything about it. When I finally left the abbey, I discovered my family had died of the sweating sickness and their land had been claimed by the Church. They said that my father had made it so by a deed of will. It was then that I heard of the Holy Order of Knights and became a camp follower. That's when I first saw you." Paul smiled. "By then I was used to laying with men and when I became valet to Sir Estienne de Quincey, he took me to his bed. I think I loved him." At the remembrance of Sir Estienne, Paul had a faraway look in his eye. "You don't appear shocked, Master Clay."

"Nothing the Church does shocks me," replied Robert. Entering the hut, Paul lit a fire and after it had blazed for some minutes, he offered Robert hot broth from an iron cauldron, just like the one in the cottage in the woods on the St Malo road.

"I am happy to join the Brotherhood. Being an outlaw may help dispel the rumours of me being a sodomite. You can understand that, can't you, Robert?"

"I can," he lied. "You have nothing to fear from me divulging your secret, Sir, I will never betray you if you keep faith with me and maintain your pledge against the Church."

"Robert Clay, I hate the Church with every fibre of my being… especially now as you've put the thought in my head that it was the Church behind the slaughter of the knights in Poitiers Castle."

"I don't recall seeing you at the time we took our revenge on the King's men. Where were you? In hiding?"

"In a manner of speaking. I was sent away by Sir Estienne as he had his eye set on another that evening. He ordered me to keep other company… an old friend of his in Poitiers."

"That was a stroke of luck for you!"

"With my life being as it is, I wish I'd have died at Sir Estienne's side."

"You were saved for a purpose, Paul."

"A purpose? I thought you didn't believe in God?"

"I don't… but I do believe in fate and fate has put us together, and we must make the most of it."

"Will you stay the night? It is late and I hear that there are marauders abroad on the roads."

"Aye, I will. Besides, we have much to discuss, you and I."

Robert Clay hid the disgust he felt inside himself at forming an alliance with a sodomite. He recognised, however, the power that he had over this person, Paul Martin, who yet might prove useful to him in his fight against the Church; and if he did not, then he would sacrifice him for whatever advantage he could gain. What did he care for the life of a sodomite?

THE RISE OF THE BROTHERHOOD

After four months, the Brotherhood had enlisted twenty new recruits; Duane Catchpole had progressed so well in his reading and writing that Margaret believed he'd been able to read and write all along; and John Clay continued his slide into madness, exacerbated by being undermined in everything he tried to do to advance the aims of the Brotherhood. Not all those undermining him were strangers, nor were they external forces; they were the very people he thought should have been bending to the will of his leadership.

For John Clay, it began the day his sister Margaret threatened the life of Duane Catchpole should he prove to be a traitor. *This is not how it was meant to be,* thought he at the time. He had expressly forbidden the use of violence, especially in dealings with those approached as recruits. Since that first meeting in the barn, four people who'd been approached to become recruits had gone missing, with the remains of one of them turning up in a feeding trough in a pig sty. When Brethren sought advice, they seldom went to John Clay; instead they went to either Margaret Clay or Duane Catchpole, who'd become so close during their reading and writing lessons that Lorence Blackstone punched Catchpole on the nose during a fit of jealous rage.

Attacks on aristocrats and their property were taking place weekly, sometimes twice weekly, with the plunder from the raids being hoarded in secret locations. People were now refusing to work for aristocrats or supply them goods for fear of angering the Brotherhood, the mere mention of whose name struck fear into the hearts of those who should be fearful of them. Ordinary people began spreading rumours about the Brotherhood, linking their name to every escapade that took place in the six parishes. Peasants would carry out crimes and blame them on the Brotherhood, those uncovered performing this ruse were brutally dealt with by the Brethren. To have done all the things they were supposed to have done, the Brotherhood would have needed to number more than one hundred.

"This was not how it was supposed to be," mumbled John Clay. "We were to be a secret society, a Brotherhood, set on breaking the hold of the aristocracy in the six parishes, not attacking them or burning their property to the ground. They will not stand for it; they will seek revenge and then we'll be for it." After a few moments further thought, John Clay continued his rambling. "In our actions we sin against God and His laws. They've ruined everything… we're sure to finish at the end of the hangman's rope. How I hate them… how I hate them all… especially…" He couldn't say it; he could not bring himself to say his sister's name lest it lead him where he did not want to go.

The day following, the fourth official meeting of the Brotherhood was convened, as usual, in the barn by the stream on what remained of the Clays' estate. Duane Catchpole proudly read out aloud the *Constitution of the Brotherhood*, which he'd written with his own hand, a hand guided by Margaret Clay. Then a cry rang out from the Clays' house: "She's started… baby's on her way," howled Marion Marley, her voice carrying to all parts of the farm.

The women of the house gathered in Margaret's bedroom to help with the delivery. The hours passed without any sign that the baby was wanting to be born. Margaret became weaker and weaker and after thirty hours she had hardly the strength to lift her head from the bed, let alone deliver her child into the light. Mary whispered to Marion that she'd seen this before when she'd attended at the Frost family birthing a few years earlier. She said the family had to decide whether to save the baby or poor Mary Frost, and in the end they lost both. Marion replied saying surely it wouldn't come to that with Margaret. "She's young... so strong... so..." Choking back tears prevented Marion from completing her sentence. Not wanting Margaret to see her so distressed, Marion left the room to fetch water. In the kitchen, she explained the situation in the birthing chamber to the men. Lorence then wanted to join the women attending to his Margaret, who he regarded as his wife even though the Church did not. Marion held him back, saying that if the baby would not be born of its own accord before the middle of the afternoon then he, Lorence, would have to decide whether they should save the child or Margaret.

Lorence broke down crying at the prospect of having to make a choice between losing his wife or his baby child, and through sobs so deep that they shuddered his shoulders he whispered hoarsely, "Margaret... save my Margaret... in God's good name, save my Margaret."

Marion returned to the birthing chamber with a craggy-faced old hag of a woman by her side. She stared at the old woman for a moment but could not think where she had come from. She did not recognise her, nor could she recall the old hag joining her company. Lorence Blackstone, having decided that his place was at his wife's side, entered the room behind Marion and upon seeing the old hag, he made to remove her from the birthing chamber. On touching the old hag, Lorence slumped in a heap to the floor as though his bones had turned to jelly. He could move only to turn his head upwards to look at the old woman. She was glowing with an aura and waving her arms around inside her black shroud and shouting something, but the sound she made was incoherent to him, it just echoed in his ears. The old woman stooped and blew some powder into Lorence's mouth. Moments later he felt himself being lifted up into the air and once outside the room his strength was restored to him. Galen Spurling appeared and asked Lorence what was going on. Pushing Galen aside, Lorence attempted to re-enter the birthing chamber but no matter how hard he tried, he could not reach to touch the door. Mystified, Lorence turned to look back at Galen who, to his eyes, appeared to be in a trance. As he shook Galen violently by his shoulders to wake him a black darkness descended on them both.

Kneeling beside the birthing bed, the old woman rocked back and forth chanting soothingly to Margaret, though none of the others there could make out anything of what she was singing. Then, bending over, the old woman opened her bag and produced a green glass bottle, from which she poured some milky liquid into Margaret's mouth. Then everything in the room went silent, soundless and black. That was all anybody could recall when they woke some time later at the shrill cry of a newborn baby. Looking around the room, the old woman was nowhere to be seen. The birthing bed was covered in blood and the baby, a girl, as predicted, was lying wrapped in a brilliant white cloth next to her mother. Margaret, peering down adoringly at the baby feeding at her breast, asked for Lorence. The moment Lorence saw his baby for the first time, he involuntarily uttered her name: "Alice."

Thanks to the timely arrival of a wise old woman of the woods, who'd materialised after being summoned up in response to the incantations of Robert Clay, his sister Margaret survived a childbirth that otherwise would've killed her.

That evening, the whole family gathered around Margaret's bed to pray for her recovery. Some there secretly prayed for her immortal soul as she looked as though she was about to pass from this life. Exhausted from a lengthy birth and loss of blood, Margaret lay motionless, drifting in and out of a deep dreamless sleep. Her breathing was laboured and her whole body dripped with sweat. Things were looking bad for Margaret but Robert said he had faith that she would survive.

"And where does this faith of yours spring from, brother?" asked John Clay in a menacing monotone.

"From Him on high, dear brother... I know that He will answer my prayers."

"Tell me, brother, did you hear of the old woman who suddenly appeared at our sister's birthing bed at the precise time when she was most needed?"

"I did, brother, I did," smiled Robert serenely. "I swear, brother, that she must have been an angel sent from heaven above in answer to my prayers for our dear sister."

"Some are saying that she was a witch, but you say she was an angel. Tell me, brother, do angels render men so weak in their bodies that they lose their strength to even stand? Do angels cast knowledge or memory from the minds of witnesses? Do angels—"

"Who can say how an angel will act?" responded Robert with a smirk. "Are you complaining that the angel saved the life of our beloved sister?"

"What is this you are saying?" asked Lorence Blackstone, overhearing the conversation.

"Robert says the old woman who came to the aid of your wife was an angel sent from heaven in answer to his prayers. I say she was a witch or worse. What do you say, Lorence Blackstone? You have some recollection of events, do you not? You have told how you were floated out of the birthing-room and how you could not re-enter it no matter how hard you tried. Is this the work of an angel... or a devil? Such a devil as we met on the road to St Malo!" This last sentence was screamed by John Clay, spraying spittle into the face of Robert Clay.

"How can such women be devils, dear John? Did these women perform evil or good in both circumstances? I ask you, is their way of work the way of a devil or an angel? It can only be that of an angel," argued Robert Clay, wiping his brother's spittle from his face.

"What if it's just the work of a wise old woman of the woods, like many have already said? It need not be divine work at all... just the wisdom of centuries passed down through their line," offered Lorence Blackstone as a possibility.

"Then why did Robert summon up the old woman through the chanting of pagan incantations? You were overheard, brother, so do not deny it!" John Clay was now incandescent with rage.

"What the eavesdropper overheard, dear brother, were my prayers to our good Lord God above asking Him to intervene to save our sister."

"Do not make a mockery of Him that rules all mankind from His throne on high in the heavens. You summoned the Devil and He came... Lucifer came! It was Lucifer who answered your heathen call, attending our sister in the form of one of his vile disguises."

"His? His! Dear John, it is abundantly clear that the Devil is female... as are all her servants," spoke Lorence Blackstone sincerely.

"Are you mocking me, Master Blackstone? The Devil... Satan... the Fallen Angel... a woman? Are you suffering some delirium of the mind after your recent trials?"

"Pay him no mind, brother; Lorence believes God himself to likewise be female," said Robert Clay, purposely adding fuel to the fire of John's rising rage.

"Of course the Devil is a woman. Look at the evidence..."

"Prepare yourself, brother; Lorence's argument for God being female was extremely entertaining... but be ready to be convinced!" Robert Clay could not contain a derisory snort from his nose, which further inflamed his pious brother.

"I will not tolerate heathen talk taking place under my own roof!"

"Dear brother, it is not heathen to debate whether God or the Devil be man or woman... Go ahead, my outlaw brother, explain your theory to brother John."

"It stands to reason that Lucifer... the Fallen Angel... is female. Look at Her behaviour. There She is, sitting at the right hand side of the Lord our God in His most sacred place..."

"Enough! I will not stand by while you make mockery of me and my religion. As soon as my sister is able, Lorence Blackstone, you are to leave this house, taking her and your Devil daughter with you; and you, brother... you thought that you had tricked me with your returning to the fold but you did not... I was wise to you all along. You are to return to living in the barn by the stream. I would banish you altogether but we are shorthanded and the seasons keep coming round." That said, John Clay stared wild eyed at every corner of the room as though spying sprites and spirits. He then turned on his heels to leave his brother and Lorence Blackstone staring at his disappearing back. They seemed content with their work.

The raging argument between John, Robert and Lorence did not go unheard by the others in the house and was at the root of many bitter family quarrels over the ensuing days.

★

At the meeting of the Brotherhood following the birth of Alice Blackstone, John Clay informed the gathered Brethren of Margaret's difficult labour and her subsequent poor health, saying that she was recovering in her bed and, as soon as she was able, would be leaving the Clay estate along with her husband and child.

The gathered Brethren were surprised at the announcement, and no less so when they noticed the absence of Mary Spurling, Galen Spurling, Marion Marley, Jethro Marley, Lorence Blackstone, Charles Leclerc and Samuel White.

Duane Catchpole stood and told John and Robert Clay, on behalf of all those others there, that they were relieved to hear that Margaret and her baby were okay, adding that if there was anything any of them could do to help around the farm while they took care of her and the newborn, they were only to ask. John Clay gave a slight bow in acknowledgement of the kind offer. "Now, brothers and sisters," he began. At 'sisters', Duane Catchpole and some others looked round the barn, as no sisters were present. "Let us get on with our business here before the sheriff comes down on us." Duane's nervous laugh at John's 'joke' was joined by others in the barn.

John Clay described to the meeting how well his plans were going for breaking the hold of the aristocracy over the 'good people of the six parishes'. According to him, several parish councils were coming under his influence and moves were underway to have Brotherhooders voted onto them, though he presented no evidence for this. Plus he was petitioning the good lady wives of aristocrats to form a society to provide care for tenant farmers who were no longer able to work their lands. Furthermore, John Clay claimed that the good lady wives of his society could be influenced to act in ways beneficial to the aims of the Brotherhood. It was as though the other activities carried out by the Brotherhood weren't going on at all. John Clay was simply ignoring them, no doubt hoping they would go away. Everybody in the barn sat listening patiently for nearly half an hour before John Clay finished speaking, at which time Robert Clay asked if there was any other business to be discussed. Duane Catchpole took to his feet again. He'd been primed to bring up a difficult subject.

"To the best of my knowledge and belief, there are no others who we can recruit to our Brotherhood left in all of the six parishes… there's not one left who is suitable. Brothers, tell me if I am mistaken." Heads shook no and mumbles passed around the gathering. "To grow our Brotherhood, I say that now is the right time to go beyond the borders of the six parishes." John Clay was quickly to his feet.

"Brother, it is for me as leader to say what we should do," responded John Clay with no little anger in his voice. "I will contemplate your idea before giving you my decision." Duane Catchpole bowed, saying that was all he could ask for or expect. Robert Clay smiled inside at his own cunning.

As the Brethren made their way from the barn following the meeting of their Brotherhood, Robert Clay held John back by his elbow, whispering into his ear for him to remain a while. With everybody out of earshot, Robert said to his brother that if he wished to dilute Duane Catchpole's growing influence, what was needed was more recruits, and as the area was exhausted of suitable men they would have to be found beyond the boundaries of the six parishes, exactly as Duane Catchpole had said. Stroking his bearded chin between thumb and forefinger, John Clay contemplated his brother's words. After considering Robert's advice, John Clay conceded that the Brotherhood should indeed expand beyond the six parishes and said he would order Brethren to go out and seek new recruits. Robert asked John if he should inform Master Catchpole of his decision but John said he'd do so himself. Not wanting to find himself marginalised in his own scheming, Robert Clay ran and caught up with Duane Catchpole to give him the good news personally.

"Master Catchpole!" shouted Robert Clay, signalling those with him to continue on their way without the company of their ringleader.

"What do you want, Master Clay? Hasn't your family done enough today to spoil my designs?" spoke Duane Catchpole loudly for all to hear.

"Master Catchpole, believe it or believe it not, I want what you want but I set about achieving it in a different way to you." Duane Catchpole was uninterested in hearing any more of what Robert had to say and so continued on his way. "Know this, Master Catchpole," shouted Robert Clay at Duane Catchpole's back, "I can convince my brother to agree to expanding the Brotherhood beyond the boundaries of the six parishes." These words stopped Catchpole in his tracks.

"So what? I was going to do that anyway."

"I thought as much," lied Robert, not wanting to appear naïve, "but to avoid war, a war that neither of us wants, you should listen to what I have to say. Believe me when I tell you that John will come with orders for you to travel throughout the middle lands to recruit new members for the Brotherhood."

"So what? I repeat, I was going to do that anyway. I will recruit men of action, men who will do my bidding and not sit on their arses contriving trivial plots... plots that depend on the wives of aristocrats for their success."

"If it is 'so what' that you say, then you are a fool, Master Catchpole. Where will you find sanctuary from the hangman's noose while engaging on this rampage of yours?"

"Mind your mouth, Clay. I've thought this through and the others are with me."

"Then, Master Catchpole, tell me this: have you thought how you will evade capture? Where will you hide out? Lorence Blackstone was in the company of a band of fierce outlaws when I met him in Rennes Forest, but when the captain of the King's Guard and a knight called Sir Aldred Benz set their minds to it, they flushed them out and slaughtered all they found. The same will happen to you if you set yourself upon this course."

"Tell me, Master Clay, what is your design in all this?"

"I have no design in this other than for the Brotherhood to do its work unhindered by internal strife."

"Why then are you set against your brother?"

"I am not set against my brother. He is a good man and once he sees his schemes failing, he will come around to your view of things. He is stubborn so it may take some time. In the meantime, grow your influence while his diminishes."

"And what of your sister, Margaret? She has her own ambitions and ways of thinking and they are not along the same lines as my own."

"You are correct in what you say, Master Catchpole; my sister may indeed prove to be problematic but we are family, and we will all do our best to see that no harm comes to her." Duane Catchpole shook his head at Robert Clay's interpretation of his words.

Duane Catchpole had not considered Margaret Clay problematic until Robert Clay had mentioned it and he was now concerned that she might be so, just as Robert Clay intended. The men parted with the agreement that Duane Catchpole would wait to hear what John Clay had to say about expanding the Brotherhood and would act surprised on hearing the news of recruitment being made beyond the middle lands. Robert Clay, for his part, was resolved to have Duane Catchpole killed if he did not go along with John's plan. He wasn't going to allow Master Catchpole's ambitions to scupper his own schemes.

A short time after Robert Clay's conversation with Duane Catchpole, John Clay sought Catchpole out to take him into his confidence by sharing with him his 'daring plan to expand the Brotherhood beyond the boundaries of the six parishes'. Duane Catchpole acted surprised as if hearing the plan for the first time, and manufactured delight that John Clay had sought to share it with him. As John Clay's plan played to Duane Catchpole's ambitions, he decided to stay tight with the Brotherhood for the time being and oust John Clay as leader when the time was right.

After his conversation with Duane Catchpole, Robert Clay sought out his sisters to discuss 'concerns over Master Catchpole' with them. Perceiving Catchpole as a man of great energy and a natural leader, it was no surprise that Margaret was in favour of him, while Mary and Marion were not. They felt, as had been said by many people several times, that his recklessness would lead them all to the gallows or worse. Speaking later with Lorence Blackstone, it was apparent that he held a deep and abiding hatred for Master Catchpole, largely out of jealousy for his closeness to his wife. Robert took the opportunity in his conversation with Lorence Blackstone to reassure him that everything was going according to plan and though its fulfilment would take a while yet, it would all be worth it when they two would rule the Brotherhood together, having let Catchpole do all the work to build up its numbers. What Lorence Blackstone couldn't know was that he was at risk of death until such time as he unequivocally denounced the Church and all who served it; only then would Master Blackstone be reliable in Robert Clay's eyes.

Having stirred his pot of schemes, Robert Clay mounted his favourite horse and rode to the hut of Paul Martin. On his arrival he found Master Martin in the company of a young man called Simon Sparrow, who Robert knew well. They'd never seen eye to eye in the past but if Robert's suspicions about Sparrow were correct, that he was indeed a sodomite, he now had Master Sparrow exactly where he wanted him. A thought then occurred to Robert Clay: *Having seen me arrive alone at Paul Martin's hut, what if Master Sparrow suspects me of being a sodomite and believes he has me exactly where he wants me? If he alludes to that possibility I will order him killed... What good, right-thinking man would weep over one less sodomite in the world?*

"Master Sparrow, good day to you but leave us now, we have business to attend to."

"By chance is your business to do with the band of outlaws known as the Brotherhood, Master Clay?" spoke Simon Sparrow. Robert Clay passed a deadly glance at Paul Martin.

"Good Master Clay, I was just saying to Master Sparrow how this so-called Brotherhood makes life so much worse for everyone and he was just saying how the sheriff has been given the task of rounding them all up. They say his spies are already picking up loose talk."

"Is that so?" enquired Robert Clay.

"It is indeed, Master Clay," interjected Simon Sparrow.

"And so, good Master Sparrow... Simon... away with you until next time," spoke Paul Martin, the two men whispered and hugged before Simon Sparrow finally took his leave.

"What the hell is going on?" sputtered an exasperated Robert Clay.

"You have your contacts and I have mine, and it's just as well for you that I have, otherwise we wouldn't have uncovered the sheriff's scheme to capture the leaders of the Brotherhood."

"Is there a reward?"

"There is indeed a reward... the good sheriff will be allowed to keep his job and not lose his head," laughed Paul Martin.

"How so?"

"It's just the way things work. Master Sparrow told me that several prominent families have put upon the sheriff to rid the six parishes of the Brotherhood. According to him, there is promise of some paltry sum of five silver coins, but Simon doubts it will ever be paid... you know what aristocrats are like."

"How well acquainted is Master Sparrow with the sheriff?"

"Quite well, I believe... well enough to have his ear, at least."

"Is that the only part of the sheriff's body Master Sparrow has access to?" asked Robert Clay with a sour taste in his mouth. Paul Martin blushed before replying.

"The sheriff's preferences are, as they say, to go both ways."

"And you can prove this?"

"I cannot… but Simon and others can testify to it." Putting aside for a moment the scheme he was conjuring up in his head concerning the sheriff, Robert Clay changed the subject.

"There are big changes on the way for the Brotherhood. As you noticed at the meeting, there were empty places where my family should've sat. My brother has estranged himself from them and so Duane Catchpole's star will rise while my brother's will fall. Very shortly, Master Catchpole will expand the Brotherhood into the middle lands."

"To what end?"

"My brother will never attack the true enemy… the Church. Duane Catchpole, on the other hand, will do so after he realises just how much easier it is to steal gold from churches than the well-guarded homes of aristocrats."

"And what of the others?"

"Which others?"

"All those in the Brotherhood who are religious… they will never go against the Church under any circumstances."

"That is why we need new recruits… carefully chosen recruits."

"I am not following your line of thought."

"It's simple enough. When the Brotherhood expands into the middle lands, we will help Master Catchpole choose the new recruits… recruits who are prepared to act against the Church."

"How will we be able to tell which recruits will be so inclined?"

"We will listen to their stories."

"Listen to their stories?"

"Yes, as I listened to your story, so shall we listen to theirs and make our choices then."

"And if we choose badly?"

"Then that will be the end for them." Paul Martin became aroused as he drank in Robert Clay's dark ruthlessness.

"Is that it?"

"The plan is somewhat incomplete but, in essence, we will leave the property of aristocrats in the six shires unmolested, thus providing us a safe refuge there while leaving Catchpole to rampage throughout the middle lands."

"The Brotherhood is not going to attack Sir John Belcher?" gasped Master Martin in disbelief.

"No, not under any circumstances. I have other plans for him."

"So, let me understand you… the new recruits must be against the aristocracy and the Church, but mainly the Church? How many reliable men will we find with this as our criteria?"

"Enough. I will not be diverted from my quest of destroying the Church! It is an evil empire that must be brought down. It is a big task that will not take a week or a year, or even a hundred years… it may take generations, but in my lifetime I will set in motion the wheels of the Church's demise."

"There are precious few men who would dare to think as we do, let alone act against the Church. The power of the Church is great. It preys on the feeble-minded, of which there are many as far as religious worship is concerned. I would counsel you this caution: that you carry out your quest incognito. Be a wolf wrapped in sheepskin… roam inside the flock, mix, act as one of them, and this will allow you to strike the Church with impunity. Everybody will soon enough know that the Brotherhood is against the aristocracy… nobody will suspect that a faction of it is set against the Church. Think carefully on what I counsel, Master Clay."

"A faction operating within the Brotherhood? That would be a most perfect refuge and disguise!"

"We must choose our marks well as our existence will not be tolerated by the Brotherhood. Recruits must have a good reason to enrol, otherwise we should not entertain them."

"We should name our faction."

"What shall we call it?"

"Call it what it is… The Faction For Those Who Wish To Act Against The Church."

Unimpressed by Robert Clay's naming of the Faction, Paul Martin had another suggestion. "What about calling it the 'Anti-Church Faction' and using the letters ACF to confuse eavesdroppers?"

"I'm not sure how confused eavesdroppers will be with just three letters to decipher the meaning of, but ACF sounds right somehow... ACF it is, Master Martin." The two men shook hands to seal the naming.

And so, in that brief transaction, the Anti-Church Faction was born. Over the centuries, the ACF would inhabit the shadows within the shadows of the Brotherhood. It would bring the Church to the very brink of extinction before the twentieth century was out.

★

Over the four years following Robert Clay's conversation with Paul Martin, the Brotherhood went from strength to strength under the stewardship of Duane Catchpole. Catchpole expanded the Brotherhood far beyond the borders of the six parishes, and in Robert Clay he found a man sufficiently trustworthy for him and his lackey, Paul Martin, to recruit new members. There were some instances, however, of men Catchpole had thought of as suitable recruits disappearing, several of whom were subsequently washed up on riverbanks or found lying in the woods with their throats slit, leading Master Catchpole to become wary of many of those around him. Little could he suspect, however, that the man responsible for disappearing his recruits was the puny Paul Martin, acting under the orders of Robert Clay; the unfortunate recruits having failed the ACF test and with neither Clay nor Martin being able to afford to have them go blabbing to Catchpole they had to die.

Over that same four-year period, John Clay's power diminish to the point where he was reduced to carrying out minor tasks for the sake of simply having something to do. In his madness, John Clay convinced himself that the tasks he was carrying out were something other than trivial, and he would hold court with himself to say how well he was doing.

The constitution of the Brotherhood decreed that leadership elections would be held every five years and John Clay's time was nearly up. He feared for what may lie beyond that anniversary. Having trusted his brother to keep watch on Duane Catchpole, John Clay had neglected to keep his own eye on the activities of Master Catchpole; and, if the rumours were to be believed, those he'd recruited were loyal only to him. Catching the whispers of others, John could guess what would happen next. He'd lose the upcoming leadership vote, and then what? He shuddered at the prospect. *Maybe I'll start anew by creating a version of the Brotherhood dedicated to acting in Godly ways,* he thought, but no, he recognised that its existence would not be tolerated by the original. Downcast as he was, John Clay refused to accept defeat as inevitable, but he was at a loss as to know what to do to change his fortunes. The one shining light in John Clay's life was that he'd taken a wife and she'd produced two pairs of twin boys. John had fantasised that his sons would grow to lead the Brotherhood one day but he now believed they'd have to content themselves with running the family estate. During intermittent periods of lucidity, John Clay prepared himself for the worst. Most of the Clay clan had long believed he should not continue as leader of the Brotherhood anyway, though none of them said anything of the kind to him.

During that same four years, Duane Catchpole ensured that John Clay remained occupied with refining his policies and forming societies such as the *Charitable Wives of Aristocrats* for the benefit of obtaining information for the Brotherhood. This work confined John within the borders of the six parishes. Catchpole knew, of course, that John's schemes were fanciful, existing only inside his head. In all their years, there had been no progress whatsoever with John's policies. *What a waste of time*, thought Duane Catchpole, *but it keeps him out of my way!* To keep John Clay further occupied, Catchpole handed him menial tasks dressed up as essential to the Brotherhood's future success. John Clay wasn't so crazy as to not recognise what was going on but he never complained, he just got on with them. While John Clay was busy buzzing around inside the boundaries of the six parishes, Duane Catchpole was up to every kind of mischief outside them. Necessarily, he and his cronies took periodic sanctuary within the six parishes whenever things got too hot. Over the years, Catchpole grew the Brotherhood to a number of around four hundred. He became the gang-master of all the recruiters and organised the Brothers into regional lodges. Each new recruit was sworn in personally by Duane Catchpole during Brotherhood lodge meetings. At swearing in ceremonies, the new recruits recited the oath of allegiance, the one that Catchpole and Margaret Clay had written together and which he had amended over time to suit his own purposes. After the taking of the oath of allegiance, Catchpole would read out the latest version of the *Constitution of the Brotherhood* so all would be reminded of it. Like the oath of allegiance, the brotherhood's constitution was tweaked over time to suit Catchpole's purposes. These ceremonies bound the loyalty of all Brethren outside the six parishes to Duane Catchpole, which was his intention. The Brotherhood being split into regional lodges as it was had the advantage that very few men knew all members. Accordingly, if any recruit was to betray the Brotherhood, they could not wipe it out more than a handful. Under Catchpole, the reputation of the Brotherhood became such that the mere mention of its name, which was now only ever made in whispers, was enough to strike dread into the hearts of every aristocrat and feudal lord across the middle lands. The Brotherhooders themselves were content with Duane Catchpole's leadership; none wanted a change because they were all getting rich, with many of them now occupying the class of landed gentry.

The Brotherhood was fast turning into the thing it was created to destroy.

All the while the Brotherhood was growing, Robert Clay's machinations grew in proportion. He quite understood that fate, Fortuna, human nature and other factors that lay beyond his control meant it was impossible for any plan to succeed as first envisaged; plans need to be nurtured and so long as they go in the right direction, the only important factor is that they end up at the intended place. Constant adjustments must be made to plans to keep them on track, keep them alive, keep them to their purpose. To ensure his plan did just that, behind the scenes Robert Clay operated the strings of each of the main players. It was he who advised Duane Catchpole to become the gang-master of the recruiters in order to pull power away from John to destabilise him. He suggested to Catchpole that he form regional lodges, with each holding its own monthly meeting at which he would induct all new recruits personally and read out the *Constitution of the Brotherhood* to ensure those attending knew who their master was. Robert even counselled Master Catchpole on amendments to the oath of allegiance and the Brotherhood's constitution documents to make them more to his own liking. At the same time, Robert was whispering in his brother's ear about how Duane Catchpole was turning the recruits to his ways, never paying mind to John's leadership and holding secret meetings with them. Meanwhile, Robert was keeping Lorence Blackstone informed of the progress he was making even though he was resolved to finish Master Blackstone's life if he gave him cause. In any case, Robert only let Lorence know enough to keep him compliant, so in reality, Lorence couldn't do any real damage to Robert's plans if the two fell out. In the background, Robert had prevented Lorence and Margaret, who were now lawfully wed in their new parish, having baby Alice christened in church by ensuring the record of her birth in the Clays' home parish declared her illegitimate. Having such a record, Alice would forever be deprived of the things in life that the Church held sway over. This infuriated Lorence and Margaret to such a degree that Lorence planned to have the priest meet with an unfortunate accident one dark night, but Robert convinced him that the timing was not yet right. When asked when the time would be right, Robert replied, "Soon, my outlaw brother... soon." How Robert congratulated himself on the forming of the ACF, even though those few he'd recruited to it so far would abandon him if their existence became common knowledge.

★

In the early fourteenth century, the Church was all-powerful and knew well how to wield the power it possessed to best effect. Owning more than half the land in England, as it did, the Church controlled the lives of the vast majority of ordinary people and if any of them did anything to attract the Church's displeasure, they'd find themselves homeless and with no land to feed themselves. Accordingly, Robert Clay and Paul Martin went about the work of selecting recruits for the ACF very carefully lest they be betrayed for rewards; rewards that never came the way of betrayers as they were loathed by both sides. Robert Clay's grand plan was to destroy the Church; not its buildings or those serving it, but to destroy its purpose so that it had nothing to offer people and consequently there would be no reason for it to exist. The part of the plan that he wanted to achieve in his lifetime was for him to grow the ACF to one hundred devotees, spread throughout its host, the Brotherhood. The ACF would latch on inside the Brotherhood like a parasite... mimicking how the church was a parasite on society. He would often laugh at thoughts of the imitation game he was playing. *Being like the thing you want to destroy makes it all the easier to destroy it*, was Robert's thinking. Despite the cleverness of his thinking, his scheming and planning, Robert Clay could not get certain things out of his head, things that he knew could destroy the ACF. More than anything, he wanted to see the crow priest dead. See him dead by his own hand. He wanted to look into the crow priest's eyes as they turned milky and lifeless as his life drained from him.

★

Four months before the vote was to be held for who would be elected leader of the Brotherhood for the next five years, Robert Clay sought out his brother as he was travelling to a meeting of parish councillors. Again and again John's candidates were defeated in ballots for admission onto the parish councils, the results of which were only ever seen by those sitting on parish councils.

"How goes it, brother, how goes it?"

"It goes as ever it did," replied John, the tic in his eyes now wildly uncontrollable. "What do you want? Are you coming to gloat over the successes of Master Catchpole? If so then save your breath, he tells me of them himself... every day if he could!"

"What is this? Do you believe me to be in favour of Catchpole? In his service, perhaps?"

"You are a recruiter for him, are you not?" Robert nodded. "Then what have you to say to me? Are you come to give me news that Master Catchpole has decided not to stand against me in the election, perhaps?" Robert shook his head. "Then I ask again, what do you want?"

"As you have mentioned the election, we are best to begin there... let us stop riding a while and take a seat on the felled tree over yonder." The brothers dismounted, tied their horses to the bushes, as they'd done that night while on the run in France, and sat, not looking at one another, on an old felled tree. "The election... you must win it, brother."

"Really? You say that after all that's happened? All that you've done to undermine me, going against me and my Brotherhood?"

"I see now that you are the best man to lead us forward… but you must strike an agreement with the Brethren. They need to live… to eat… to raise a family… and none of it is free. You must reach a compromise that all can live with."

"So far all I've heard is words with nothing in them."

"Then hear these words, brother: we must work together to defeat Master Catchpole. He will, as many have said over many years, lead us all to the gallows and I have no desire to visit them. Hence, Catchpole must be done away with."

"Done away with?"

"Killed! Not that we would do it ourselves, of course, but die he must and die he will… and don't give me any sermon about sins and sinning; it is not a sin in my eyes to rid myself of a rabid dog before it bites me, and so it is with Catchpole."

"You'll get no such sermon from me, brother!" Robert Clay could hardly believe his ears. "The truth be told, I've thought about killing Master Catchpole myself many times over the past year or more." John Clay stood and stroked his bearded chin, deep in thought, or so he wanted to make it appear. "I've been pondering God's creation and in it I see death everywhere… why, more men are slaughtered in His name than for any other reason I can think of. So, I can only conclude from this fact that God recruits souls to heaven as we do for the Brotherhood… it is only our method that differs. I am happy, therefore, to give Master Catchpole up to God and commit him to His merciful care and love." On hearing John speak thus, Robert wondered whether his brother's mind had completely gone, but as their needs aligned to suit Robert's purposes, nothing now stood in the way of his plan to remove Catchpole and his closest accomplices.

"I am glad to hear it, brother, very glad indeed. We will set the Brotherhood on a course to work for our purposes, and in doing so we will rule its future."

"Aye, brother, we will rule it… rule it with a rod of iron! How then shall we set up to be rid of Catchpole?"

"Alas, brother, if it were only Catchpole that we needed to rid ourselves of; there are those he has recruited who will never take orders from anybody else, they are his men to the last."

"Who are they?"

"Fret not, brother, I have a list. While we are cleansing the stain of Catchpole from this good land, there are others we might attend to at the same time." John Clay looked at Robert in anticipation.

"Sir John Belcher! What do you say about adding him to the list?"

"Now… and hear me out, brother… now, what do you think about adding the…" Robert hesitated to allow John to complete his sentence.

"The crow priest… You were going to say the crow priest, weren't you?"

"I was, brother, I was," smiled Robert in triumph.

"For what he did to our family, add him to the list! Behaving as he does, he cannot be a man of God! Add him to the list!" The look in John Clay's eyes took on more madness than evil; they were wide and glaring, tic-blinking, darting here and there with sparks reflecting the light of the moon.

"What would you say if I told you I have a plan for Belcher and the crow priest to do our work for us?"

"I would say all the better, so long as we kill them as soon as their work is done."

"Let us leave our talk there, brother. I will consult with others and bring you in for your part in the scheme."

"Tell me, brother, and tell me true, if I didn't concur with your scheme… would you have killed me here this night on this lonely road?"

"Brother… brother mine…" whimpered Robert in a hurt voice, "how can you say… how can you think such a thing! No brother, no! Of course not!" lied Robert Clay, returning his dagger to a sheath hidden beneath his cloak as he mounted his horse.

PACT WITH THE DEVIL

Robert Clay and Paul Martin were deep in conversation when they stopped at the sound of an approaching horse. It came to a halt outside Paul Martin's hut. The door edged slowly open and Simon Sparrow's grimy face appeared through the gap. He asked if all was safe. They told him, "Yes, friend Simon, all is safe." He then put his fingers to his mouth and whistled so loudly that his horse bolted. He cursed his jittery steed rather than his own stupidity at not securing the animal. Then came the sound of horses galloping up the lane toward the hut. The riders dismounted and pushing Master Sparrow aside they made their way into the hut.

"If what Master Sparrow tells me is true, I should arrest you."

"Who have you brought with you, Master Sheriff? Can you vouch for them?"

"There be no need for any names. Give me one good reason why I shouldn't arrest you for treason."

"For one thing, Sir, we are not traitors, we are fighters for freedom; and for a second thing, if we are molested in any way, word will get out that you, good sheriff, are a Molly." The sheriff's companions were not thrown by this accusation; they seemed accepting of it, boastful almost. The sheriff cast a glare at Simon Sparrow before continuing.

"Scurrilous accusations apart… why have you requested this meeting?"

"For the last several years, Sheriff Judd, you have been seeking those of an order known as the Brotherhood."

"You tell me what I already know you three to be a part of. I should arrest you and have done with it, then perhaps I'll get Sir John Belcher and his like off my back!"

"We are but small fish in the Brotherhood's pond, and you'd do well to listen rather than act. Besides, we might have a dozen men within earshot who'll come running with sword in hand if you act against us."

"Have you?"

"No, of course not! It's a matter of trust. We need one another…"

"What do you need me for?"

"I need you to break the Brotherhood, Sheriff Judd. Nothing more, nothing less."

"Break the Brotherhood? That sounds far-fetched. You're setting me up."

"I can understand you being suspicious at being handed such an opportunity, so I will tell you of a small raid that is to happen on the morrow night so that you might be certain that we mean business."

"Give it me, then!"

"After I've proven to you that I am sincere in the opportunity I present to you, you will need to do something for me."

"What?"

"You will guarantee me that neither you nor those that take on the Brotherhood will ever come for me or seek out any of my family or their spouses, or Masters Martin and Sparrow. Do you agree?"

"This assurance you ask can easily be broken… Do you put so much trust in me?"

"No, I surely do not. If you betray me you will not see the She-Devil that comes to take you, but take you She will… First though, She will take your children one by one and you will live to see the last of them before you beg Her to take you from this life." Robert Clay's words and tone sent shivers scuttling down Sheriff Judd's spine. "Do we have an accord, Sheriff Judd?"

As the sheriff offered his hand to Robert Clay, Masters Martin and Sparrow slipped unnoticed to stand behind his two companions. Then, grabbing each of the men round their necks in a headlock, Martin and Sparrow stabbed the sheriff's companions using long slender assassins' daggers. Over and over, again and again and again, they stabbed them, piercing their hearts a dozen or more times. There was little blood to evidence the ferocity of the attack due to the slenderness of the daggers. As the victims' hearts pumped blood into their chest cavities, their bodies quickly became yielding and then fell dead to the floor. The sheriff stood motionless, paralysed in a state of terror and shock. Before he could think to act, Lorence Blackstone emerged from the shadows to hold a sword to his heart. "You should never have brought them along with you, Master Sheriff. With the knowledge they possessed they could've done for us all. In future you will act only as instructed, or it will be you who pays the price."

After Sheriff Judd recovered his composure, Robert Clay told him about the raid that was to be carried out at the home of a parish councillor the following evening. It was only a small raid, so he said, and consequently only four Brotherhooders would be involved. Robert Clay ordered the sheriff to take with him only men that he had a hold over as no prisoners were to be taken; they were all to be killed, 'householders, guests, servants and perpetrators alike!' Sheriff Judd did not feel this was the time to ask questions; it was a time to follow orders and stay alive by doing so. As he mounted his horse, the sheriff asked Robert Clay about his dead companions' mounts and what he should tell folk about them. Robert replied that the horses were now his property and that the sheriff's companions, having declared their love for one another, had fled to France to be with their kind. "Their families know them for what they are and will be glad to see the back of them and the shame they brought on their households!" Paul Martin and Simon Sparrow recoiled at these words but held their tongues. Robert Clay, sensing their displeasure, later assured them he was only playing a part for Lorence Blackstone's benefit. To their credit, Masters Martin and Sparrow chose to chastise Robert Clay for threatening to expose the sheriff as a Molly, saying that was the sort of threat they'd come to expect from the Church, usually as foreplay to priestly sodomy.

Riding away from Paul Martin's hut, Sheriff Judd felt he'd made a pact with the Devil. He sat on his saddle feverishly crossing himself while reciting the Trinitarian over and over again and kissing a crudely cast cross of the crucified Christ. With the life he'd now entered into, the good sheriff never again made these signs of devotion.

★

The following evening, Sheriff Judd and seven carefully chosen men hid themselves behind a barn close to the home of the parish councillor while awaiting the arrival of the Brotherhooders. It was Paul Martin, acting under Robert Clay's orders, who'd suggested to the four Brethren that they carry out the raid. He'd said, "The whole place is stacked with ill-gotten gains from selling off land to Sir John Belcher and his kind; land that the parish council stole from honest farmers. No need to tell anybody about this... it's just a bit of privateering, like, that's all... all the more for us this way. I can't be there with you as I have my other duties to attend to."

One of the Brethren had asked, "Why can't we do it on another night then? A night when you can be with us."

Master Martin was prepared for that one. "If we wait we'll miss out... the money's going to be shared out with the rest of the parish council on the morrow of the next day." Unhappy at Paul Martin not taking part in the raid with them, the Brotherhooders agreed between themselves that his share would be halved and 'divvied out between them what's going to do the job'.

Another had said, "Why give him any share at all?"

Shortly before midnight, Sheriff Judd saw several shadowy silhouettes moving along the line of a drystone wall, making their way toward the back of the priest's house. He signalled for his motley crew to follow him. The night was silent and all the men likewise made not a sound. Approaching the rear of the building, Sheriff Judd made himself known to the Brotherhooders, warning them not to try to escape as he had the place surrounded. Frozen to the spot, their leader tried to talk his way out of their situation.

"Sheriff Judd, they say you're a good man, so it's told. A good man should let us poor farmers go free and forget tonight's events. We've been greatly wronged by the parish council and we're just trying to get a little back... no harm done."

"So, poor farmers trying to get a bit of natural justice, are you?"

"We are indeed, good Sheriff, we are," spoke one of the Brethren.

"In a pig's arse you are! You are all of you members of the Brotherhood and don't deny it!"

"Members of... what is that you say? The Brotherhood, you say? I've heard of them for sure and all, but I don't think they exist, if you ask me."

"They exist right enough and you're a part of them. Do you think we're here by chance? You've been given over, you fools.

We were told that four of you would be coming here tonight and lo and behold, what do we have? Four of you! We already know what your business was here tonight… plunder and murder." At being accused of conspiring to commit murder, another of the Brotherhooders broke his silence.

"Good Sheriff, that is untrue! We would never murder a priest; we just want some justice by taking back what the thieves on the parish councils have stolen from ordinary folk like us."

"And what were you going to do with the stolen booty? Share it with the unfortunates of the parishes? I doubt it… the Brotherhood only thinks of itself." Turning to his deputies, the sheriff said, "Take their swords and knives from them." The sheriff's men moved forward and disarmed the Brethren.

As soon as the Brotherhooders handed over their weapons, they were set upon and killed. The commotion caused a stir inside the priest's house and brought several men from within to appear at the back door. The sheriff and his men knew some of them to be Mollies and assumed likewise of those they didn't know. As Sheriff Judd was explaining the situation to the priest, he beckoned him in close to whisper something in his ear and as he did so, stabbed him through his heart. The priest slumping was enough to signal to the deputies to dispatch all in the house. As soon as the killing was over, the sheriff and his men entered the priest's house and removed all the gold. A couple of deputies took some other items against orders and were killed. The sheriff, having not followed orders once, wasn't going to make the same mistake again.

When Sheriff Judd reported the night's events, he told a tale of dozens of Brotherhooders rampaging through the priest's house, looting and murdering as they went. His tale told too of the heroism and bravery displayed by himself and of his men in chasing them off at great risk to their lives, as testified by the unfortunate deaths of two of his own men. The good sheriff told of cornering a group of four Brotherhooders, who fought them desperately and ferociously with their backs to the wall... but he and his men prevailed. Sir John Belcher and the rest of the Council of the Middle Lands loudly applauded the Sheriff for his bravery and devotion to duty. One of them asked Sheriff Judd how he had come to be at the home of the priest when the Brotherhood came calling. He was prepared for the question. He said his tavern spies had heard rumours of a raid in the area and it was by the merest chance that he and his men came upon the Brotherhood, catching them in the act of robbery and murder. The same questioner noted that it was the first time that the Brotherhood had been known to steal from the clergy, let alone murder one of them. Again, Sheriff Judd had an answer prepared for the question: he suggested that this might, perhaps, 'be the beginning of a new phase... a change of policy of the Brotherhood... and now everybody is under threat." The sheriff's words greatly alarmed all in the room. Satisfied, though, with the sheriff's answers, Sir John Belcher proposed a reward of four gold crowns be paid to him, and he was, at his discretion, to share it with his deputies and the families of the two men who'd fallen. This was an unusual gesture from Sir John and one which he had no intention of fulfilling.

★

"You and your men did well, Sheriff, very well," acknowledged Robert Clay. "We must be fair to those who serve us well, otherwise we will lose their loyalty and their silence. Tell your deputies that they will each receive a bonus of two gold crowns, but it can only be paid to them slowly, over time, otherwise such sudden wealth will attract attention. Each will receive a groat a month."

"There's no need to pay them anything, good Sir; they're accomplices in the murder of a Priest... they won't say a word."

"I understand, good Sheriff, but when their consciences prick them when they lay alone in the dark of their hovels, the gold will be their comforter and keep them from the confessional. Do you understand, Sheriff Judd?"

"I do, Sir, I do." After a brief pause, Sheriff Judd continued. "What next for us, then, Sir?"

"We wait, good Master Sheriff, we wait for time and torment of the mind to do their work for us. Soon they will panic. The good barons of the six shires will see danger and demons everywhere and will demand the destruction of the Brotherhood."

"Won't that mean you and your kin…"

"No, Master Sheriff, it will not. I have a scheme to see us right. See all of us right. But for the now, we must not be seen together. Be gone." The Sheriff departed as quickly as he'd arrived.

"You are too loose with your tongue with that one, my outlaw brother."

"I sense your meaning and I forbid you to act against our good friend the sheriff… I still have use of him. Fear not, he is so full of the terrors I planted in his head he will not dare betray us."

★

Following the slaughter of the priest, his guests, his servants, the four Brotherhooders and two of the sheriff's men, the whole of the middle lands was placed in virtual lockdown.

Duane Catchpole was furious that four of his men could have been so stupid as to murder a priest. "Murder a priest?" It just didn't make sense to him and didn't sit well with what he knew of those who'd carried out the raid. "Why did they do it? It was so out of character for them." Catchpole couldn't understand it as plans had been made to steal the gold when it was being transported. Finally, after a suggestion from Robert Clay, he conceded that, "Maybe they just got greedy… but how did they know that the gold was being held at the priest's house?" Master Catchpole had more questions than answers... all of which he shared with his inner council, including Robert Clay.

For the time being, the Brotherhood ceased all its activities, including the meetings of the various regional clans set up by Duane Catchpole. It didn't take long, however, before some of the Brotherhooders ignored the order to keep a low profile and went into business for themselves. They'd become used to the lifestyle that their thievery had provided them, a lifestyle that depended on a regular flow of money to support it. This was what Robert Clay was waiting for. He made his way to the diocese of the crow priest who'd led the inquisition in the six parishes. When receiving Robert Clay, the crow priest kept a dagger beneath his cloak as these were dangerous times and people like Robert Clay were not to be trusted.

"Master Robert Clay, come in, do! I must say that I am surprised to see you here. I'd have thought that your brother, John, would've made such a trip to see me and not your heathen self. You look prosperous."

"As indeed do you, good priest."

"And what brings you here, so far from the six parishes?"

"I understand that you are soon to return to the middle lands to hunt down the Brotherhood and that you will have for company a knight of the French King named Sir Aldred Benz..."

"Pray tell me where you heard of—"

"It is just a rumour, good priest, that circulates in all the taverns round our way... nothing more. But by your reaction there must be some truth in it."

"What do you want? What are you doing here? Plunderer! Murderer! Sodomite!" spat the crow priest with venom.

"I am none of the things you accuse me of, as well you know, and have always been guiltless of all such acts. You ask what I want… what I am doing here… why I have travelled so far? I have information that will aid you in your mission to rid the middle lands of the Brotherhood once and for all time."

"And what is your price?"

"My price is simply that you will leave me and my family unmolested, and that, if fingers are pointed our way, then you will ignore them."

"I will make you no such promise, Master Clay, and as you have been so foolish as to enter my keep I have no need to make any transaction with you… plunderer!… murderer!… sodomite! that you are!"

"What, then, is your next move, Crow Priest? Have me taken away and tortured for all that I will give you freely if you would but just look the other way?"

"Look the other way? I will never… I will not! It is well past time for you and your family to pay the reckoning… it is time to settle the score!"

"Settle the score? And what score is that? You and your Council of Parish Commissioners took all that we had, so rather the score needs to be settled the other way round, I would say."

"You are brazen for somebody in your situation, Master Clay. So much so that I will take the trouble to conduct your inquisition personally as the price for your impudence!"

"How unfair is it that I am prepared to look the other way and yet you, good Father, you are not?"

"You speak in riddles!"

"Let me speak clearly then, Crow Priest that you are… let me speak of you as a boy-lover… yes, and a philanderer with women of loose morals… or, more particularly, of Beth Harley… Beth Harlot, as she is more popularly known." The Crow Priest stared at Robert Clay in shock horror at the words his burning ears were hearing. "Aye, and more besides… like a certain good widow of this parish who's had nigh on a dozen of your bastard children over the years. What do you say? Struck dumb, are you?"

"You must be possessed by the Devil to make such accusations against a man of God."

"A man of God?" sputtered Robert Clay in a mocking choke-laugh. "A man of God? If you were a man of God, as you claim, She would disown you." The crow priest was so shaken he failed to notice that Robert Clay had referred to his God as a female.

"These accusations you make are mere fabrications. What proof do you have of any such—"

"There is no need to go on so, good Priest," spoke Robert soothingly, "but rest assured I have proof aplenty... and of many more indiscretions besides those already mentioned."

"I have no need to listen to any more of this... this! I will have my guards remove you to the dungeons, from which you will never again see the light of—"

"Good Priest, if I am not at my rendezvous before midday, four riders, along with proofs of your acts, will ride to London and Canterbury and pass their papers onto those who will be glad to ruin you." At these words, the crow priest began nervously fingering the dagger hidden beneath his cloak. "You may want to use that dagger you have hidden beneath your cloak to rid the world of your own worthless soul rather than spill blood," Robert Clay said with a sneer. Dazed, the crow priest removed the dagger from beneath his cloak and flung it across the table.

"I knew it would come to this some day... I am ready to accept God's justice." Beaten though he was, the crow priest was far too cowardly to take his own life.

"God's justice? It need not come to that, good Priest," said Robert, again soothingly. "In fact, nobody need ever know anything of your... indiscretions." The crow priest made to interrupt Master Clay but he held up the palm of his hand for him to remain silent. "There is a way for you to make amends in the eyes of your God, by ridding these lands of the scourge of the so-called Brotherhood." At these words the crow priest's ears pricked up. "I am your salvation, good Priest. I will give you all you need to destroy the Brotherhood, and all that I ask in return is that should those inveterate liars name any of my family or their spouses… you are not to move against them."

"Is that all, young Master Clay?" responded the crow priest in a hollow choking voice.

"No, good Priest, not quite all. You will petition Sir John Belcher for him to restore the lands and possessions of all those he has wronged in the six parishes; furthermore, you will dissolve the parish councils."

"But how can I, a mere priest, convince Belcher to restore the land to the people of the six parishes? It is an impossible thing that you ask of me."

"Nonsense; it is the simplest thing for someone like you to do. You will simply do like all good crow priests have done for centuries… you will promise Sir John everlasting eternal life basking in the glory of God's good kingdom as reward for returning his ill-gotten gains to the poor people of the six parishes… tell him his path to salvation came to you in a dream… tell him the Archangel Gabriel spoke to you in this dream." The crow priest smiled at Robert Clay's cunning. "And besides, news has reached me that King Edward grows impatient with Sir John for the lack of results in ridding the middle lands of the Brotherhood. He will grasp this opportunity with both his greasy fat hands."

"But, good Sir," spoke the crow priest grovellingly, "you know Belcher, as do I; he is a welcher and will, most likely, renege on any such promises he makes. What then? Do I fall with him if I do my part well?"

"Do not concern yourself with such details, good Priest. Sir John must first restore the lands to the people of the six parishes before any information is handed over to you. Now, I must be gone, otherwise my riders will be away to London and Canterbury delivering the documents of your doom in default of me not showing up."

Robert and the crow priest agreed to meet in one month's time, when he would pass over to the priest all he needed to know to destroy the Brotherhood… so long as Sir John Belcher did his part by handing back all ill-gotten lands and possessions to the good people of the six parishes.

★

"It is all done then?"

"Aye, it is done."

"And what of my part?"

"There is nothing more you need do. Go home, brother, return home."

"Brother… or you, Master Blackstone… tell me truly, who will lead the Brotherhood after all this is done?"

"Why, you will, of course," chorused Robert Clay and Lorence Blackstone in unison to John Clay.

"Dear brother, there can be no other… how could there be?" affirmed Robert Clay. "For you are the eldest brother. Just as William was, so you now are, and as head of the family it is for you to lead us all."

John Clay was ecstatic at the prospect of once again being the one and only true leader of the Brotherhood. *There'll be changes this time around though!* he thought as he conjured visons of majestic magnificence in his mind. *Things'll be different this time around… mark me… they'll obey or they'll suffer the consequences.* What those consequences would be he wasn't sure but the one thing he was certain of was, *There'll be consequences!* After all he'd been through, after all the guilt he'd suffered over the years, John Clay's mind was finally broken. He walked around with that faraway look in his eyes that all true madmen have; a look that everybody recognised and feared as the look of a man capable of carrying out any act without a second's separation between the thinking and the doing.

After John Clay left the company of his brother, Lorence Blackstone and Sheriff Judd, the three men plotted revenge against the crow priest and Sir John Belcher, but first, Lorence Blackstone had a question.

"Robert, my outlaw brother, what has entered your head that you would back John as leader of the reformed Brotherhood. Surely it must be you that leads us?"

"Why, Lorence, my life brother, isn't it obvious? Our faction will not be tolerated by the Brotherhood; many Brethren will demand our doom… we shall have to tread most carefully, you and I. As we have said many times before, it's one thing to attack the aristocracy, which will be popular amongst ordinary folk, but it is entirely another thing to attack the Church." Lorence Blackstone and Sheriff Judd nodded their tacit agreement. "We three shall ensure that the reformed Brotherhood constitutes itself as a shadow organisation, hidden from the prying eyes of the outside world, and our faction will inhabit its darkest recesses. No light will ever shine upon us."

★

The crow priest's men came in the dead of night. Duane Catchpole and forty of his closest Brethren were bound, gagged, beaten and hooded before being spirited away to an isolated glade in the forest, where they were handed over to the inquisitor and his men, each of whom had been specially selected for the task to be performed. As their hoods were removed, the Brethren beheld before them eight men in monks' cowls and a dozen or more knights whose shields bore coats of arms that none of them recognised.

Even before any questions were asked, Christopher Cole was dragged by his hair from the Brotherhooders' ranks to stand before a large fire, whereupon his belly was slit and hot embers shovelled into the opening. A large leather belt was slung round Cole's middle and pulled tight to close the vent in his abdomen. He was left writhing on the forest floor to die in screaming agony and convulsions. None of those in monks' cowls or any of the knights looked at Christopher Cole's death gyrations; they kept their eyes fixed firmly on the line of Brotherhooders, as though choosing their next victim. Duane Catchpole spoke before the choice of who would die next was made.

"Holy Fathers... good knights... I beg you... pray tell us what is going on here... why are we being treated so? We are just poor land workers and—"

A voice, speaking from the shadows of the forest, interrupted master Catchpole's entreaties. "Is that Duane Catchpole I hear whining?" The named recognised the voice immediately as belonging to the same crow priest who'd led the inquisitions of the Council of Parish Commissioners all across the middle lands.

"It is indeed I, Your Grace. Can you enlighten us as to—"
"Save your breath, Catchpole. You are here because you are the leader of the notorious band of outlaws known as the Brotherhood... don't bother denying it... and these here with you are your familiars. I have witnesses against you all, and in my hand I hold their statements."
"They speak falsely, Your Grace, I am no outlaw... we are not outlaws."
"If you persist in lying I will have the bellies of your compatriots filled with embers for each and every lie that comes out of your soon-to-be toothless mouth... Do you understand me, Catchpole?" The named realised he was doomed... but who was it that had fingered him? This is what he wanted to know more than anything.
"Your Grace, I openly confess to you that I am a member of the so-called Brotherhood. All we here are but a collection of

random fools and miscreants creating minor mischief, more for amusement than anything else... we are not at all the people you think us to be. My Lord, whenever anything happens, rumour has it that it was the Brotherhood that carried it out... This is nonsense! The true culprits attach their acts to the name of the Brotherhood... I swear it, Your Grace. Nevertheless, my Lord, as God is my witness, I am not its leader, that title belongs to another... Come close, Sir, and I will whisper his name to your ear alone." The crow priest stepped from the shadows, walked toward Duane Catchpole and stooped to hear what he had to confess.

"Tell me truthfully, Catchpole, and do not deceive me."

"Your Grace, if I tell you the name of the leader of the Brotherhood, will you let me go and—"

"What? You try to strike a bargain with me?" screamed the crow priest. Then, pointing at the next of the Brethren in line, he shouted to one of the knights, "Take him, and fill his belly with embers." The poor man screamed for mercy but there was none to be had. "Do not attempt to make bargains with me, Catchpole, you are not in a bargaining position. Now, the name!"

Duane Catchpole gasped in horror at the sight of his cousin's belly being opened up and filled with hot embers. He hurriedly whispered, "The man who leads us is John Clay... I swear to you, my Lord, he is the one you want."

The Crow Priest hiss-whispered his reply. "Tell me something I don't already know!"

Returning to the shadows, the Crow Priest nodded as he passed a knight who drew his sword and, plunging it into the flames of the fire, shouted, "I stand here before God and swear that I will have the truth out of each of you. Confess all to the brother monks and you will be offered a last confession... take it or take it not, it is up to you." Sir Aldred Benz motioned his King's Knights to close in on the line of bound men. "Begin the inquisition!"

The Crow Priest wanted the names of each and every member of the Brotherhood. He intended on adding some names of his own to the list as settlement of vendettas with aristocrats, members of the King's court and others who'd crossed him in the past. He'd ordered the monks to extract the information by whatever means they wished but, in order to earn their bonuses, they had to keep the Brethren alive for at least two days and nights under torture. He, of course, had no intention of paying the monks any such bonuses, and if he was forced to, he planned to recoup the payments by way of taxes.

★

As soon as the news spread of the taking of Duane Catchpole and his inner circle, panic gripped the Brethren. Many of them simply sat in their homes waiting to be arrested while others left their families to flee to the north and the west. Margaret Blackstone, Mary Spurling and Marion Marley, and their husbands, children and farm serfs made their way to the Clay estate to take refuge there. Paul Martin and Simon Sparrow arrived shortly after. Nobody remarked on their unexpected appearance.

"Do you think they will come for us?"

"No, I shouldn't think so."

"Why do you think not, Robert?"

"Because Duane loves us far too much to betray us. Besides, why should anybody come looking in the six shires? There hasn't been any trouble here."

"Indeed not, thanks to John."

"Robert… why do you think it was that Belcher returned our lands and possessions to us?" asked Margaret Blackstone, suspicious over recent events.

"I heard say that the Archangel Gabriel appeared to him in a dream and told him to return all his ill-gotten gains to the good people of the six shires."

"What about Belcher's ill-gotten gains from beyond the six shires? From the middle lands? What about the good people of the middle lands, brother, do they not deserve their property returned to them?"

"I am not privy to another man's dreams and so have no notion of whether the Archangel Gabriel mentioned the returning of property to the people of the middle lands."

"You make jest at a time like this? What kind of man are you?"

"Hold your tongue, sister, he is our brother and will do his duty in all things necessary to protect us, so speak no more on the matter lest our talk wanders where it should not go," spoke Margaret Blackstone menacingly.

"What is next for us then, Robert?"

"Well, as it's about six, you should attend to cooking our evening meal and then we should all be off to our beds." With that, the Clay sisters retired to the kitchen to prepare the food for the evening meal.

★

In the forest glade, the Brethren gave up names of Brotherhooders one after another under agonising torture. They'd have given the names up freely but the Crow Priest's orders were for the monks to torture the men for two days and two nights if they wanted their bonus. Some of the names given up by the Brethren were not in fact Brotherhooders. They gave names to the list as revenge or out of spite or to ensure the women they were leaving behind wouldn't marry somebody they'd despised in life. Some names were added to the list by the monks themselves; and by the King's Knights, some countrymen they hated, but they were later removed by Sir Aldred Benz because he felt certain King Philip would not believe them.

With their work taking its toll on the Brethren, the monks were concerned that the Brotherhooders wouldn't last two days and two nights under torture. Well before the forty-eight hours was up, monks and knights alike were physically, mentally and emotionally spent. Many could stand it no longer. Sir Aldred Benz was the first to quit the camp, taking the list of names with him along with half his knights. With their leader gone, many of those who remained behind wanted to put the Brethren to death immediately; their moans and plaintive pleadings were driving them to madness. It was only payment of their bonus that drove the monks to continue with the torture. Schemes were concocted between the torturers to preserve their sanity: "Let us kill them all now and agree between us to tell His Grace that we did as he had commanded", and so on. But in such a band, nobody trusted anybody to keep their own counsel.

Only at the final second of the final minute did the suffering of the Brethren end. An argument then broke out as to who should dig the graves. The remaining knights didn't want to bury the men but the monks insisted. "We cannot just leave them for anybody to come along and discover their bodies. They must be buried... not only to conceal them but also for the sake of their immortal souls." One monk suggested weighting the bodies down with stones and casting them into a local river for the fishes to do their work on them. The problem was transportation; it would not be an easy task moving forty bodies, especially over such terrain.

"Let's burn them! Cremate them! That'll do the job."

"Good idea... Let's do it quick, while it's still dark... no smoke to attract attention."

"Let us first search them and remove items that might identify them."

"Why bother? By now, everybody'll know they've gone missing and who it was that took them, so why—"

"We'll search them and remove any items that could identify them. If people know for certain the fate of these men that is one thing, but if their disappearance forever remains a mystery then their families will always have hope. We can spread rumours that the men have been taken to France at the behest of Isabella, having been accused of committing crimes against her father's person… King Philip."

"That is a very good idea. Shall we vote on it?"

"Vote on it? What are we going to vote on? Let's just get on with it! You lot, go and collect wood and bring it back here," ordered a knight to the monks.

Being in a forest, a large pile of wood was soon collected, brought to the glade and made into a mound resembling a massive funeral pyre. The monks continued gathering wood as the knights, in pairs, picked up the Brethren one at a time and swung them as far as they could into the flames. Some Brethren groaned or moaned as they were lifted up from the ground but the knights ignored any signs of life in them and threw them, with their dead brothers, into the very heart of the fire where their lives were finally extinguished. Before the dawn, forty bodies had been cremated and their ashes scattered to leave no evidence of what had happened in that innocent glade.

Arriving at the lair of the Crow Priest to claim their bonus, the monks found no sign of him. Instead a lowly friar was there to greet them and to tell them that His Grace had been called away to London at short notice and he'd 'settle up with the good monks anon'. Furious at not receiving their bonuses, the monks cursed and berated the friar and the Crow Priest in his absence. The friar told them that he'd noted the curses uttered against his master and looked forward to telling him who'd said what the next time they met. Badmouthing any member of the clergy in fourteenth century England was risky, but badmouthing somebody with the

Crow Priest's reputation was life-threatening. One of the monks took the friar aside and explained to him that he and his brother monks had been working for two days and two nights for his master and so, due to lack of nourishment and sleep, had been rash in their remarks, and said he hoped that the good friar could 'see his way to taking that into consideration and not inform his master of the regrettable remarks that had been made against his good and Holy person'. The friar held the monk in his gaze, and with a sly smile he replied that he would consider his plea upon promise of some future favour. The monk assured him that he could ask any favour and it would be done. "In that case, no more need be said of this tawdry matter."

As it was Duane Catchpole who had built up the membership of the Brotherhood outside the six parishes, and because those taken with him were his lieutenants, they knew, between them, all the names of those who'd been recruited into their society. Consequently, the list of names handed over to the Crow Priest by Sir Aldred Benz was complete and entire. The Crow Priest studied the list carefully before removing some names while adding others, including that of Sir John Belcher.

"A man like him would be their leader, wouldn't you say, Sir Aldred? Why, it stands to reason that it would be him as there has been no trouble in the six shires… no trouble on the doorstep of Sir John Belcher! I dare say, for uncovering such a traitor, Kind Edward will reward the Church with his lands." Finishing his words, the Crow Priest emitted a snort of satisfaction.

"I care not for your petty squabbles. I want the esquire brothers. They evaded me in France but I will return them there to receive the King's justice in Orléans. Then and only then will I be satisfied."

"I care not for your petty squabbles, good Knight!" replied the Crow Priest in mocking repetition of Sir Aldred.

"The esquire brothers must have a terrible hold over you for you to be so lenient with them!" remarked Sir Aldred.

Ignoring Sir Aldred's remark, the Crow Priest continued, "The Clay brothers are nothing, but you would lose all that you should hope to gain to satisfy a trifling vendetta? They escaped from you in France... so what? Forget it! There's land aplenty to be divided up after Belcher has gone, and some of it is set to come your way, my friend."

"What makes you think your King will believe your story? Or the men who gave up his name under torture?"

"I have been preparing the ground. Not only is Sir John unpopular at Edward's court, as he's so seldom there, I have spread rumours about him wanting the crown for himself and, more recently, that he is a sodomite."

"Hah! That last part will not sway Edward against him, even if only half of what I've heard about him is true."

"It is a fact that Edward's tastes are diverse, but they serve to help us in this. In condemning a sodomite, he frees himself from being tainted with that same brush. Ingenious, am I not?"

"You would freely and so easily conspire to deceive your King, and yet you would have it that I should trust you?"

"My dear good Knight... my dear good Knight," spoke the Crow Priest, putting a comforting arm around Sir Aldred's shoulders, "we are bonded together in this. Besides, you have your knights to aid you and the power of France behind you. How then could I renege on a pledge to you? What would be the purpose? There's land aplenty to be shared out."

"You said the land would go to your church..."

"Aye, Sir, and some of it will, but... and this is where you come in... most of it will not. It will go to an Order, which you and I will found and lead."

"This is risky business."

"No, good Sir Knight, this is the middle lands and it is my domain now."

After his meeting with Sir Aldred was over, the Crow Priest wrote out the entire list of the Brethren in his own hand so it would appear genuine to anybody questioning its authenticity.

★

"What news?"

"Master Martin says the Crow Priest is on his way to the six parishes."

"And how does he know this?" asked John Clay, his eye tic rebounding from one to the other.

"When he was in servitude at the abbey he formed a... special friendship with some of the monks there, some of whom were present at Catchpole's inquisition. They went to claim their blood money from the Crow Priest but he had departed for London."

"London is not the six parishes!" spoke John as a sprite might speak.

"Patience, brother. Another of their kind in London sent Master Martin a messenger pigeon carrying notice of a meeting between the Crow Priest and a French knight, after which the Crow Priest assembled an entourage for a trip to the middle lands."

"The middle lands is not just the six parishes; it is all of the middle lands, as the name itself implies."

"Why are you in such a contrary mood today, brother?"

"I am impatient to begin the resurrection of our society!"

"You must believe me, brother, when I tell you that all is in hand. Soon we shall leave this place and wander as we will without fear of arrest."

"When will this be?"

"After my parley with the Crow Priest."

"Then you must have known he was coming here."

"Aye... but when was the question, and now we have the answer. I must prepare all before his arrival."

"And what of Belcher?" enquired Lorence Blackstone. "He's grabbing back the lands he'd previously returned. The Church is at it too. It's a race between them as to who is going to come out on top."

"There is no need to worry about Belcher... or the Church, for that matter."

"What do you mean?"

"I cannot say until I know it to be true."

"What game are you playing with us, Robert? Are you striking out for yourself?"

"You words sting me, sister. Have I not always been straight and true with each of you?" Though they knew he hadn't been, none would speak up for fear of raising Robert's increasingly dark nature. "If you feel otherwise then let you speak out against me."

"Easy, my outlaw brother, we have no need to fight among ourselves when victory is so near. Let us speak of other things."

"Aye, you shall speak of other things, but for me, I am away. There's something I must do that none can aid me in."

"Shall none accompany you?"

"No, brother, no. If it goes ill then my life will be forfeit, not yours. Master Blackstone, this is the time we have spoken of. You and the others know what to do." Robert's sisters entreated him not to go, not to endanger his life, but he ignored their pleas.

ABSOLUTION

Arriving at a church on the southeasternmost boundary of the six parishes, Robert Clay entered through the main door of the chapel to find the Crow Priest and a knight, whose coat of arms he did not recognise, waiting for him. Instinctively he knew the knight to be Sir Aldred Benz, the same knight that had pursued him and his brothers after they'd fled the slaughter of the knights of the Holy Order at Poitiers Castle. Robert sensed some change in the Crow Priest's demeanour from their earlier meetings, and, by his posture, the knight seemed ready to do battle with him.

"You are alone?" asked the Crow Priest, peering over Robert Clay's shoulders.

"Aye, that I am."

"That is... foolish... or brave... or cunning. I know not which, nor do I care."

"What do you mean by these words? They sound to me like—"

"There must necessarily be a change in our agreement. Do not misunderstand me, Master Clay, I am forever indebted to you for betraying your Brethren but as they are soon to be no more, then what further need do I have of you or your kin?"

"You seem to forget—"

"I forget nothing. Leave us, Sir Aldred, but stay close at hand;

I must have private talks with this sinner." Sir Aldred moved to stand just inside the open door of the chapel, out of earshot of the whispering priest.

"What is your game, Crow Priest?" hiss-whispered Robert Clay through gritted teeth.

"How I have come to relish that epithet… Crow Priest… aye, and proud of it!"

"If you renege on our agreement then the documents of which I spoke—"

"These documents, do you mean?" said the Crow Priest, waving a wad of documents in Robert Clay's face.

"Are you sure they're all there?" responded Robert, though realising that the Crow Priest looked to indeed have possession of all the statements.

"Yes… I am sure of it. And now I have the names of my accusers. You see, Master Clay, the Molly network has many mouths and many mouths cannot keep secrets. When I pondered how you came by, let us say, certain information about me, the realisation came to me that there can only be one source… a Molly."

"A Molly as you are yourself, Crow Priest?"

"There is nothing for you to gain by slandering me."

"It is only slander if it be untrue… which it is not."

"I am left with the vexing problem of how to dispose of you. Obviously I cannot have a hand in such things myself, but my friend knight over there is only too willing to execute you and your verminous kith and kin."

"If I am to die, then I will have a final confession to be heard by you so that my words will haunt you for eternity."

"Entertain me for eternity, I think you mean," mocked the Crow Priest. "I heard that your return to God's path was a ploy but let me hear your confession, my son, as I have no wish to deny a condemned man his final request." Robert knelt in front of the confessional booth.

"Forgive me Father, for I have sinned... it has been two years since my last confession..."

After the Crow Priest heard Robert Clay's confession, he made the sign of the cross over him and ordered him to carry out a penance of one hundred Hail Marys and four hours of contemplative prayer before taking his last breath. Not wishing to witness Master Clay's recitations, the Crow Priest departed the church to visit a widow of the parish he held long acquaintance with. Sir Aldred, overhearing Robert Clay's chanting, felt a twinge of sorrow rush through him. *He was only following his way as was his right to do*, he thought.

"Hail Mary, Mother of God, pray for us sinners now and at the hour of our death. Amen. Hail Mary, Mother of God, pray for us sinners now and at the hour of our death. Amen. Hail Mary, Mother of God, pray for us sinners now and at the hour of our death. Amen. Hail Mary, Mother of God, pray for us sinners now and at the hour of our death. Amen. Hail Mary, Mother of God..."

"Esquire!" called Sir Aldred Benz.

"What, Sir Knight, are you in such hurry to dispatch me from this life that you interrupt the penance ordered on me by the Crow Priest?"

"Why do you call him 'Crow Priest'?"

"Is it not obvious to you? You have them in France also."

"I have never heard this name before."

"It is a name given to priests who attend the bedside of those about to depart this life and convince them that, for a heavy payment of tribute to the Church, they are guaranteed entry into the kingdom of heaven. Sometimes the tribute is their entire worldly possessions, thus robbing the rightful heirs." Sir Aldred was deeply shocked by Robert Clay's accusation. "The Church and the aristocracy are in joint enterprise to oppress the common people as their familiars... on payment of a tribute in gold of course... there is nothing ever performed without tribute in gold unless it be land."

"Tell me what acts you speak of, Esquire Robert."

"The Church uses its power to benefit the aristocracy. If a feudal lord has problems with his tenant farmers, the Church will say to them that they are committing some sin or other... it's always the same. Everything is a sin when it is convenient for it to be so. Peasants will willingly take up arms against feudal overlords, but not so the Church. The Church is unassailable. I'm certain you can bring to mind where the Church has interfered on behalf of an aristocrat in his dealings with his serfs or the peasantry."

"I can but I see things different to you. I see the Church intervening where the aristocracy would act with rapaciousness to the detriment of the peasantry. I see only good in the actions of the Church."

"Then you, Sir Knight, are blind. The Church is an evil empire... but what good will it be for me to convince you?"

"There is no convincing to be done. I serve God and my King." And having mentioned God and his King, Sir Aldred bowed his head before continuing. "In you, Robert Clay, I see a misguided, delusional man, but a man who followed his beliefs in becoming a devotee to the Holy Order of Knights. A man of honour serving men of honour."

"Then why were you party to their slaughter?"

"I was not there. I was set on your trail by my King but you and your brothers escaped me. That failure fell hard on me; it did my reputation a great deal of harm. Tell me truly, Master Clay, how did you escape my men on the road to St Malo?"

"By a miracle, Sir Knight, by a miracle."

"You claim divine intervention?"

"It was intervention, but whether it was divine or not has been the cause of many an argument between me and my brothers... between me and my brother."

"Tell me your tale."

"But what of my penance?"

"We both know you to be a non-believer, so what does penance matter to you?"

Robert smiled and told the knight his tale of the wise old woman who'd tended his wounds after a bear had attacked him in the forest, and how afterwards the esquire brothers had joined the St Malo Road to find it clear to the north but blocked to the south.

"I have heard of such women... one such healed the broken arm of a brother knight when I believed it beyond saving. I was certain he'd lose it, or perhaps die! There are many mysteries in life and I am not at all sure I understand any of them, as it is with the mystery you retell. I am going now, Robert Clay. Do what you will with your freedom and your life. Farewell."

With that, Sir Aldred Benz left Robert Clay standing alone in the church and wondering whether this was some cruel jest on the part of the knight. It was not. The knight mounted his horse and rode south. A few miles down the road he passed Robert's supposed rescuers dragging a gagged and bound Crow Priest behind them at the end of a rope. The Crow Priest made grunting noises through his gag and stared with frightened eyes toward Sir Aldred, but the knight heard and saw nothing. The group hurried to the church to see what they might find there. When they arrived they found Robert Clay sitting on a stone wall chewing on a long stalk of grass. They asked him what he was doing and he replied, "Contemplating the mysteries of life and death... justice and injustice."

"Any longer in my rescue and you might've been rescuing a corpse... or was that your intention?" Robert Clay asked his rescuers, partly in jest but with a hard voice.

"My outlaw brother, I swear to you that I would never—"

"We meet again, Crow Priest," spoke Robert, ignoring Lorence Blackstone's words. The Crow Priest made no attempt to grunt an answer through his gag. Instead he closed his eyes in silent prayer. "Remove his gag. I will speak with this man of God." Galen Spurling ripped the gag from the Crow Priest's mouth so roughly that it brought four teeth with it.

"I see Benz spared your life, and now if you would be so good as to return the compliment?" spoke the Crow Priest without the slightest sign of fear in his voice.

"Oh, I think not, Crow Priest. For all you have done and for all you would have done and for all you would come to do, you must die and die you will... here... today... and by my hand." Samuel White winced at these words but the Crow Priest showed not the slightest change in his demeanour.

"What, Robert Clay? You expect me to beg? I will not. If you kill me, a man of God, you and your motley crew will spend an eternity of suffering impaled on the fiery spears of Satan's disciples."

"Do you recall how the Brethren died in the forest?" The Crow Priest, for the first time, showed some reaction. "Two days and two nights under torture. How does that sound to you now, Crow Priest?" Samuel White was about to intervene when Lorence Blackstone held him back. "It seems justice to me that you should go the same way."

"I will have no part in this," spoke Samuel White in fear of holy retribution.

"You, Samuel, you? You who led the slaughter of the assassins? You... scared of a little black work?"

"But he is a man of God, Robert! A man of God!"

"He is no more a man of God than Robert is," spoke Jethro Marley.

"If you've no stomach for it, Samuel, you may stay or leave as you wish." Realising that to leave would doom him, Samuel White went and sat on the wall where Robert had sat moments earlier.

"I'll perch myself here until it is done."

"Come. Bring the Crow Priest into the house of his God. It is a fitting place for him to end his days." The others went to grab the Crow Priest but he shook them off and made his own way, unaided and unbowed, into the church.

Searching the Crow Priest, the men came across the list of names hidden in a secret pocket at the hem of his cloak. They handed the list to Robert, who looked at it momentarily before folding it and placing it in his boot. Robert Clay had no intention of torturing the Crow Priest for two days and nights. As soon as the man knelt in prayer, he took a sword and drove it deep into his body at the point where the neck joins the torso. The Crow Priest's death was instantaneous.

As the group left the church, Paul Martin asked Robert why the knight had let him live. He simply replied that he did not know the answer to this question, though he felt he did.

★

With the list of names in their hands, the men returned to the Clay estate to arrange the next phase of the revival of the Brotherhood. Arriving through the door of the house, John Clay threw himself on his brother and hugged and kissed him while weeping uncontrollably and saying that he thought he'd seen the last of him. John's behaviour was becoming more and more bizarre. The family were concerned for the safety of his children as he'd taken to putting them through trials to test God's mercy. John's wife was scared to intervene, though Robert had a plan to distract his brother. Specifically, John was to become the inquisitor for the resurrected Brotherhood and would sit in judgement over new recruits.

"The Crow Priest is dead," said Robert as an aside.
"What! Who killed him? Who killed this man of God?"
"Nobody, John, nobody killed him… it was an accident, he

had a fall from his horse, that's all. Damn thing stalled going over a jump and threw him off sideways. Neck snapped, so they say."

"He'll be in God's kingdom now," John sighed as he swayed in a rapturous trance.

"Aye, that's right, John, that's right. Robert here did well though. He met with the Crow Priest…"

"Can we stop calling him that? The poor man's dead, for God's sake!"

"Robert met the good Priest at the church, you know, the one on the border with the middle lands. He handed Robert the list of names of those given up by Catchpole and his cronies under torture."

"Why would he do that?"

"He felt the black heart of the Brotherhood had been cut out when Catchpole and the others were ended and that he need not act against the rest of us."

"Aye, brother," interrupted Robert, "it is true. The good Priest himself handed me the list, saying to me that I should do with it what I will."

"And what will you do with it, brother?" asked John slyly. "Surely it is for me, as leader of the Brotherhood, to decide what is to be done with the list."

"Indeed, brother, indeed. And what would you have me do with it?"

"Burn it! Burn the thing before it sends us all to hell! The Brotherhood needs a fresh start and that is impossible with old names."

"Wait on that a while, brother. First look upon the list and tell me what it is you perceive in it," John stared at the list for several minutes.

"I see our names there… and those of our sisters and their husbands… all of whom would otherwise have perished had it not been for the Christian goodness of the priest's holy heart and kindly spirit. The world is poorer for his passing."

"You speak truly and well, brother, but look again upon the list and tell me you do not see the makings of a resurrected Brotherhood in its number?"

"But their names are known by our enemies! How can they—"

"But who can recall the names other than those who hold the list? And look here... there are names in the good priest's own hand that give us power over those who could seek to destroy us."

"Who is named there?"

"Sir John Belcher, for one... many parish councillors, too. Belcher is stealing back the lands he returned to their rightful owners and he must be stopped. His name being on the list will do that. How long would he evade the hangman's noose if King Edward saw his name written on the list in the good priest's handwriting? He's unpopular at court; they'd hang him in a trice!"

"Let me contemplate your words and I will give you my decision before the day is out," spoke John in a sermon-like manner. "Hand me the list to assist me in my deliberations."

"Brother, the sanctity of your deliberations shouldn't be influenced by the names on the list. Let me hold it for you and should you decide that it must be destroyed, then we will destroy it together, as brothers."

"Robert, God bless you, you are the best of brothers," said John, patting Robert on his head. "Now, all of you, leave me so I can give my best to my contemplations." Outside the room the discussion continued.

"He's completely mad! We cannot allow him to destroy the list! Robert, you have to take over as head of the Brotherhood; John is too incapacitated in his mind for such a job."

"Lorence, as I have said to you before, John is the most perfect person to lead us. If I... or you... or Master Martin were to lead the Brotherhood, our faction couldn't exist. We need the cover of the Brotherhood for us to carry out our work."

"But the list—"

"Worry not! I will copy the names on the list and if John decides that it must be destroyed, then it'll be the copy that will be given up to the flames. We will then recruit those named on the list into the resurrected Brotherhood."

"Aye, and at the same time we can scout them for the ACF," added Samuel White.

"But what if they are against our faction? What if they give us up to John?" asked Jethro Marley. "He will not tolerate our existence... he will kill us all. I say let us not be too hasty in growing our ACF."

"Jethro, Master Martin and I recruited many of these men into the Brotherhood and in doing so we got to question each of them about their past. We know which of them the Church has wronged. They have reason enough to go against the Church and will make perfect recruits for our ACF."

Jethro Marely was barely unconvinced. "It is my belief that few of them will actually go against the Church when called upon to do so. They will give us up and then we will be killed."

"Worry not, Master Marley. John doesn't know these men; he didn't recruit them, I did. They will follow where I lead. We will first take care to seek out Mollies to join the forces of our ACF."

"Why so?"

"Being treated as they have by the Church, they have more reason than most to hate them... as you do..." said Robert Clay, pointing at Paul Martin, "as we all do. Tell me, Master Martin, that you do not live in fear of a fiery death for simply being as you are?" Paul Martin felt crushed at being singled out by Robert Clay's words but gave no outward sign.

"Hate is akin to love, Master Clay, and people love God even if they have cause to hate the Church," Paul Martin cautioned. "Do not rely on somebody aligning themselves with our ACF, Master Clay, simply because they are Mollies. Molly temperament is capricious and what suits one day doesn't suit the next." All the group nodded agreement.

"Let us leave our talk there, I have much writing to do," spoke Robert Clay as he gathered up his writing box to copy out the list of names.

That evening, John Clay called everybody together, telling them that he'd completed his deliberations and was ready to hand down his decision that the list of names must be destroyed and the Brotherhood would start anew with new names. He said that even at the risk of Sir John Belcher stealing back the lands he'd returned to the good people of the six parishes, he would destroy the list with Belcher's name written on it in the good priest's hand. Robert Clay bowed to his brother and said, as promised, that they would destroy the list together. John looked deep into Robert's eyes and joined hands with his brother as they tossed the list of names into the flames.

★

First thing the following morning, Robert Clay rode out from the Clay estate with several of his cronies in tow: Lorence Blackstone, Samuel White, Charles Leclerc, Paul Martin and Simon Sparrow, who he now referred to as his 'Inner Council of the Anti-Church Faction'. They'd sworn an oath of secrecy to the ACF, which was no less binding than the one they'd taken when they'd joined the Brotherhood. The main rule was that for anybody betraying the ACF, there was only one punishment: death. Despite knowing this, they willingly took the ACF oath of allegiance while kneeling, head bowed down, to Robert Clay, their sworn leader.

The Inner Council of the Anti-Church Faction laid in wait for Sir John Belcher as he and his party were out hunting on some land he'd recently grabbed from a widow of the parish, whose husband was one of those tortured to death by the monks. The hunting party consisted of fourteen men, all of whom were known to Paul Martin. At a prearranged signal, the fourteen moved away from Sir John, leaving him alone in a small copse. He called for them to return and then shouted at them to wait for him, but they ignored his cries. Angry at being left behind, Sir John mounted his horse, but before he could make a single stride the animal's bridle was snatched from his fat hands by Lorence Blackstone, and the burley Samuel White pulled Belcher from his saddle and flung him to the ground. Staring up at his assailants, Sir John could only concentrate on the sword points pressing against his face. Then a face came into focus that he knew well; it was that of Robert Clay.

"You will pay with your life for this attack upon my person, Master Clay. Your family will be ruined as I turn them out of their home and they will have to rely on—" Robert Clay stamped his boot into Sir John's chest and pressed him into the mud.

"Silence! Do not speak, you fat turd," screamed Simon Sparrow, inches from Belcher's jowly face.

"Well, Sir John," continued Robert Clay, "we've come a long way, you and I, haven't we? We've seen a lot of changes... especially with your fortunes! I think it's fair to say that you have done rather better than us Clays. But all that is about to change." Sir John made to speak but Samuel White piled into him, reining blow after blow upon him until the assault was halted by Robert Clay. "You were told not to speak. Now is the time for you to listen. I will tell you when you may speak. Nod your head if you understand." Sir John nodded his head vigorously to emphasise just how much he understood Robert Clay's instructions. "Your good friend, the Crow Priest, is dead." This was already known to Sir John and he was delighted at the fact. "He was killed by me. I killed him," said Robert Clay with emphasis, his eyes shining. Sir John didn't like where he thought this was going. "I tortured him to death... it took him hours to die... but not as long a time as the monks inflicted on the Brethren they slaughtered." Robert took a moment to look into Sir John's eyes and drink in the fear he saw in them. "Horrible way he went in the end... having his privates stuffed down his throat so he couldn't breathe... but by then all the fight had gone out of him anyway. Now, good Sir John, what shall we do with you, eh? What shall we do with you?"

"Hand him over to the women of the six shires! They'll know what to do with the fat turd!" The cruelty of women-mobs being well known, Sir John lost control of himself and defecated in his britches. "Dirty bastard!" yelled Simon Sparrow, kicking Sir John in the groin. A signal from Robert Clay told Master Sparrow to go more lightly.

"Do control yourself, Sir John, and try to save your energy... we've hours yet to go." At those words, Sir John swooned. He was awakened by his head being plunged into a cold stream. "You don't get off that easily, Belcher. About the Crow Priest... a friend of yours, wasn't he? You may answer."

"Yes... no... I wouldn't call him a friend... he was more of a... I don't know how to put it."

"Well, friend or no, would you have expected him to add your name to the list of names extracted from the Brethren?" Sir John understood the point immediately. "Yes, look... see... there it is," said Robert Clay, pointing to Sir John's name written on the list in the Crow Priest's hand.

"His Majesty will never believe..."

"Wrong, Sir John, wrong! His Majesty will believe, especially now with the Crow Priest dead, murdered within the boundaries of the six shires while his assassins remain at liberty. Around our way it is said that you are unpopular at court and there are many there who would condemn you out of hand for being responsible for the Crow Priest's death. I would not be in your shoes, Belcher... not for a thousand gold crowns."

"What do you want of me?"

"Sir John," spoke Robert Clay in gentle tone, "I will come to you as often as I wish and you will receive my petitions and you will agree to them without delay."

"Agreed!" replied Sir John hastily to conclude this business.

"Wait, do not be so hasty, Sir John, there's more yet. You reneged on your agreement with the Crow Priest and so you will return all your ill-gotten gains to their rightful owners right throughout the middle lands, and you are never to take them back. Finally, you must promise to leave me, my family and my friends in peace… and in return, His Majesty need never see your name on the list. Do not come looking for the list. If you do, it will find its way to our good King Edward."

"You are no fool master, Clay, you would not dare show His Majesty the list; your own names are on it. It is your death sentence as much as it is mine."

"Well now, Sir John, is it one list or is it several?" Sir John did not comprehend Robert Clay's meaning. "I see you are puzzled. Allow me to demonstrate." Robert Clay took a knife and carefully cut the list into eight separate sheets. Showing them to Sir John, he tore up three of them and threw them into the stream. "As you can see, Sir John, there are no Clays on the list, nor any of our kin, or our friends or associates." Sir John finally realised he was beaten.

"Is our business here concluded?" Sir John Belcher asked despairingly.

"No, it is not!" interjected Lorence Blackstone. "You will have the birth deeds of my daughter changed as being legitimate." Sir John nodded agreement and slowly, carefully, raised himself from the mud. Wiping himself down, he looked around.

"I note that my hunting party did not return to check on my safety. They are your men?"

"We have the eyes and ears of people everywhere who gladly do our bidding. So be careful what you say and do, Belcher, as it will come back to us."

"And what of the other names on the list… those of the Brotherhood? What of them? Is the Brotherhood to be reformed?"

"No... no, Sir John, it is not," Robert Clay lied. "I can guarantee you that all will be quiet and there will be no trouble in the six shires. You can tell your King that there never was a Brotherhood... it was just a small disparate group intent on creating mischief and used the myth of the Brotherhood to build its reputation and to torment the minds of simple folk. They are now all dead on the orders of the Crow Priest. Tell King Edward that the crimes committed in the name of the Brotherhood were more often committed by others, and that good Sheriff Judd is on their trail. Now go, Sir John Belcher... go but do not ever forget what happened here today." Sir John needed no second invitation to leave as he leapt, as well as such a fat man could leap, onto his horse and galloped away.

★

"What news, brother, what news?"

"Great news, brother, great news."

"Belcher is finally dead! Hurrah! Praise be to God!"

"Better than that, brother, much better than that. Belcher is our man... he rests in our pocket and has agreed to do our bidding."

"But how? How? The list is destroyed! What hold could you have over him that he would do our bidding?"

"Aye, the list is destroyed, brother, but a note left by the good priest condemned him, and the sheriff has it in his possession. Belcher is ours! He will do our bidding for the remainder of his worthless life. He has agreed to return all his ill-gotten gains to the folk of the middle lands and will receive your petitions whenever you choose. Do you see the benefit?"

"I am not so sure about this. I need to contemplate this unexpected development... have the good sheriff bring me the note that would condemn Belcher."

"Would that I could, brother, but it is away to France for safekeeping with a familiar of the sheriff in the court of the French King."

"France," spoke John Clay in a dream-like trance. "France. Bastard heathen France. William still lies there, you know? At least we have Thomas at home. At least we have that." Sobbing and wailing at the thought of his dead brothers, John Clay left the room.

"His mind is deranged, Robert, you must take over…"

"I will not!" replied Robert Clay as John Clay suddenly re-entered the room, his eyes wide and wild.

"A throne. That's what I meant to talk with you about; building a throne for me when I hold ceremonies to invest new recruits into the Brotherhood… my Brotherhood!"

"A throne, brother?"

"Aye, Robert, a throne. I must have a throne to establish my authority over all that come… and a crown… yes, a crown."

"Brother, those trappings will condemn you should our gatherings ever be uncovered by the King's men. Please, brother, I beg you, be modest in your regalia, as was our Lord Jesus, and—"

"You need say no more, brother… yes, I must be modest… as was with our Lord Jesus Christ. Maybe a chair?… A panelled chair… a High Chair of Office… high enough to be seen by those standing at the back of the barn. It should have our family coat of arms on it, on each of the eight panels… adorned with gold leaf… not too much… a modest amount only. Have carpenters construct such a chair in time for our next gathering; it will betoken my authority. Now, Robert, how goes the recruitment?"

"It goes marvellously well, brother, marvellously well. By happenstance, some of those recruited already know of our Brotherhood."

"How so?"

"Duane Catchpole attempted to recruit them but they never liked him, never trusted him."

"But will they follow me?"

"Of course they will, brother, of course they will. Some have already taken the oath of allegiance, declaring fealty to you and you only. You have nothing to fear on that score, brother."

"They've taken the oath of allegiance already, you say?"

"Aye, brother, they have, and glad they were to know that it is you who leads us."

"But, Robert, it should be I who conducts the oath of allegiance and reads out the constitution to recruits at their first gathering, should it not?"

"You make a good point, brother, and you shall take the oath of allegiance from new recruits at their first gathering."

"And read out the constitution to them."

"You have written a constitution?"

"Aye, brother, I have. Here it is." John Clay produced a copy of the constitution that Duane Catchpole and Margaret Blackstone had written. "What do you think of it?"

"It is a marvellous work, brother. Very fine work." Nobody dared to say that it was the work of Catchpole and Margaret; they just smiled and nodded approvingly.

"I will make a drawing for my throne... my High Chair of Office. It will have eight panels in its high back. Those standing at the rear of the barn will be able to see it and they will understand from what they see that I am a man of great importance and authority." Lorence Blackstone and Samuel White were looking particularly uneasy; it seemed to them that John was descending further along the road into madness.

"I will see to the construction of your Chair of Office, brother, from which you will take the oath of allegiance from the new recruits and read to them the Constitution of the Brotherhood," said Robert Clay. Then, turning to Blackstone, White, Martin, Sparrow and Leclerc, he said, "Come, men, we must away. We have work to do." With that they departed the room, leaving John Clay pawing over musty documents.

★

It was some fourteen months before the inaugural meeting of the resurrected Brotherhood was held. In between times, the barn by the stream had, under John Clay's supervision, undergone massive transformation. A platform had been constructed along the back wall, on which was placed John's High Chair of Office; on either side of it, on two lower platforms, sat smaller versions of John's Chair of Office. On the other three sides of the barn were four rows of benches that could easily accommodate one hundred or so backsides. The rows of benches were covered by an internal roof, making them look like theatre stalls. The walls, roof and walkways of the barn were decorated with symbols of the Society of the Brotherhood, as designed by John, and the floor in front of the raised platform was set out in black and white squares set diagonally to the walls, making them appear diamond shaped. In the middle of the open floor area was a kneeling stool, covered in black and white checked plush fabric, next to a tall, narrow lectern that had two scrolls on top of it. With the hold Robert Clay had over Sir John Belcher, neither he nor his familiars dared to come nosing around, especially on the Clay estate, and so the works were carried out uninterrupted. Now that all was ready with the barn, John Clay was impatient to use it for its purpose of ensuring that all who entered there knew that he was the leader of the Brotherhood. John had amended the Brotherhood's constitution so it read that he was its leader for life.

In the intervening fourteen-month period, if John Clay had been busy with renovations, Robert Clay had been even busier recruiting suitable candidates for the resurrected Brotherhood. Suitable candidates, as far as he was concerned, meant they were also likely candidates for his ACF. In interviewing those on the list of names given up by Duane Catchpole and his cronies, Robert Clay and his cronies discovered myriad reasons why people hated the aristocracy, with some having reason to hate the Church. It was frustrating to Robert that many of those having good reason to hate the Church did not bear any grudge against it. It was just as the learned men of the knights of the Holy Order had said: 'Faith is stronger than proof', and the proof of wrongdoings by the Church held no sway against the power of faith. Robert interpreted this phenomena as 'fear of the unknown'. The afterlife, being unknown, held the people in fear of harming their immortal souls and consequently they were unwilling to go against the Church. The one ray of hope was the sheer number of reasons people had to hate the Church. It wasn't just the persecuted, such as Mollies, who hated the Church; it was people with ideas, people who asked questions about life, the firmament and the sciences, people who thought beyond the stars in the heavens. They lived in perpetual fear of being branded a heretic and burned alive at the stake for harbouring 'sacrilegious' thoughts. The Church's Holy Christian Code was harsh and suffered no contradictions or contradictors. These were the people Robert Clay hoped he could, over time, persuade to join his ACF as the vanguard of the destruction of the Church.

On the evening of the inaugural meeting of the resurrected Brotherhood, the barn was packed to bursting. The overspill was seated in the walkways and on the roofs over the benched areas. On the two smaller High Chairs of Office sat Robert Clay and Margaret Blackstone, both looking embarrassed at being seated how they were. Then, at the sound of mighty hammering, the barn doors flew open and in entered John Clay, followed by an entourage of lackeys dressed all in black and gold from head to toe. To the audible gasps of the audience, the entourage walked in slow procession across the black and white diamond patterned floor. Robert and Margaret couldn't believe their eyes. John was dressed in a black monk's cowl trimmed with gold and blue and red and on his head, and this is what mainly caused everybody to gasp, was a puffed-up dark red headpiece of plush fabric, around which was, interwoven in gold thread with red droplets, a crown of thorns. After John took his seat, with a movement of his right hand he gestured everybody to sit, despite them already being seated... and open-mouthed.

Robert Clay took to his feet and, demanding silence, welcomed everybody to the 'Inaugural Oath of Allegiance Ceremony of the Brotherhood'. After introducing the proceedings, Robert Clay invited John to speak.

"Friends!" proclaimed John Clay, surveying his audience. "Brothers! Welcome! Welcome! Thrice welcome to all! It has been a long road… a hard road… a trying road… but here we are. We have overcome many adversities, suffered treachery upon our person and yet we have come through all trials unscathed. Unscathed, I say! Now is the moment of our great rebirth. To be born into our Brotherhood we must pass pledges of fealty… formed as an Oath of Allegiance… an oath of your allegiance to me, and me alone! I will now read the Oath of Allegiance and you will all repeat it after me." John Clay paused to whisper to Robert Clay and then, taking to his feet, walked to the middle of the chequered floor to stand behind a lectern. Once there, he signalled his brother to speak.

"John Clay, our avowed leader, will now take your Oath of Allegiance. In doing so, you will repeat, after me, the words I will speak, thence to proceed to kneel on the stool… there," said Robert pointing to the stool next to the lectern, "and kiss the ringed finger of our great leader, John Clay." At those words there was shuffling and murmuring from the audience. Sensing the rising displeasure of the gathering, Robert Clay made a signal to Lorence Blackstone, who jumped to his feet.

"Robert Clay, my outlaw brother, let me have the honour of being the first to take the Oath of Allegiance and thence to kneel and kiss the ring on the hand of our beloved leader."

"Aye, then me," chimed Charles Leclerc.

"Then me," shouted Mary and Galen Spurling together.

"Then me!" shouted, in turn, Margaret Blackstone, Marion Marley, Jethro Marley, Samuel White, Paul Martin, Simon Sparrow and Sheriff Judd.

Twelve, including Robert Clay, took the Oath of Allegiance to John Clay. Afterwards, each in turn knelt on the kneeling stool to kissed the ring on the proffered hand of their leader. Robert Clay then resumed his position on the lower platform to continue with the ceremony.

"All, say after me... I, then state your name." The gathering muttered their names in a cacophony of murmurs. "Do solemnly swear..." The assembly spoke in unison and some conviction. "That I will uphold..." These words were repeated as a loud throng. "The laws and customs of the Brotherhood..." These words were repeated with righteous zeal. "Upon pain of death..." These words were repeated rapturously, as though the audience were possessed of demons. "And offer my unwavering fealty to our leader, John Clay." After reciting these words the audience spontaneously cheered and chanted the name of John Clay... their leader.

After the Oath of Allegiance was complete, the entire gathering proceeded to kneel, one at a time, on the kneeling stool to kiss the ring on the hand of their sworn leader, after which John Clay returned to sit on his High Chair of Office from where he read out the Constitution of the Brotherhood.

"Are they not just the words of Duane Catchpole?" asked one of the Brethren from the benches.

"No, they are not!" screamed John Clay, glaring wild-eyed at the speaker. "Robert, dear brother, are the words of the Constitution of the Brotherhood the words of the poor departed Catchpole?"

"No, brother, they are not... they are your words and your words alone." With a contented look on his face, John patted Robert on the shoulder and pointed to the middle of the floor. Robert rose from his seat, bowed to his brother, and walked to stand in the middle of the floor to address the gathering.

"As you all know," he began, "names were given up, under torture, to a Crow Priest," Robert looked toward his brother for signs of disapproval of the expression but there were none, "by our erstwhile compatriot Duane Catchpole and his inner council of Brethren. This must never be allowed happen again. Accordingly, we will abide by the following rules to keep our society safe and incognito. Firstly: no Brother shall know by sight, or by name, more than five other Brethren. Second: no brother shall..."

The Brotherhood's 'Rules of Engagement', as they became commonly known, were amended over time to take account of changing circumstances; political, economic, societal and, from the twentieth century, technological. For the next seven hundred years, the Rules of Engagement were rigorously observed. Had they not been, the Brotherhood would've met its end long before the challenges the future had in store for it.

★

The day following the inaugural meeting of the resurrected Brotherhood, a meeting of the ACF was held, as was becoming usual, in Paul Martin's hut. Having grown to twenty-two members, nineteen men and three women, the space in the hut was cramped. It was standing room only, except for Robert Clay and Paul Martin, they sat in the seats reserved for them.

"We'd better look for larger accommodations; there's no elbow room in here."

"We grow rapidly. What say you, outlaw brother?"

"I say we have enough crew for now. Recruiting for our cause is risky business and every risk we take is one that brings us nearer to the holy fire."

"That's right enough, Robert, well said," spoke Samuel White, the self-appointed enforcer of the ACF.

"What were Brethren saying after yesterday's meeting at the barn?" asked Robert.

"I think you can guess, Master Clay."

"I can, but I want you to tell me what you know for fact and not hearsay."

"Many are nervous, you know, of John's ways. They say he's… they say that he suffers from an incurable malady of madness."

"Will they stay?"

"Why not? So long as John doesn't interfere in their dealings against the aristocracy… and they have you to rely on."

"We must ensure that all keep to the rule of no more than five or six Brethren associating one with the other. We will be safer that way. If they can keep to that then all well and good, but if not they will answer to us. I will not have our ACF jeopardised by the greed or ambition of men… or their folly."

"We're all with you on that one," spoke Sheriff Judd.

"Both we and the Brotherhood must only operate our schemes beyond the boundaries of the six parishes; this will keep Belcher quiet and John ignorant of our activities. We can roam where we will throughout the middle lands but we must not recruit others to the Brotherhood. Nobody must mention the name of the Brotherhood and none shall whisper our name! To all intents and purposes, neither exists. The deeper into the shadows the Brotherhood goes, the more secure are we."

"We're all with you on that one," spoke Mary Spurling, a recent and surprising convert for the ACF.

"Thank you, sister. Now to our business. I shall say, for the edification of our newer members," which Robert meant to serve as a reminder to the older members, "that nothing… nothing!… is ever to be written down. There's no written Oath of Allegiance; it must be learned and recited from the heart. There's no written constitution; it is built into the nature of our very being. The ACF's single and only purpose is the destruction of the Church. This does not mean killing a priest or burning down an abbey. Such actions will only bring about our ends. Our task is not a small one, for the Church is great in size and number. We will not achieve our end in a month, a year or even in our lifetimes… it will take many generations. It is my hope that it will be achieved within two hundred years. We must starve the Church of the things that give it life. We must devise schemes to take away its power over people. The Church bleeds the poor dry through its collections and its demands of them to hand over bond servants from families working hard just to survive." Robert looked around the room to gauge how his words were being received. Though these people had signed up to the ACF, Robert knew it would be hard for them to hear such open anti-Church talk. He continued, "Do you ever see a thin Priest? No, you never do! Do you ever see a monk poorly attired… or a bishop? No! They have full bellies and clothes on their backs, not to mention fine roofs over their heads!"

"You speak the truth, Robert!" shouted the room. That was the sort of thing he wanted to hear.

"I trust to hope that we will get unlooked-for help along our path. I trust that some monarch or tyrant will come along that shares our views and assists us in our task by curbing the power of the Church in every way." Even though the Brotherhood was against the monarchy, the ACF would welcome help from any quarter. "We must at all times blend in with the Brotherhood. Only in that way can we remain hidden from view. We must appear indistinguishable from the Brotherhood in every way. We must not raise our heads above it as our existence will not be tolerated. We must adopt its methods as they will kill us all if we are found out."

"What do you mean by 'adopt its methods' then, Robert?" Simon Sparrow asked in a pre-planned question.

"We will organise ourselves exactly as the Brotherhood does. No ACF member will know or associate with more than three others. None shall openly act against the Church. We must appear to love the Church if we are to survive. Orders for actions against the Church will only come from the inner council. Do not expect to be employed in ACF business every day or week, or even month.

You will only be contacted when you are needed and you must do as instructed without hesitation or question. We will never embark on schemes that will put your lives in jeopardy. Never! I promise you." How Robert could keep such a promise was a question on everybody's mind. "Thinking to the future, and our continued existence, it is the responsibility of the inner council to ensure continuity by planning the succession of each of us and to grow our ACF through new blood. We must ever be mindful of…"

And so Robert went on and on, longer and longer, as more things occurred to him. Having no written constitution meant, over time, the constitution of the ACF became "built into the nature of our very being." The nature of 'our very being' changed with each new generation as the ACF adapted in order to survive.

★

Within a year, Robert Clay married a woman from within the ACF. They were regarded by everybody in the six parishes as the perfect couple. Just like his brother John, Robert fathered two pairs of twin boys before going on to father six more children. John likewise fathered ten children in all and, despite child mortality being over fifty percent during the early fourteenth century, every one of the offspring of the Clay brothers survived childhood. When their time came, each of the offspring, in turn, fought for control of the Brotherhood. But there can only ever be one leader. And so all but two of the children were killed during the war of succession. One to lead the Brotherhood and the other to be at her side as her lieutenant… and the first female leader of the ACF.

End instalment one.